SCOTLAND BEFORE THE BOMB

Introduced and edited by

M.J. NICHOLLS

With Illustrations by Alan Lyons

Sagging
Meniscus

Printed in Great Britain and the United States of America.
Set in Williams Caslon Text with LaTeX.

ISBN: 978-1-944697-80-8 (paperback)
ISBN: 978-1-944697-92-1 (ebook)
Library of Congress Control Number: 2019942816

Sagging Meniscus Press
www.saggingmeniscus.com

For my very Scottish parents

Contents

Editor's Introduction   *vii*

"A Report on the Uptilting of Cromarty" [*ROSS & CROMARTY*]   1

"The Potential Country" [*ARGYLL & BUTE*]   8

"The Last Man in Skye" [*ISLE OF SKYE*]   16

"Festival ∞" [*EDINBURGH*]   20

"The Republic of Hugh" [*MORAY*]   25

"InfoJog" [*CLACKMANNAN*]   33

"Q+A with Hank Righteous" [*SUTHERLAND*]   41

"Trip Advisor Reviews" [*SPEAN BRIDGE*]   44

"The Fictional Village of Echt" [*ECHT*]   48

"Vestibule Chairs" [*ANGUS*]   64

"The Sound of No" [*PERTH*]   69

"Just a Lifetime" [*BRAEMAR*]   72

"The McCulloch Inheritance" [*BANFF*]   80

"Tickertape of Misery" [*FIFE*]   85

"I'm Still Sorry" [*SELKIRK*]   92

"The Cleft of Hate" [*ORKNEY*]   97

"The Sport of Kickballs" [*LANARK*]   103

"The Really Real" [*DUNDEE*]   110

"Why the Camels?" [*AYR*]   116

" " [*ROXBURGH*]   120

"The Mnemoshop" [*PEEBLES*]   121

"The Smog" [*STIRLING*]   127

"The Courting of Tchuh" [*BERWICK*]   129

"Kibbitz from the Kibbutz" [*ABERDEEN*]   134

"The Literary Utopia" [*WIGTOWN*]   138

"Pictures of Presidents" [*DUMFRIES*]   142

"In Session with Kristin Sump" [*INVERNESS*]   151

"Prawn Confusion" [*SHETLAND*]   158

"Diary of a Pineapple Holder" [*KIRKCUDBRIGHT*]   162

"Realm of Sapo" [*LOTHIANS*]   166

"When Four Tribes Live Peacefully in Punctuation" [*KINCAR-DINE*]   174

"The Misanthropists" [*KINROSS*]   176

"Tetris in Thurso" [*CAITHNESS*]   182

"Quiz" [*DUNBARTON*]   186

"Aleatoria" [*NAIRN*]   192

"Textual Dysfunction" [*GLASGOW & RENFREW*]   196

"Appendix: The Isles" [*SEE ABOVE*]   233

INTRODUCTION

IT IS A WELL-DOCUMENTED historical fact that on May 12, 2060, the country formerly known as Scotland was completely destroyed in a series of merciless nuclear missile strikes from Luxembourg. To this day, Luxembourg's reasons for the calculated vengeful murder of over five million people remain unknown, as those responsible fled the country and have never been seen since. However, sources close to the Prime Minister at that time Xavier Clunker blame a series of unsolicited emails sent by one Douglas Kelly from Armadale, West Lothian. Mr. Kelly is believed to have sent over nine thousand emails mocking Mr. Clunker, bypassing the various spam filters and firewalls, delivering hateful invective to his inbox on a daily basis. Those close to the Prime Minister claimed that these messages, filled with vicious personal abuse, mostly pertaining to Mr. Clunker's untrimmed nasal hair, arriving two or three times a day, sent him into a state of temporary apocalyptic lunacy, at which point he ordered that one atomic bomb, known as "The Foreigner Fixer", the centrepiece of the country's suprisingly vast arsenal, be trained on Douglas Kelly's house at 27 McCallum Court, Armadale, and that Scotland be blown from the map. To prevent the blast from destroying parts of England, the military tweaked Mr. Clunker's orders, and spread the attack across the country, ensuring that the entire landscape was indeed blown from the map with rigorous precision. The events of that horrific afternoon are still impossible to contemplate, and are commemorated by Annual Scotland Remembrance day, where people the world over observe a minute's silence for the slain. This book is about the fascinating period leading up to this moment: 2014 to 2060.

❋

In 2014, the First Minister Nicola F. Sturgeon staged an independence referendum to remove Scotland from the United Kingdom. The no vote won 55.3% to 44.7%, and the matter rested until increasing tensions between left-leaning Scottish voters and right-wing Westminster rule led to a second referendum in 2019. This time, the vote was 65.2% to 34.8% in favour of yes, and Scotland became an independent country. The new nation, still named Scotland, was triumphant for several years, and showed unity until two council boroughs began squabbling over the penalty for dog fouling in public. Two ministers came to blows on live television. It was then that Steven Horse, MP for Dundee, proposed that Dundee separate from the rest of the country, and demanded an independence referendum for his constituents. The people of Dundee, known for their staunch isolationism, had proposed a border wall several years earlier, and had their request refused. This was the perfect opportunity to make themselves aloof from the rest of Scotland. The referendum was permitted, the result 87.9% to 12.1% in favour of the ayes. Passports and border checks were soon made compulsory when entering the proud nation of Dundee.

The parliament became a chaotic and unstable place, with fistfights a common sight between ministers refusing to compromise on policy matters. The MP for Perthshire put the MP for Highland North in a headlock when the latter blamed increasing deforestation on the rise in Dutch elm disease, and not the cottage industry of celebrity golf courses. The MP for Aberdeen South headbutted the MP for Glasgow Central when the former opined that artificial insemination was the solution to the red squirrel shortage, as it had worked for the pandas in Edinburgh

Zoo. The MP for Edinburgh East chinned the MP for Hamilton and Motherwell when she suggested that the residents should dredge the local ponds of scum themselves, rather than waiting for the understaffed park ranger service to perform this task. Sessions often ended with MPs sitting with their arms crossed, refusing to address one another. The new First Minister, Alasdair Gray, bowed to pressure to allow further referenda.

After requests were made for independence by Glasgow, Aberdeen, East Lothian, and Stirling ministers, Mr. Gray suggested that separation be offered by county, i.e. for each county to become a country, if desired. The next to leave Scotland was Aberdeen. The others followed, and by March 2026, Scotland was no longer the name for a country, but a new continent encompassing thirty miniature countries, a number that was to increase over the next year, when several isles and villages "went rogue" and illegally declared independence. It is my ambition in this book to present a portrait of a fractured continent across these tumultuous years, to chart the various, wayward turns each country, bewildered and intoxicated by its constitutional freedoms, took in the years leading up to Scotland's destruction.

Many invaluable historical resources were destroyed along with the continent. To help me in assembling this eclectic mosaic that I present to you now, I have scoured the world for first-hand accounts, trawled the university libraries for archive material, and made visits to the scorched landscape that remains above England, to present eye-opening portraits of how these countries functioned post-referendum. I have arranged the countries in the order in which I received or located the necessary material: in some cases, facts were scarce, in others, all too plentiful. The material here ranges from detailed accounts of new political orthodoxies, to reports on incidents in individual villages or towns that allude to what might be taking place across the nations. The material is simultaneously trustworthy and untrustworthy, illuminating and obfuscating, so I ask the reader to maintain a sceptical eye when reading. The presence of several former villages (the aforementioned "rogue states") might confuse some readers: Spean Bridge, Echt, and Braemar are the aberrations here, each having removed themselves from their countries through illegal means. Since each country boasts a striking and incredible account of how its inhabitants lived, I have allowed them to stand alongside the legitimate nations. I have included brief prefatory explanations for the more obscure material, referenced my sources at the end of the excerpts, and included a short appendix on the isles, each of which have wonderful stories to tell, perhaps for another book. For counties formerly sporting the '-shire' suffix, i.e. Ayrshire, Banffshire, these have been removed, having lost their -shire status upon becoming countries. Please note that the titles refer to each country name, and not towns or cities of the same name in that country.

I hope this small volume brings you closer to understanding the enigma that was Scotland before the bomb.

—M.J. Nicholls, 2113, New Jersey

Scotland
Before
the
Bomb

"A Report on the Uptilting of Cromarty"
[ROSS & CROMARTY]

INTRODUCTION

I N AUGUST 2036, Civil Parish of Cromarty intelligence officers became aware of suspect noises emanating from the port of Invergordon. These noises, reported by various locals as "harsh rustling" and "vicious creaking", were subject to an intense investigation by Chief Intelligence Operative Paul Woolman. Mr. Woolman maintained a three-week vigil atop the border wall with a powerful telescope, and observed unusual movement involving a chain of citizens rustling crisp packets in front of microphones, and stepping on loose floorboards hooked up to operational amps. The incidents increased in their frequency, with locals reporting a "persistent uptake in rustling" and a "more severe campaign of creaking" over a two-month period. A vote was taken in parliament to forge communication with the notoriously troublesome Invergordon mayor, Astrid Boathouse, whose acts of provocation had been notable: among them, a sustained campaign of flan bombardment over a two-week period, leaving the village flooded in custard, and the pumping of Laura Marling songs through the water supply, causing untold aural torture on those who sought a shower or sustenance. Our pigeon missives, seeking an explanation, were ignored. Mr. Woolman recorded, after a further three-week assault, that the human chains had increased in length, and that the noises had become audible across the entire town. An historic decision was then taken.

OBJECTIVE

After a vote of two to one, the Parliament implemented its plans to up-tilt Cromarty to a 75° angle in order to maintain a constant watch over the hostile port of Invergordon, and prepare for potential retaliation in the event of unceasing provocation. The chief civil engineer overseeing the project, nicknamed Operation Askew, was Sólveig Hallason, a world-famed figure from the Icelandic firm Volcanic Constructions. His reputation had been made building vibrant conurbations on the slopes of volcanoes and on mountain ledges, known as 'Lífborgs' ('Vivicities') as part of the means to control the ballooning immigrant influx in that country, and to create Global Villages containing microcosms of all world cultures. His expertise at helping sustain small villages amid continual geodetic shifts would prove invaluable. Mr Hallason arrived in the winter of 2036 to outline his plans to our members. In his polite and efficient manner, he estimated the operation would take up to a decade, and that the following resources, as a bare minimum, would be required for a successful uptilting:

15,000 JCB trucks
45,000 cranes
60,000 construction workers
4,000,000 tonnes of concrete
3,000 transportation vehicles
4,000 support workers
43,000 lengths of rope
200,000 shovels
30,000 pneumatic drills

EXECUTION

Before construction, it was necessary to ensure that all existing structures were rooted in strong and lasting foundations, before the deeper foundations were unrooted. All four hundred and two structures would require "expert pinning", in Mr. Hallason's words, to ensure the uptilt would not cause them to collapse and "tumble" down the slope. In addition, each structure had to be mounted on a concrete plinth to place them on the correct plain of elevation, i.e. not pointing downwind. This meant pre-tilting each structure at an unusual elevation in anticipation of the new angle. The residents of the Civil Parish were evacuated to a special camp at the east coast (the "foot" of the new uptilted Cromarty), where basic facilities, meals, and activities such as korfball were provided for the decade of their encampment. Before the uprooting of the landscape, a concrete dam was erected around the surrounding sea to prevent flooding. 45,000 poles were driven into the landscape, and 45,000 vehicles positioned to commence the "industrial tugging" procedure, where the terrain was pulled upwards several inches at a time towards the 75° angle. Each exposed area was blasted with 54,000 metric tonnes of concrete. This slow process of "tugging" and "filling-in" to create a stable concrete gradient took place over a period lasting from April 2037 to September 2047, with a rolling workforce at task twenty-four hours a day. During this stressful decade, various problems such as malnutrition, lice, and dysentery occurred in the camps, and emergency "pop-up" hospitals were required. The poor living conditions in these damp and cold tents led to severe depression and various instances of suicide, and by December 2047, half the population mounted an expedition to Fortrose and were reported missing.

AFTER THE PROCEDURE

The Civil Parish of Cromarty was introduced to the new 75° angle on April 2048. To facilitate habitation, a network of cable cars had been constructed between several "floors" equalling fifty steps per stop, and residents could move between streets and houses with the assistance of interlinked step-paths. Cars were no longer functional in the village, and the pre-existing roads were coated in Velcro to prevent accidents. (Those who fell onto a road could blow one of the special whistles and wait for the fire brigade to unstick them). For those with mobility problems, a lift was added between the "floors". A new council office, and special observation point, was built at the summit. A telescope from NASA, strong enough to view individual follicles on Invergordon scalps, was purchased. The remaining citizens were returned to their homes, and an advert was placed via pigeon to attract newcomers to move to the abandoned properties. The new uptilted town became a vibrant and thriving place, with thousands of tourists arriving to experience life on a 75° uptilt. Hotels and restaurants were added to the infrastructure, in addition to museums, pubs, and galleries.

During the construction procedure, the original rustling and creaking noises coming from Invergordon had ceased. The non-stop earth-shattering racket from the industrial vehicles uprooting the landscape and causing immense seismic frictions had been interpreted in the rival village as a form of violent riposte, and a serious retaliation to the minor irritations of Astrid Boathouse and her legion of impish followers. A mole in the construction team had smuggled intelligence to the Boathouse government outlining our plan. In response, Invergordon planned and executed an expensive operation to lower itself into the landscape by 5,000 feet and cover itself in a enormous strip of tarpaulin. This rendered our telescopes useless at monitoring their movements and, in retrospect, the entire £700,000,000,000 operation a waste of time and money. After completion, the Civil Parish was peaceful for six months. A pigeon-missive arrived with the words "a huge mistake", signed Astrid Boathouse.

CONFLICT

Tensions arose in the town between the residents, whose taxes had been raised by 550% to help repay the costs to uptilt the village, and the MPs, who had been humiliated by the futility of their costly surveillance measure. In September 2049, a fleet of black airships appeared over the village, each with stadium-size speakers, broadcasting the same bothersome rustling and creaking noises that had sparked the uptilt. These transmissions were constant from 5PM to 5AM every day, and caused intense frustration to those attempting to unwind or sleep. The airships, totalling eleven in number, hung over the village, restricting the sunlight, and forced the tourists to abandon their trips in sheer irritation. Noise-cancelling earphones were shipped in to prevent the residents from succumbing to madness. This rendered all verbal communication void. A unanimous vote was taken among the residents to shoot down the airships at once. This amounted to an outright declaration of war with Invergordon.

After the missile strike (the missiles were purchased from a Dominican dictator at a reasonable exchange rate) a swan of peace was sent to the rival village (no doves being available) pleading for cessation. There was no response. Several weeks later, an extraordinary sight emerged from the clouds. An even larger fleet of aircraft appeared, pulling the world's largest vacant crisp packet. The aircraft, in under four hours, shrouded the entire Civil Parish inside the large purple-coloured wrapper, causing immediate darkness, and a repugnant stench of pickled onion that permeated the atmosphere for months. The action proved disastrous. A state of emergency was declared, and tunnels were carved in haste to escape its oily packaging. Several people suffocated under the airless shroud of bagged pickle. The echo of internal rustling inside the packeted Cromarty caused the loss of hearing among dozens. In total, it cost approximately £4,000,000 to remove the crisp packet from the town. The buildings and landscape were left with such a strong smell of onion that no visitors would enter. The town became bankrupt, and debtors from the World Bank demanded payment. At this point the Parliament was forced to sell Cromarty to Texas as a nuclear testing site.

CONCLUSION

The Civil Parish was cleared on March 2050. I stepped down as Prime Minister on the 4th of that month and made this brief speech: "I would like to thank the residents of Cromarty for their patience and persistence over the last twelve years. Our vision to uptilt this wonderful Civil Parish to a 75º angle was not successful, but we achieved a stronger, more personal victory: the bonding of a community, the collective struggle for survival in the face of unspeakable oppression. This is not something to be ashamed about. I leave my post as Prime Minister not as a failure, not ashamed by my actions, but buoyant in the knowledge I served this town with an intensity and passion rarely seen in politics." At this point I had to leave the stage, as the residents began to revolt and tear down the town hall. I managed to escape in a private helicopter. I offer this personal account to anyone interested in the history of our former Civil Parish, and hope a lesson might be learned that leaders think twice before realigning their towns, cities, or villages to 75º angles. The evacuated residents were compensated with £30,000 per head and were advised to seek shelter in Fortrose—however, it came to our attention several months later that all carbon-based matter was vaporised upon contact with Fortrose, so this struck a seriously tragic note to the already seriously tragic tale.

BREAKDOWN OF EXPENSES STILL OWED TO THE WORLD BANK

Sólveig Hallason Fee	£110,000,000
Cost to uptilt Cromarty (resources, workers fees)	£700,000,000,000
One cocker spaniel crushed under a JCB (compensation)	£30,000
Velcro to coat the roads	£900,000
Emergency Velcro rescue whistles	£30,000
New council offices and observation point	£7,000,000
NASA telescope	£32,000,000
Training pigeons to send messages	£70,000
Missiles to obliterate airships	£34,000,000
Fee to Dominican Dictator Elvérez Mùan	£2,000,000
Crisp packet attack clean-up	£4,000,000
Crisp packet attack fatalities and injuries (compensation)	£299,000,000
Erection of and maintaining of "pop-up" hospitals	£3,000,000
Swan of peace	£3,400
Compensation to evacuated residents	£630,000

Total: £700,492,663,400

['A Report on the Uptilting of Cromarty: The Logistics, Repercussions, & Consequences, By the Right Honourable Prime Minister, Mr. M. Westlake' in *The Book of Lost Places: Accounts & Documents*, Phyllis Strang (ed.), Vulpine Press, 2090.]

"The Potential Country"
[ARGYLL & BUTE]

A SERIES OF SCHEMES *to shape life in the indecisive nation of Argyll & Bute were implemented over a span of three decades. No scheme was adopted as the accepted modus operandi: instead, the country became known by its persistent, fruitless experimentation. —Ed.*

Children by Committee

First pioneered in Eastern Slovenia by Minister for Families Cvetko Dančar, the purpose of this scheme was to keep the breeding rates at a more respectable ratio of one child per one hundred people (i.e. fifty couples). One couple, selected from a randomiser, had the honour of providing the sperm, harvesting the foetus, and birthing the child. Passed into the nurse's hands, the birth couple would relinquish their right as sole mother and father, and enter into a contract with their fellow committee members to be "collective" parents of the child. All aspects of its upbringing would be resolved by votes at committee meetings, from choosing a name, bottle- or breastfeeding, the absorbability of nappies worn, to the choice of nursery, primary school, and so on. Each choice had to reflect the financial means of the collective: children born in poorer neighbourhoods would have to suffer some parents being unable to contribute to college funds, or help with Christmas presents. The child would live with fifty mothers and fathers at approximately 7.3 days per couple per year, among whom he would experience a series of personalities, opinions, dysfunctions, hobbies, passions, and acquire knowledge. When practiced in Argyll & Bute, the children raised in this scheme ended up as schizophrenic polygamous adulterers, seeking love and appraisal from multiple partners, and assuming multiple personalities to cope with the demands of their endless parents. The scheme was scrapped when six-year-old Tim Finn waged fifty lawsuits against his fifty parents and won nine million in compensation.

Double-Barrelled Obscurantism

The writer Paul Shishkin in his book *Blinkering the Bad* practiced self-hypnosis for nine months whenever he was faced with facts or situations that caused him intense mental stress or suffering. He found that when confronted with a news item that made him miserable, or a fact that spoiled his afternoon, he could improve his happiness by 97% by inducing a mental block using keywords planted in his mind under hypnosis. During a recession, the Finance Minister Bill Greeboll proposed this as a solution to Argyll & Bute's lugubrious air. In tandem with this was an idea from Tamara Volt's book *Die Hard with a Vengeance*, showing how the pressure to understand tough intellectual concepts made people sad, and if encouraged to bluff their way through based on their abilities, people were 94% happier. These two forms of obscurantism worked together: a challenging situation presented itself, and citizens had their mental blocking techniques in place to overcome them. Henceforth, Argyll & Bute was ordered to hide its lack of substantive knowledge on various topics, and reorder their discourse into strings of inconclusive, ungraspable verbiage to mask the knowledge of the things that had been blocked out. As a consequence, people walked around oblivious and unresponsive to the tangible suffering around them, and spoke in infuriating intellectual gibberish to maintain a pretence of things being fine. This scheme was scrapped when a sailor, blocking out the fact that his vessel was about to hit a prominent crag, offered his passengers an informational and inaccurate lecture on rock formations and coastal erosions as the boat capsized.

Ayn Rand with Ocelots

First posited by Gordon Gano, lead singer of The Violent Femmes, this notion twisted Conservative Russian-American novelist Ayn Rand's theory of objectivism into a more palatable form. In Rand's writings, the ultimate purpose of man is to spurt with vim towards an heroic state of priapic self-interest, whereas in Gano's version, man's moral purpose is to ensure that all ocelots everywhere are as happy as possible, and to take personal pleasure in ensuring this is the case. Prime Minister Wilmot Popple had several thousand noctural wildcats shipped over from their South American rainforest habitats, and released into Argyll & Bute's sprawling forelocks. These beautiful spotted cats, with their sleek bodies, regal postures, graceful pounces, and mercurial eyes, made their home in the unspacious peaks and depths. Citizens were then encouraged to incorporate some form of ocelot-loving activity into their daily lives, whether releasing rabbits, opposums, and lizards into their habitats for them to snack on, or helping protect their homes from poachers or other predators like pumas and bobcats. The community felt happy devoting their lives to these creatures, until human life became miserable thanks to the millions sunk into ocelots instead of them. The ocelots began hunting the homeless population, terrorising impoverished people on the streets, and eating the weak. The scheme was scrapped when a girl scout group were ambushed and devoured while bringing the ocelots homemade cookies.

Masks

Pessimist philosopher Ivor Leibniz observed that people became bored and frustrated at themselves and the people around them extremely quickly, and posed the solution to have people wear a series of masks showing the faces of less mediocre people instead. As an example, Ivor used Alex Bog. An audio technician in a rap studio who wanted to be *Swordfishtrombones*-era Tom Waits, Alex Bog bought a Waits mask and wore this to the rapture of his girlfriend, fed up with the sallow sag of his face. Alex asked his girlfriend if she would wear a *Mulholland Drive*-era Naomi Watts mask, which she sported with pleasure, replacing her previous expression of sour indifference. This scheme was adopted in Argyll & Bute. Parents put masks of less irritating children on their offspring, and wore smiling masks over their own unsmiling faces. People met Mel Gibson in their bakeries; Nana Mouskouri in their surgeries; Linda Perhacs in their offices; Yoko Ono in their cafés; Greg Kinnear in their nightclubs; David Hyde-Pierce at their bus stops; Steve Punt in their airports; Lillian Gish in their haberdashers; Colin Mochrie in their swimming pools; Harvey Keitel in their prisons; Penelope Shuttle in their subways; Catrin-Mai Huw in their sewers. Mischevious kids sported provocative masks, like the one scamp who walked around as Joseph Merrick, or the imp who strutted around as Jean-Bédel

Bokassa. The scheme was scrapped when the mask supplier only had Tony and Cherie Blair faces for sale.

Crime & The City Solution

It was observed in a sardonic tweet from humorist D.M. Nicols that the volume of crime dramas and novels had vastly overtaken the number of actual crimes being committed. The Ministers for Crime and Entertainment checked the stats and found this to be true. For every new season of a murder serial containing three to five murders, one real-time murder was committed. Other series showing rapes, assaults, thefts, and so on, contained higher volumes of these crimes than their real-time versions. As a cure for crime, it was suggested by ministers that those thinking of breaking the law should apply to work for the production companies making these dramas and turn their actions into profitable ideas. This worked for several seasons. However, the production companies complained that without actual crimes to inspire their writers, their shows were lacking in original flair, and passed over for awards. The production companies took it upon themselves to pay the criminals to commit real-life atrocities so they could write down what happened when these went awry. It was not an uncommon sight to see writer taking notes while a hoodlum knived an old lady for her pension book. The scheme was scrapped when everyone involved was arrested. A serial about this episode was soon aired.

The Critical Mirror

To keep citizens humble, and to prevent egotism ruining the country, a critical mirror was to be installed in every home. The mirror was invented in Hungary by Laszlo Gimmer. A black box containing a computer program with information about each reflectee was built into the back of the custom mirrors, to provide morning criticism on cue. The nature of the criticism was based on the Insignificance Principle, which treats each human life as of little value in itself, and views collective decency as more important to maintaining the species. This meant one morning Morag Filmore awoke to the message: "You are a mediocre trainee programmer for an uncompetitive tech firm." Paul Virgins: "Your swaggering gait and outgoing air fails to hide the frightened little child you are inside." Dennis Postula: "That waxed moustache and cropped bob is no compensation for your complete absence of wit." Simon Ethel: "Up again to sell cars and fail to address your deep childhood trauma." Eric Staadhoff: "Those vapid brown eyes, like swirling pools of fetid nothing." Francis Wheem: "You work in accounts. You are 40." Tyrone Smiddy: "A dusty stinking cravat of a man." Dobbie Coll: "Your prose lacks the basic competence to command a cursory glance from the most tolerant reader." Erin Quiz: "A slow trickle of cold yellow sick." Alison Pettigru: "You are simply a dull woman." Valerie Wym: "Oh! God! No!" The scheme was scrapped when the suicide rate went up by 175%.

Scandanavian Shadows

For decades, commentators had used the countries of Sweden, Norway, and Finland as exemplars of liberal, well-educated societies uncorrupted by big business that treated their citizens in a fair and dignified manner. Since Argyll & Bute had been hitting the skids corruption-wise, with thousands set aside for forest conservation siphoned into ministers' trousers, and millions set aside for mental health provisions wired to a Swiss bank account, the populace voted that Scandanavians come to the country and shadow everyone, from ministers to trash collectors, and teach them how not to be complete pricks. Colin McGregor, a baker, was shadowed for two months by Kjell Eriksen, who lectured him on not helping himself to cream puffs, charging the same for day-old pastries, or masturbating in the back room. Iain Macquarrie, the finance minister, was shadowed by Linnéa Nyberg, who lectured him on not pocketing the OAP winter heating allowance to build an extention on his seafront cottage so his son Malcolm could move in with his new partner. Alasdair Adair, a single parent of two, was shadowed by Aki Heikkinen, who lectured him on not singing unionist folk songs to his seven-year-old son, thereby implanting a factually incorrect history of the trade union movement into his baby's ears. Erin Stewart, a reporter, was shadowed by Jørgen Solberg, who lectured her on not arriving too early at crime scenes and interrogating traumatised victims minutes after their ordeals. Arlene Galt, a hairdresser, was shadowed by Tove Ek, who lectured her on not leaving people too long in the dryers, causing acute burns on their scalps, and not trimming her nails to a tolerable length for washing procedures. Callum Brotchie, a GP, was shadowed by Armo Järvinen, who lectured him on not letting off stink bombs under the table to force his chattier patients to leave.

Iona Archie, a shepherdess, was shadowed by Aku Hämäläinen, who lectured her on not whipping the sheep with her riding crop when her patience with the flocculent ruminants was tested on windy, rainy afternoons. Jimmy Crae, a hobo, was shadowed by Alfhild Rønning, who lectured him on his poor begging technique and limited repertoire on the zither. Helen Galloway, a senior management accounts executive, was shadowed by Ake Larsson, who lectured her on not talking complete bollocks from the minute she entered the office to the minute she left the office. The scheme was scrapped after the Scandanavians had substantially improved the populace.

The Sham Castle Initiative

The market research wing of the Argyll & Bute tourist board noticed that people complained about the dearth of accessible, complete castle ruins. "These historical structures are in fields miles from hotels, and we have to book bus tours or hire cars to see them. All that expense later, and there's nothing more than a pile of bricks covered in birdshit," the tourists whinged. So the tourist board invested millions in sham castles—structures built in sandstone, blasted and chiselled to appear time-beaten, with bogus histories presented in the brochures. These castles were within ten minutes of towns and villages, with cafés, restaurants, and soundproofed areas for children to run around in screaming. The first, near Lochgilphead, was called King McCullan VII castle, a residence for the fictitious king in the era of the fictitious skirmish between the Bute Battlers and the Argyll Arsonists. The King was a prolific shortbread manufactuer, and sold his tartan to local clans, modern versions of which were available in the gift shop. In addition to the castles, other popular new historical artifacts included the Crying Stones of Carradale, which leaked water on cue from small "pores"; the Bouncy Bog of Bonawe, with springloaded soil for people to partake of history in a mildly bouncy fashion; the Tattoo Tapestry of Tarbet, a spurious tapestry with tattoo-like inscriptions to appeal to the under-twenties attendee; the Goblin Glen of Gometra, where holograms and projections of goblins periodically flashed on trees and thickets; and the Squirrel Safari of Succoth, where squirrels were fired towards passing cars on the trails, so the passengers inside could make this noise: "Ooowwwooo!" The scheme was not scrapped, even after a brutal exposé in *The History Review*, as people preferred these to their real counterparts.

Liquid Imp Removal

It had been reported (by Al Ubik) that citizens had been periodically walking into the woods at night for hours and hours without rest and collapsing dead. Their exhausted bodies were found frozen in copses the next morning (by Al Obec). These spontaneous strolls into suicidal oblivion caused a huge amount of inconvenience for the local police force, who had not been trained in the sort of forensic work required on fresh corpses, or the grief counselling required to console the families, so a special taskforce was imported from Belgium to root out the cause. Gert Harrf located a semi-transparent liquid imp knuckling around in a forest clearing shooting Gloom Pellets at passing walkers from a peashooter in its maw. The creature, believed to have been hiding inside the underdrawer of a porcelain cabinet, had lapsed into primitive malfeasance, and required a chronometric tilting procedure to bring it in line with modern imps. To perform this, Gert Harrf asked local resident Colin Pamp to hold a parallelogram and think about broccoli. The semi-transparent liquid imp would, at the mention of such a noble vegetable, return to his feet and, with light fructal coaxing, over the course of two weeks, become fully transparent. Once invited to tea with a well-spoken and entertaining family (the Ibixes), the imp would solidify, and return to its usual state of rock-hard visible friendliness. This scheme was adopted across the land and seven hundred liquid imps were saved before standing trial in the criminal courts for their vicious murders.

Legalising "Drugs"

Following the blanket ban on narcotics and recreational intoxicants, the PM observed that if people even heard the word "drugs", their cravings were prone to increase by an incalculable integer. The use of the word "drugs", in speech or in print, was therefore verboten. This state of affairs continued for twelve years, until the new liberal PM, Shepp Salvop, overturned the policy and legalised the word "drugs" forever. Euphoric citizens celebrated with street parties in which they listed the varieties of drugs that people could take, using the word "drugs" in their sentences, such as "Drugs like fluoxetine, drugs like abecarnil, drugs like kebuzone, drugs like quifenadine, drugs like necopidem, drugs like iodixanol, drugs like escitalopram, drugs like paroxetine, drugs like gestodene", and so on. In the shops, cottages, and coracles of the nation, children and teengers and adults and the dying were using the word "drugs" in public and private, and the rise in strong recreational use of the word "drugs" became steep. In the course of four months, hundreds of "drugs" addicts—people who used the word "drugs" in every sentence—were recorded. One man was found in a shop doorway, completely incapable of saying any other word than "drugs", and taken to an emergency speech therapist immediately before he swallowed his own tongue. The new PM refused to reverse his choice, explaining that although the word "drugs" had invaded the popular lexicon and become a temporary linguistic sensation, and that some unfortunates, caught up in the hysteria of saying the word "drugs", would need help coping with their newfound freedom, it was more important that people had the freedom to say "drugs". Help was provided to the hundreds of "drugs" addicts who, in a couple of weeks, were able to reduce their use of the word to three or four hundred instances a week, and exercise a normal and varied vocabulary. The scheme was scrapped when a shipment of cocaine was accidentally leaked into the water supply, and everyone became rabid and desperate for that particular narcotic. The word "drugs" was never uttered on Argyll & Bute again.

[From *The Big Book of 1001 Failed Schemes*, Peter Weep and Walter Pepp, Eds, 2047, Hahaha! Books.]

"The Last Man in Skye"
[ISLE OF SKYE]

JANUARY 25

I amble across a lumpen knoll. I swerve the terrace, the lime-bird, the stag-beetled recrudescence, and the twig. A curled corner of *Cutter and the Clan* peeps into my perceptory, I bag the fragment. The swirling opera singer reappears in a lamé waistcoat with a seeping viscus in a plastic container. I emit words from my sound-hole, I re-emit words from my sound-hole, I stop emitting words from my sound-hole. The day drops.

JANUARY 29

In a fever, I hear the strains of 'Abhainn an T-Sluaigh'. I see Casio chords like the spooked face of the re-animator. I see intermittent timpani fills like the beasting vision of an unlaunched missile. I see the lilting Gaelic vox like an alphabet inked in the nihilistic night. I waft towards a crateload of sold notions and upcount the stock-take. You allow sweet pencil shavings to fall into my ears, and for that I am thankful.

FEBRUARY 5

Before the twigs, the twigs, the twigs, the twigs, I observe cold cattle. One bovine bump, two bovine bumps, and a third. I picture the screaming in that mattress, and raise a colder compress to my temples which are, of course, not there. "Might we open our clavicles to the accommodate the night?" I ask. The response, that is now patent pending, is worth reciting word for word.

FEBRUARY 9

A faded sticker that reads "Reduced" is found on a fragment. I lick *The Big Wheel*. The posit tastes like seven bags of rice in the pouches of a sclerotic kangaroo. "Kerry, was that you, in the mosque, limping towards a shard of someone's metaphor?" I ask the kopje. The sun looms over towards the sky, almost as if a bald man had forgotten his cane and impressed upon a wall. We pray, and why not.

FEBRUARY 19
Is that you, Donnie Munro? Is that the skitter-skatter of an ovoid plane, landing in a strop of hot noodle? Is that you, Calum MacDonald? Is that the arched lemon pie, as seen on TV's Hot Lime Dinners? Is that you, Blair Douglas? Is that a sense of polity, viewed from the half-blind mind of a mud-caked villager? Is that you, Rory MacDonald? Is that a raw snip of tennis on the low pitch? Is that you, Bruce Guthro? Is that the cauterised dream clipped from the wing of a TB-ridden tinkerbell? Is that you, Peter Wishart?

MARCH 3
I return to the backend. The crabs retreat. I nuzzle the CD shard *In Search of Angels*.

MARCH 5
Overhead, the bolt hole closes, and opens. "Hmm," I think in words, "I will need a pontificate to urge this scenario across." I sometimes eat the remnants of former afternoons. I won't spring a plate of pesto upon thee. Gone, along the perforations, are the scissors that lifted us to victory, some long pint of wonder ago.

MARCH 26
"I was a walnut," a voice remarked. This has nothing of significance. On an escarpment, the bust modulation in 'Alba'. "I might opine," I opined. "That was a cult vestige," a remark voiced. This has something of insignificance. "I opined that I might," the walnut revoiced. That was a lot of ballyhoo.

APRIL 2
I lump across a stumbled knoll. Smells like January, tastes like Saturday. In the wrap, a song. 'Cutter'. Look, we aren't here to accuse each other of mutual fragmentation. A clinamen wraps things up.

APRIL 5
Memories of violence. Memories of the expendable, unlovable other. This swarm of hot mess. The aftermath of a lightning stroke. We roll across the turpentine hills, swatting the demons. I love the soup, I love things. If we were a

braver man, you might believe in the refrigerated middle. As this stands, I can only swim.

APRIL 18

The lute, the fiddle, the croaking whore of time. We will never complete the set. These fragments of Celtic MOR. These shards of trad-pop. These songs never to be re-sung. In lucid moments, this pain is the most. I span evermore into the internment of the colloquial insane, and make a nest there, with painless feathers.

APRIL 30

YOU SEE? "I was at a loss," the gain said. "I never gainsaid," the loss gained. How we curl into our darkened wings. How the sharp tip of Gabriel's sword perforates our limbs. How like atoms we are, in a spinning lager. Cross-pollinating ourselves, with the exuberance of bumblebees, our sacs stuffed. How the seedbed accumulates small, fervid eclectic shocks. "I gained a loss," the never said. I SEE!

MAY 5

Swishing kestrels care not. Yes, we see. The opal crescent unfurled and along the translucent tongue was the picture, 'Cnoc Na Feille'. Placed into a burlap satchel, the mother was not concerned with the haircut motes. Drachma alterations, please. One: a cold press. Two: a building semi-erect. Three: an oubliette omelette. Four: fairweather exaggeration. Five: a sestina on twelve breads. Six: the hour, sliced.

MAY 17

Is there anyone, mortal or flautist, who communicated like a salamander? In the curt half-light, a slowly inflating yoghurt. Is this the epicentre of our pain? Is there anyone, mortal or piper, who blew their stacks like a lemon? In the unforeseen chancre, a lummox of sorrow evaporates. Is there anyone, mortal or harpist, who could equivocate with the shoulders of a multicoloured priest? Is that the bus?

MAY 30

So, in the flaming hour, I notice. I up and notice, and I insert the fragments into a rowboat. I hum the last note of music, and prod. The melodies float to sea. The songs and sounds are silent. I listen to the birds. I listen to the waves. I listen to the wind. A serenity, a heavenly serenity, invades my soul, and I stagger towards something like clarity.

[From *Diary of the Last Man in Skye*, Author Unknown, Graham Butters (ed.), Historicoloco Press, Manchester, 2059.]

"Festival ∞"

[EDINBURGH]

I RETURNED TO RECLAIM a stapler I had left on the News Steps twelve years
ago. Stepping from the train at Waverley, a tall and flexible blonde chap
said: "Have you a marble in your eyes?" He produced from under his right lid
a pebble and offered it to me, cackling in a backflip retreat. The Mystical Marauders, a troupe of trapeze artists, tumblers, and beaming circus performers,
were at work in the station. I had made a point of arriving in late September to
avoid the festival and the clean-up, and was most irritated at this extravaganza
of commuter torture. At the station concourse, a tightrope walker was showing
off, and assorted fire-eaters, lion-tamers, and pole-spinners were performing
at full pelt. I noticed people at the ticket office throwing their money into a upturned bowler hat and receiving tickets from a mime, who fattened the queue
by pretending to be trapped in a box before handing them over. I inched forward at the exit, bunched together with harassed travellers and people shoving
flyers into my face, muttering "free show", until it became apparent that there
were only about two people trying to move forward, and the crowd was com-
posed entirely of flyering nuisances, imposing their loss-making productions
on us. I copied the man in front, and climbed over a pile of lapsed flyerers,
who had collapsed into a breathless heap, some probably expiring below the
mound.

On Waverley Bridge, I stopped the other man. "Is the festival running for
two months this year?" I asked. He replied curtly, "Edinburgh *is* the festival."
I would learn later that several years earlier, on August 31st, a band of enraged
performers, having sunk thousands into their failed shows, staged a coup on
the city, inciting the hundreds of comedians, actors, writers, and entertainers
to violent revolt, refusing to leave the former capital until the ill-bred public
had acknowledged their brilliance and let them turn a profit. In the meantime,
I walked towards the News Steps, passing the beggars who were actors (one lu-

natic was performing the Lucky monologue from *Waiting for Godot*), the human statues (one man was meta-miming the statue of Walter Scott), and performance artists with various parts of their anatomy nailgunned to the pavement. There, I encountered another impediment. On each step was a comedian, reciting their routines to the middle side of the step. Each step was roped off with a bouncer-cum-ticket collector on the right side. The first performer was Gordon Harriet, a nervous Welshman who mispronounced every second word. His bouncer informed me the price of admission to the middle of the step to listen to Gordon perform the show thirty centimetres away from me was £10.

"I only want to advance one step. Are you telling me that each step will cost a tenner?" I asked.

"My show is only £7.50, and I have rude balloon animals!" Step 2 said.

"Only £6 for mine, with a free sticker with my catchphrase on, 'Syrupy virtues, m'lud!'" Step 3 said.

"I'm the anti-comedian's comedian's auntie. Only £4 for me!" Step 4 said.

"I'm £11.50. But it is two hours of non-stop laughters and a moving song at the end, inspired by recent events in Yemen," Step 5 said.

"Are you intending to pay, sir?" Gordon's bouncer asked. My stapler having been left on the fourth set of steps, I calculated that to reach that level would cost between £250-350, depending on the prices set. I might also have to suffer a heckle from each of the performers for "walking up" on their shows, and I loathed being the person singled out for attention. I would have to contrive another method of stapler retrieval.

Curiosity compelled me around the city, first to the castle. Here, writers from the book festival had holed themselves up, reactivating the cannons and threatening a bloodbath if anyone came near. This hadn't stopped the American tourists, who had camped outside in the belief that the Queen opened the castle whenever she felt like it. Over a loudspeaker, poets recited their terse elegies on topical themes, novelists read amusing scenes from their crime capers, their eye-opening memoirs, and first novels about the war and families and wartime families at war, to an uninterested audience. These were punctuated by the public executions of critics who had been rounded up across the city. A gallows had been erected overlooking Princes Street Gardens, where sanguine writers read out their negative reviews, invited the critics to respond, and let the rope take their necks before a regretful oral noise could be made. I was horrified to see the corpses of Joyce McMullane and Stuart Snelly being pecked clean by pigeons, the latter for a criticism of Liam McEwen's "recycled tropes."

On Princes Street, the usual parade of hoopla took place, except inside shops performers lurked in ambush. In the coffeehouses, baristas were free to showcase their talents, reeling off soliloquies, hopping about in suits of armour, and singing a capella renditions of Kraftwerk. In the clothes shops, clown assistants would squirt water from their bowties when you inquired about a loose-fitting pair of slacks. In the police stations, officers would refuse help until the victim watched an agitprop reworking of *The Threepenny Opera*. In the hospitals, surgeons would perform operations while making incisive observations on the clangbirdishness of modern technology. I could tell that the citizens, with their crushed expressions, had been pummelled into submission over the years by the relentless fighting spirit of these performers, hoping to be spotted by any talent-scouts in the vicinity (no talent-scouts remained in the city, the festival having been technically over for two and half years), and that many people had lost their livelihoods. In fact, thousands had to pretend to be struggling actors in order to blend into the fabric of the new Edinburgh. And the fact that performers had made so many people unemployed meant no one had the funds to see their shows, making the possibility of profit impossible. I could see this place had become an unbearable living hell.

Down Fleshmarket Close, I was pulled into an alley and held at knifepoint. "What skill?" my attacker barked. "Nothing . . . I'm here visiting," I said. He released me. "Hop it," he said. "Why the knife attack?" I asked. "We're the Critic's Biteback. We're working in tandem with the People's Revolt to take the city. Are you interested in becoming a member?" At that point, he produced a flyer, the seventy-fifth I had taken that morning, and I skimmed their manifesto. Their main mode of attack was to surround a performer at night and bludgeon them with bad reviews then escort the broken and weeping person to the London train or the North Bridge, whatever option they preferred.

"I need a stapler reclaiming from the News Steps, perhaps I could help," I said.

"A tough one. But I have an idea. Listen." He unravelled his plan for me to distract the performers on the steps, while he crouched in the foliage and whispered excerpts from their negative reviews through a microphone. I would pretend not to hear anything and the frail comedian's egos would explode.

Back to Gordon Harriet. "Listen, I feel terrible for walking off like that," I said. From the bushes: *tiresome, incoherent taff-chaff.* "I would like to hear more about your confessional show, Cardifferent." *Obsessed with masturbation and leering at girls in the audience.* "Growing up weird in Cardiff must have been hilarious." *Relies on spent Welsh stereotypes, and reduces the audience to yawns.* "So what was that ticket price, £10?" Harriet's lip quivered. He dropped the mic and muttered "I have to . . .", howling as he ran towards the 12:52 to Crewe for the connecting train to Cardiff. And on to Step 2: *this talentless bore wilts like the unfunny balloon penises he ties on stage.* And Step 3: *a diabolic diabetic sentences us to an hour of boredom.* And Step 4: *the comedian's auntie would be funnier.* And Step 5: *the laughters never start, the torture never stops.* And in this manner, we sent the chuckle-meisters and their bouncers packing. The hardest to crack was Alan Bongo, with whom we had to resort to personal attacks. We remarked that his wife had a flat face, and that was done.

I found the stapler untouched on the original step. I produced a sheet of paper from my satchel to test. "Some bastard's stolen the staples," I said. "The former capital is seething hotbed of criminal stink." I punched a man named Tristan on a pogo stick to relieve the stress. A gang of pogoing students followed in pursuit, hopping their Oxford revue show *All About That Bounce* around the streets. I lost them at the station, where The Mighty Marauders set upon them with their circus ways, trapping them with ropes and hanging them above Platform 11. It was time to leave this place. I would seek staples elsewhere. I scattered coins indiscriminately to please the artists, and in this way, arrived at the safety of my train. I smiled at the mimes pretending to be snorkellers, and pushed a few pence out the window to say "yes, thank you, I am most amused by your rubbery faces." I strongly hope the Critic's Biteback and People's Revolt work in tandem to expunge these attention-seeking vermin and return Edinburgh to its proud tradition of completely ignoring all these wretched people for a month.

[From *Staplers I Have Known*, Francis Blackmoor, Virginal Books, 2034, p.23-25.]

"The Republic of Hugh"

[MORAY]

Official Senyru* for the Republic of Hugh

In this Republic
there is one Official Man.
His name is Hugh Galt!

Hugh! Hugh!

Our spectacular
Boss Man: seven feet in height—
unlimited might!

Hug Hugh!

Love him and lick him!
Kiss and touch and fellate him!
Hug Hugh for all time!

His Trade

Carpets, rugs, and mats:
no inch of flooring is left
unclad in Hugh's pelt

*A senryu is the non-pastoral version of the Japanese verse form the haiku, with the syllable pattern 5-7-5. —Ed.

His Pate

Short-cropped with cow-lick
regal brown with silver sheen:
follicular bliss!

His Gait

A faultless stride:
two shapely legs in concord
with the Hughniverse

His Mate

Her soft swanlike neck,
sunbed-bronzed, her piercing eyes
that say "I love Hugh!"

His Voice

A booming rasping
throatful of magnificent
hollers, bellows, shouts, and screams!

His Body

An impressive sphere,
BMI of thirty-five
and stately waddle!

His Demeanour

He towers above:
a stern face upon which we
stare in blissful fear!

His Temperament

Torrential rage!
No time for buffoons or fools!
Or blacks or the blind!

His Male Enemies

A man once remarked:
"Hugh is a fat balding c***."
He was beheaded.

His Female Enemies

A woman once said:
"Hugh is an angry turnip."
She was massacred.

His Essence

Heavenly onion
mixed with camphor and petrol
is the scent of Hugh

His Facial Hair

A short strip of black
across one cheek and a tuft
of white on the chin!

His Apparel

Unwashed brown blazer,
chequered blue shirt and bowtie:
GAZE UPON HIS CLOTHES!

His Second Mate

Bigger bosom and
a more bronzed complexion:
hotter than she before!

Our Purpose

Twelve hours cutting
fabrics for the Republic:
we cherish our work!

Our Duties

To absorb ourselves
into one thriving corpus
known as the YouHugh

Our Freedoms

We are free to love!
To laugh and love and pleasure
that one Great Man: Hugh!

Our Music

Mick Hucknall's songbook
comprehensively explored
by Hugh on the mic!

Our Cuisine

Fried eggs, bread, and beans
in three configurations:
our stomachs salute!

Our Minds

We channel our thoughts
along the beautiful node
toward the HughMind

Our Peasants

Building our houses,
keeping our streets clean and safe
for free: or else, Hugh!

On Seeing Hugh in a Crowd

A fleeting whisper
of brown blazer, purple tie
sends us into spasm

On His Autobiography

An infinite work—
at seven volumes per month
Book of Hugh expands!

On Forgetting to Praise Hugh One Morning

Negligent worship
I take the whip and lash hard
my arse for two weeks

On Pleasuring Hugh

An hour's light rimming
precedes a vigorous hump
and soft teabagging

On Being Overcome with Love for Hugh

Take a moment to
stop and breathe then continue
to love Hugh always

On Falling Ill

Fear not, Hugh-lover!
Loving Hugh is better than
costly medicine!

On the Hugh Tax

Ten percent is nought
when one observes that chin on
a passing billboard

On Showing Weakness in Hugh's Presence

He might not notice
or he might authorise the
flaying of your skin

Further Praise for Hugh

1

A lover supreme,
a Technicolour wet dream.
Hugh: A Man Entire

2

One man matters here.
Neither Robert nor Peter.
No! That man is Hugh!

3

From the sack of time
one man takes a colossal
leap: Hugh is his name!

4

Astronomical
super-splendiferousness!
This sums up our Hugh

5

Nice to meet Hugh? No.
You will never meet Hugh Galt.
He cannot be met

6

Take a few minutes
to stop praising Hugh to praise
him at twice the speed

7

Sometimes the best words
in a senryu for Hugh
are simply: "Love Hugh!"

[From *The Official Book of Senyrus Writ for the Praising of Hugh*, George Hughson and Melinda Hughsmith (eds.), Hugh Books, 2053.]

"InfoJog"
[CLACKMANNAN]

RACHEL RECOGNISED her slouching tendencies and fought hard to keep pace with her social jogging group, despite being three months pregnant and desperate for a triple-chocolate muffin. The leader, Jenny Plover, liked to boast that she had been running 5K when seven months along and that her kid had the most incredible energy as a result (neglecting to mention her kid had ADHD). Rachel loathed and idolised the spandex-clad super-mum—she longed for the same stamina and outlook minus the smugness and staggering absence of self-awareness that rendered Rachel's barbs useless against the power of her anti-negative agenda. Her best friend Denise was also a member. Since rising to the managerial heights of her profession she had little time for Rachel's criticism of all inferior beings on the planet or her polished anecdotes about her husband Sean's hilarious shortcomings.

"We're going for the *puuuush* here," Jenny said, sounding her extra *u*'s like a camp ghost, "are you sure about proceeding, Rachel?"

"*Yuuuuuus*, thank you." She wasn't sure—the second éclair at lunch had been a mistake and she suspected she might throw up at the cathedral checkpoint—but maintained the illusion by punching the air (and, by proxy, the face of Jenny's invisible twin on whom she inflicted mental horrors every few seconds).

Denise resumed the monologue she had started at the park entrance. Unlike the meticulously mapped jogging route, her anecdotal style took detours, heading in two directions at once, never quite alighting on sense. The sound of her pally prattle was soothing to Rachel, who had always triumphed at conciser modes of discourse such as insults and sarcastic sneers, and who enjoyed listening to people failing to communicate a single meaningful thought in the space of several hours.

"I couldn't have a tot myself," Denise said, "I couldn't bear peeling back those nappies to the horrors beneath. How can you stand that daily drool, piss, and poop? I can't be doing with screaming and shrieking and that neediness."

"You will."

"Before I forget, do you want to sign up to this new InfoJog scheme?"

"What new InfoJog scheme?"

"It's the latest thing. Joggers pass information between each other during their runs. External information exclusive to us."

"What information?"

"How do I know? It's the latest thing is all."

"It's the latest thing to exchange random information from unspecified sources while jogging? In other words, gossip?"

"No no. I have the pamphlet in my gym bag. It's the latest facts and information from the highest sources. It's kind of an incentive from the government. To get fatties off the couch and out into the park."

"I'll take the pamphlet."

"Do."

Rachel was correct in her prediction and ducked into the cathedral garden upon arrival to release her chunks in a hedge.

"Jogger down!" Jenny cried. She signalled to her second-in-command Fiona for an official stopping of the pedometer and sprinted to Rachel's aid once she'd finished her business to begin the patronising.

"I told you it wasn't a good idea in your state to make the *puuuuush.*"

"*Yuuuuuus*, I know."

"Let's find you a nice sitty place."

"Sitty?"

"You should rest up. When I was running with Gregor, I had a regime of stops-and-starts to keep the foetty fit but not exhausted. I would be sure to have breaks for breathing and flexing before pushing towards the big one. But that's not for everyone. You should nip home for a nap."

"I don't want a fatty foetty. I'll be OK."

"As leader, I encourage you to—"

"Oh fine. I actually wanted to sit on the couch gorging on chocolate and crisps this morning. I should do that."

"Funny!"

Back on the couch she opened a pack of salt and vinegar kettle chips and put her feet up, hurling invective at a mirthless chat show host who patronised his uneducated guests. If some miscreant with a shaven eyebrow wanted to resume his heroin addiction while his obese wife fell pregnant with their fourth kid, it was none of the host's effing business. She cheered on predetermination and booed the host's attempts to strangle their lives into some sort of coherence through abusing their free will like some authoritarian thug. After the break was a couple who refused to take their kid to school because they hated pompous teachers and favoured street wisdom at the School of Hard Knocks. Rachel applauded the couple when they told the host to go fuck himself after he accused them of being layabouts milking the state, and flung crisps at the audience when they ganged up on the rebellious duo.

Denise had passed on the InfoJog pamphlet and Rachel had a read during the commercial break: *InfoJog is a government-sponsored incentive to improve the health of Clackmannan. By offering joggers the opportunity to receive the latest developments in science, politics, education, and entertainment, we hope to encourage a more inclusive attitude to healthiness. Beginners can build their knowledge by taking a brief run around the block, recording their mileage on a special pedometer so we know which materials to send out to the fittest performers! These materials include discs, booklets, and CD-ROMs where the active participant can keep their knowledge base topped up.*

"What an incentive! Because the one thing couch potatoes want to do most is to *learn*," she said, scrunching up the pamphlet and hurling it towards an audience member who had served in two wars and worked in a museum for three decades despite the memory of the dead making his every day a living heck.

Rachel was into her second week of bumgrooving. She had grooved her cheeks on the left cushion, now she required another fortnight to do the right. Denise arrived for a visit during the bum's settling period and opened her dialogue with two paragraphs that were too prattle-filled to be transcribable. Rachel nodded along and offered a coffee.

"No thanks. I have my energin right here," Denise said, sipping from a hip flask.

"Energin?"

"It's a mixture of a sports drink with a wee alcoholic leveller. Lowers bubbles in the blood rate or some such thing. Oh and what did you think of the news? Shocking wasn't it? I had always been a big fan of his."

"What news?"

"You not hear? Rowan Atkinson died in a bus crash with fourteen other people."

"Mr Bean died?"

"Yes. Horrible."

"That's strange, I watched the news ten minutes ago. It wasn't mentioned."

"Oh. I heard it on this morning's InfoJog tape, not the TV. Perhaps he isn't quite so famous any more, doesn't get reported on TV? Anyway, this InfoJog programme is amazing. I learn so much information about all sorts of things as I run. It's an intellectual and physical workout. What could be better?"

"Cake?"

"Careful with that stuff. You don't want to end up a Fatty Filomena after you've given birth, do you?"

"Meh."

Denise soon cracked under threats of cake and left to sprint away the temptation. As Rachel took her second bite of her fourth slice, Sean returned home to announce that his workplace was implementing a compulsory keep-fit scheme. He had never attended a gym in his life and preferred beef dinners with extra spoonings of mash to wheezing his lungs out on a running machine. His company was being sponsored by InfoJog to keep their employees up to date on the latest business developments, meaning if Sean refused to participate, he would fall behind his colleagues and be up for the chop.

"Enforced fitness? What is going on with this InfoJog bullocks?" Rachel asked.

"Their logic is that everyone wants to be fit. So why not combine fitness with working? That's the not the whole story, though. InfoJog withholds information from the slovenly masses. It's not an incentive at all, it's a way of whipping the unfit and feckless into shape, or else. It's a Final Solution, with sweatpants."

"No kidding. Denise told me that Mr Bean died. It wasn't on the news."

"I heard it on the headset as I was panting for my life on a running machine."

"Oh poor you. Tubby men shouldn't be made to run. It just shows quite how awfully they have let themselves go."

"Thanks for that, my lovely."

"I'll polish off the cake, shall I?"

❊

Curling up on the sofa with a tub of Tummilicious Toffee was not an option under the InfoJog scheme. Rachel relied on her harassed and exhausted husband to relay the news upon his return, on those rare occasions he managed to remember half of what he heard. Business information during work hours, the latest news developments during after-workouts. Sean returned so shattered he had to slap himself awake long enough to finish his dinner, falling at the final forkful, up and alert at 2am and dreading the morning ahead. Rachel was unable to converse meaningfully or take part in any connubial activities—the twin poles of sex and television that married couples cling to before children—and forced to call up her married friends and bore them with the highlights of her day (flinging crisps at the TV) and try to glean whatever information she could about what was happening in the universe.

It soon became apparent the informational flow was being dammed up. She watched the television news daily and noticed the increasing trend for the trivial to be featured first. The bulletins would begin with relatively minor crimes—a stabbing in Sauchie or a manslaughter in Menstrie—moving on to a chip pan fire in Tullibody, ending with an extra two or three stories of kittens up trees, old ladies being cared for by neighbours, or millionaires donating 2% of their incomes to charity. One evening Sean came home and informed Rachel someone had tried to stab the Queen of Clackmannan.

"What?!"

"I heard it on the treadmill. A fanatic republican flung a knife from the crowd. It ripped her dress after narrowly missing her right thigh."

"Why wasn't this on the news?"

"I told you. InfoJog. They're saving the most important news for those who get on their bikes."

"This is mental. So those of us condemned to sitting on their lardy bums don't deserve to hear about the Queen being sliced into sixty pieces?"

"Yep. I need to sleep."

"Sean, you need to stop this. You come home and mumble facts at me, I spend half an hour poking you awake so you can shovel frozen chips into your mouth. Then you're up at 2am stomping about and too stressed to shag. This sort of pattern doesn't bode well for our future, does it honeybumptious?"

"No. I need to find something else. I'll hand in my resignation tomorrow."

"Good lad."

"After I quit, I'll have vigorous sex with you, I promise."

"You'd better."

❋

Over the next few weeks, Sean and Rachel dropped off the planet informationally. Sean resigned and spent his days frantically searching for a replacement drudge position in an office for less money. He was dismayed to notice that a new system had been put in place at the Jobcentre where exercise machines had been added to the search terminals, showing more desirable or appropriate positions to those who pushed themselves the hardest. He allowed himself to be swallowed up by apathy, exhausted at the mere thought of having to exercise for work. TV news had skinnied down to the most rudimentary stories—two cars meeting in a one-way street, a photogenic salamander posing for tourists, Z-list celebs and their toenail infections—any vapid viral content on the internet had come to dominate the news agenda to the point where newscasters were leading with clips of old ladies falling over while trying to drunkenly do the Charleston at their granddaughters' weddings. The internet was also finding ways to censor content. New InfoJog 'pantwalls' had been erected where you had to enter your miles-per-day total to access the latest news, verifiable through entering one's official pedometer number.

"There's nothing for it. I'll have to get back on the running machine," Sean said.

"Not only you. There's a scheme in place for preggos too. But look, who cares about any of this? Why do we need to be kept up to date on the news? Who cares what politician is lying this week or what rock star snuffed it last week? Can't we get on with our lives for a while until this stupidity blows over?"

"It won't blow over."

"Let's ignore it. You look for work elsewhere. I'll read books instead of watching the TV. That is, so long as they don't make you do a triathlon before you can check out a Jane Austen."

"Don't tempt fate."

The world continued unchanged until one afternoon the neighbours began sandbagging their front lawns. Sean confronted them about this weirdness but neither was willing to explain since InfoJog was for users only.

"It's The Third World War. It's been declared while we were sitting here eating Doritos," Rachel said, eating a cheese one.

"I think I'm losing my mind," Sean said.

"The world has lost its mind. We're trying to hang on to ours, without having to squeeze our fat arses into lycra."

That night, they went to bed in a dry bedroom. In the morning the place was flooded up around Sean's ankles. The thought had crossed their minds that heavy rainfall might explain the sandbags, but the skyline had been clear the day before. Marooned upstairs in their house, Sean looked out the window to the drowned village, where rescue rafts were being distributed to residents.

"Hey! Send one of those our way, would you?" Sean shouted to a man in a rescue boat. He blanched when he noticed the logo embossed on its side.

"InfoJog password?" shouted the man.

"Don't have one."

"Then we can't issue you a raft, sorry."

"Can I sign up for InfoJog then please?"

"Hang on," the boatman said. He consulted with an operative holding a tablet who made swimming gestures. Sean knew what was coming next.

"You need to do a mile-long swim."

Rachel pushed Sean aside.

"Are you fucking kidding? He'll fucking drown if he tries that."

"Sorry, then we can't—"

"What do you expect us to do, drink the water down with a straw?"

"We can't authorise a raft, sorry."

"I'm pregnant, you fucking robots!"

At which point the boatsmen resumed helping the InfoJog account holders. Rachel went into the spare room and dragged the mattress from the single bed. Sean cottoned on and came to her aid. They forced the mattress out the window and tested for buoyancy. As Rachel attempted to keep it steady against the window, Sean flung himself on face-first and gripped his hands around the two corners, keeping himself afloat by being flat. Once the rocking stopped, Rachel clambered onto his back and managed to swivel around so her body was lying in the opposite direction. Using their arms as oars, they struggled to steer the mattress towards a safe place, following their neighbours in the rafts.

"Why don't you have an InfoJog account?" one neighbour asked.

"Because we didn't realise God was going to restage The Flood right on our front fucking door," Rachel replied. She proved a more efficient paddler, and kept the mattress from spinning around on their way to shallower ground.

Having reached the unflooded portion of the village, they set off on foot to the church to join the bivouac. Sean predicted things were about to get worse. He went inside first so Rachel didn't make a scene. After thirty minutes, he emerged panting and red-faced with a few sandwiches and a bottle of water between two.

"They made you exercise for the food, didn't they?"

"Yes," he wheezed, collapsing on a verge.

They had made him run for thirty minutes on the machine while the su-perfit villagers stared at laughed as he strained to reach the target. "Work that flab, fatso!" one neighbour said. "Faster and we might give your sandwich a filling!" another added. "If you'd listened to InfoJog, you wouldn't be in this mess, lardy!"

An enraged Rachel ran inside and called them all bona fide cast-iron capital-C-words. She caught Denise laughing and chewing on a niblet of let-tuce. She ended the friendship in a glare. And flounced out.

"We'll have to camp outside, won't we?" she asked Sean.

"Yes."

"And you'll have to do that again to get us supper, won't you?"

"Yes."

"Well, at least it's shaping up to be lovely morning."

A rainbow appeared in the bright skyline, which temporarily ailed the dread that passed between them, and temporarily abated the feeling they should have drowned themselves in the flood.

The sandwiches were stuffed with cress.

['InfoJog' by Randall Bloom, a story found perfectly preserved on several sheets of A4 between two boulders in the former Clackmannan, found by the editor, March 2108.]

"Q+A with Hank Righteous"
[SUTHERLAND]

Q: Thank you for talking to us, Hank Righteous.

A: Yes.

Q: You rose to the position of PM in 2034. Could you briefly sketch the events that led to your appointment?

A: Surely, I will. As you know, I was working as a cheesemonger in the Sutherland area when news of the Great Divide broke. I had provided locals with a selection of runny or unrunny brie, cheddar, stilton, or red leicester through catalogue order or in-store purchase for over twelve weeks. The mayor at that time, Alton Kinks, had been elected PM and asked me to provide the cheese portion of his inauguration catering. I accepted. I had to provide cheese nibbles to over one hundred thousand people, so imported seven hundred truckles of the aforementioned cheeses, and set to work on creating a platter fit for one hundred thousand kings. At the ceremony, Alton complimented me on the viscosity of my runniest brie, and asked if I would like a permanent post as his cheese provider in parliament. I accepted.

Q: You had the ear of a powerful man?

A: My kitchen was next to his office. I overheard many conversations while straining the cheese through my special buttery netting. I learned that certain towns and villages in the country wanted further segregation . . . to be made countries in their own right. For example, Helmsdale wished to establish itself as a state of mind. To achieve this, high-voltage smoke machines were brought in to create a dream-like fog, and clouds were lowered from the sky with pulleys to create a strong sense of unreality, with pan pipe and harp music being pumped in from enormous PA systems on the streets. Other places wanted nothing to do with this freaky festival and complained to their MPs. Tain wished to open its doors to the downtrodden and homeless and create a communal utopia based on the sharing and not the hoarding of wealth. Dornoch wished to relocate the populace to a series of airships that would hover above the streets and forbid any land-based occupation. This created schisms.

Q: How was Alton during this?

A: He consumed a damaging quantity of my extremely arid pecorino. I was called in to perform the heimlich manoeuvre in important meetings, and on one occasion the minister for Halkirk exploded with rage after his request for an electric boogaloo was refused. I performed this life-saving manoeuvre and suggested the PM switch to a runnier cheese, like my perilously slippery edam. He refused to switch, however, and it was in a meeting with the minister for Tongue, who wished to relocate the citizens into the eye of a raging cyclone, when he choked on that fatal piece of pecorino, and perished.

Q: Could you describe the events leading up to your coronation?

A: When Alton passed, I was placed under arrest for serving the fatal cheese. As punishment, I was elevated to the post of Prime Minister, as no one else wished to negotiate between the increasingly hostile hamlets. My first meeting was with the minister for Lairg who wished to turn every building into a larger-than-life-size model of a sphincter. He spoke for nine hours with brio and passion, outlining his vision to replace prefab homes and shops with a constantly constricting and unconstricting ring of cleftal muscle. I had to concede that he spoke most eloquently, and I was moved. Once he was permitted independence, the other towns and villages had to be given the same, or they would spit at me. In Rogart, every second man had to chuckle to himself politely or risk assassination. Lochinver was moved into the cortex of Marianne Faithfull. Brora was transformed into an "ouroborough", i.e. a self-eating village. Embo painted their road markings purple in an attempt to show character. Golspie couldn't handle the spotlight and hid under a shoe. Nothing changed in Farr.

Q: And?

A: I remained the minister for Strathy, where there was an overwhelming vote to transfer the place into a softcore pornographic movie from the 1970s. This meant the constant re-enacting of scenarios such as workmen fixing appliances proceeded by seven minutes of passionless staged intercourse, punctuated by unrealistic and overly loud moans before anything erotic had taken place. I never understood Strathy's fever for this way of life, perhaps it had its origins in the one pornographic tape in the village finding its way into circulation shortly before I arrived. So at present I rule over a land of flared trousers, cheap negligees, and the echo of exaggerated shrieks from every home.

Q: Are you happy?

A: I haven't pasteurised stilton in over nine months. I cope.

Q: Best of luck to you.

A: Hmm.

[From 'Interview with PM Hank Righteous', in *The Big Book of Interviews with Prime Ministers*, Penguin, 2030.]

"Trip Advisor Reviews"
[SPEAN BRIDGE]

currylover: The Annual Porcupine Appreciation Festival was splendid. French actress Marine Vacth made a surprise appearance as a twelve-foot porcupine, and the porcupine bouncy castle was terrific larks, if a little prickly on the toes. The two-hour porcupine montage, featuring moving tributes to the crested porcupine, the long-tailed porcupine, Rothschild's porcupine, the bristle-spined porcupine, the Sumatran porcupine, the thick-spined porcupine, the brown hairy dwarf porcupine, and the stump-tailed porcupine, was amazing. The keynote speaker, Alan Sproul, was eloquent on the North American porcupine's penchant for clover, and impressed us with his theory that the first porcupine evolved in the Neogene Period, not the Miocene. The DJ was tremendous, laying down old favourites, like 'Porcupine' by Echo & the Bunnymen, and 'Porcupine' by Joseph Arthur to end the festival. A barbellate ball!

Lorna_K: We're not sure we went to Spean Bridge. It took us two hours to find the place, if it was the right place, there not being a sign towards or in the country. When we stopped to ask for directions, we were met with silent glowers, and one man said: "Don't." Most odd. The place itself was painted blood-red, like in the western *High Plains Drifter*, where the spectre of Clint Eastwood ambushes the gang who killed him. We stopped at the Mortiis Saloon for a cider, and the server, a pale man with trembling hands said to us: "I have tuberculosis". This level of service is appalling. My husband suggested we leave, so we left our drinks and headed to the museum. Inside an otherwise vacant room, in a plastic case, was a llama brain suspended in aspic, and nothing else. I was shocked. My husband looked for the curator to complain, but the backroom was filled with wasps, so we had to flee, as I have an allergic reaction to wasps, which turn my ankles septic. Avoid this place, if you can find it.

Bill_E_Bob: We stayed at the B&B. The scrambled egg was adequate.

solaceseeker: Spean Bridge prides itself on being "the most waterlogged country in the universe", not an idle boast. Located in the basin of Ben Nervous, a mountain that prides itself on "killing the largest number of backpackers in the universe", the buildings are flooded ten or twenty times a year. Frustrated locals have ripped up their homes' foundations and sewn large water wings to their walls, so the properties bob about in the frequent short-lived lakes and puddles. This provokes rage from those whose houses are bumped by the free-floating ones: windows smashed, walls dented, roofs impacted. When we arrived, two residents were firing blunderbusses at each other's children, howling: "No mercy!" It was not a pleasant atmosphere, and since we hadn't packed a canoe or swimming costumes, we moved on.

LionelMac: If Elizabethan pottery is your teacup, then let Spean Bridge do the pouring! I have never seen a more exquisite range of ceramic items in any one small nation, or a curator as passionate about pots and cups as Dorothy O'Shea!

mariecutie: Spean Bridge is not for small children. The forest trail is unsafe, excess silt ruins the prospect of paddling in water, boulders block the central walking route, loud rave music blares from student campsites, menacing mushrooms are within reach of small hands, no changing or toilet facilities are to be found, rabid dogs off their leashes roam the forests, and a naked man with a skullcap tattoo can be seen bathing on the opposite bank. I will be writing to their Prime Minster, if he ever stops bathing.

Chaz: I took one look at this place, said 'nope', and sped past. That said, it might not have been this place I sped past, and I might have said 'hope', because I am a cheery soul.

xoxo34: This country is a hoax. Invergloy, northwards, beams a hologram, southwards, in the shape of a boring village. The only thing to do "there" is browse the highland memorabilia shop, and no one ever purchases an ornamental castle, or packet of overpriced shortbread, ever. So no one has noticed, except me. (I craved shortbread).

altogethernow: Spean Bridge is a state of mind. The state of mind one has after taking a tractor's worth of barbiturates, parading up Red Square in a cockerel outfit, and howling the canon of My Bloody Valentine to the winds. Spean Bridge is sinking one's cerebrum into cool death. To visit Spean Bridge is to blow one's cosmic brains to a patternless splatter. To suicide the real and unlock the hot bubble of lies inside the prism. To slap the alabaster logo on the fruitiest uncle in the pavilion. To incite the loon to the River Styx. To orangeade the worthiest nobleman on the plateau. To coax the marvellous manic into haughty slaughter. To overuse the salt shaker on a tape recorder. To repress the magnanimous spirit of a Labour chiseller. To re-write the night into an ultra-bright striped light. Bing-boom. Visit SB.

andyhandy: Here are directions: follow the A82 to Fort William. At the time of writing, there is a £3,500 pass-toll, so please raise that sum in advance of your trip, or you might end up incarcerated in a schooner for a few decades. This happened to my sister, who was kicking herself later. Next, make a sudden left when you see the tyre tracks that veer toward a field. Drive across the field, following the tracks for two hours. When you see some twigs beside a gymnasium, stop and ask Greg Alison for directions. If Greg's not sitting on the iron-age hill fort, he might be urinating in the gym lavatories. Wait for Greg. He will direct you, in Welsh (activate your live translation app), to the forest that you need to enter to access Spean Bridge. This part of the trip takes place on foot. I have never finished the forest trek, having lost a knuckle en route, but friends say that when you arrive, there's a nice statue of someone. Bring a packed lunch and a rocket launcher in case of pterodactyl attack.

crabhandler43: We stayed at the The Bawdy Gherkin B&B on Altour Road. The room was fine, except for the manservant who insisted on remaining in the room the whole time. After a day, we were used to his presence, and his helpfulness. He passed the lubricant when were making love, and helped me recall trivia, such as who won the 1995 world snooker championship (Stephen Hendry). At night, he would sit upright in a chair and breathe heavily, muttering the name "Alison" over and over, which was strange at first, then helped us sleep. I always pictured the lovely actress Alison Steadman from the Mike Leigh films. Apparently, the B&B burned down soon after our stay, which is a shame.

applecore24: I can clear up the confusion. This "country" is called Spleen Bridge, and is in fact a bridge made from the columns of former *Daily Mail* content writers. When the newspaper invaded Kent in 2020, that robust Anglo-Saxon county mounted a merciless retaliation, spearing over four thousand proofreaders, sub-editors, columnists, and interns, and executing the editor Paul Ducker on live television, to the merriment of one billion viewers. The paper's archives were used as ballast for various structures, among them Spleen Bridge, which contains over two thousand columns from the likes of Richard Littlejohn, Katie Hopkins, Quentin Letts, Rod Liddle, and other choleric commentators who struggled with basic human empathy, before the residents of Kent speared them in the brains. I worked on the construction of this fine edifice, which has become a popular attraction for nice people.

abstractnotions: There's nothing here except a single bowl of soup balanced on an upturned coracle. Leek and potato.

[Reviews of Spean Bridge from tripadvisor.com, accessed via the internet archive, October 9, 2108.]

"The Fictional Village of Echt"
[ECHT]

FOREWORD

T HE VILLAGE OF ECHT *in 2057 was transformed into a "fictional village", with the 300-odd residents turned into characters in an ongoing work of fiction. Although there are no plans to publish the work in its unabridged form (i.e. to render into prose every waking hour of every 'character' in the village), certain vignettes in the lives of these 'people' have been committed to print. The following represents a selection of these. As you will see, the residents struggle daily to conform to their 'character' labels, and to remain eminently readable. Readers who find these stories inconclusive, unsatisfying, or pointless, should bear in mind the village of Echt only has one resident writer, THE LITERARY CHARACTER, who at the time of this foreword is at work on 298 abridgements of the lives of the Echt populace.*

THE LIKEABLE CHARACTER

Victor is the Likeable Character. Victor is popular in the fictional village of Echt. Victor has two daughters, Claire and Nora, and works as a ticket inspector on the local rails. Victor has a line in humorous repartee and inoffensive banter on the trains, in the pub, and in the shops and streets. He remembers little details about his passengers and is polite but firm when handling fare dodgers. His wife is a soft-spoken woman who people think is too sour and unattractive. He seeks nothing from people and keeps to himself and is never too smug or too humble or too omnipresent or too hilarious or too boring. He was eating soup with his sour wife Alison when he popped a notion on her fleece cardigan.

"I think I might start up a skiffle trio." Alison ceased blowing her minestrone.

"What?"

"I've been tweeting these chaps from Dunecht. I have long nursed visions of frotting the washboard on a stage."

"Honey, we've nibbled on this rotten beef before. Your likeable character will be compromised if you're seen on stage stroking a mangle like a washer-woman."

"Stop calling it a mangle. You can't tease rhythm from that awkward washing apparatus."

"And you call that sheet of ribbed metal an *instrument*? You'll humiliate yourself if you step on stage with that. Your likeability will be vaporised the minute everyone in the village watches you in mid-hunch fingering those ribs."

"Pass the salt."

"Honey, you—"

"SALT."

Alison overrode their saline safe word to ram the point home. She painted a visual Hieronymus involving Gillian Gordon the village halfwit snickering into her egg cream and Daniel Vim the village intellectual staring in open contempt at the sight of a once-liked figure of solidity making a musical buffoon of himself to achieve some ridiculous ambition that yielded no commercial or personal dividend. During their routine coitus that night she broke her promise that she would never (since that time) nag into his ear several moments before climax to imprint her point on his sexual recall. But she inserted 'forget the skiffle' into her mmms and ooohs, causing him to cancel his oncoming coming in favour of a fast withdrawal and an artless squirm from the duvet to the floor to dressing gown to the bathroom and an enraged erectionless return to spew vitriol into her sour ear. This tactic ensured that for several weeks, before climax, Vic would remember this painful nag and shrivel up with contempt for his annoying wife, and lose his ardour entire.

THE (NON-)BLOGGING CHARACTER

The most authentic form of self-loathing blog is never written. Damon wrote this on his blog. He was seeking a compromise between not writing to express his true contempt for the act of blogging and the need to reach out and communicate a message to someone somewhere. As he explained to his mother:

"The self-loathing non-blogger community, who have no qualms about expressing themselves in the comment section, have roared up in hate. Nothing2Say said: 'Your blog is a lie. You want acknowledgement for a statement we all know to be true, but never speak out of collective understanding. You have violated the one rule in the non-blogging community, and that is never to blog. You are banished forever.' H8M8s said: 'Fail. You tried to wangle some loophole in writing this obvious statement. But in writing this, you have placed yourself on the streets with the other word-whores seeking validation for their pointless utterances.' Paul_Si said: 'I will urinate on this blog in a violent frothing stream until the end of time.'"

"Such hateful spume," his mother said.

"I made a mistake. I had such a craving to express something and receive positive feedback I couldn't control myself." Damon spooned scrambled egg into his sad non-blogging face. He was the character who didn't blog.

He had wrestled with the prospect of writing things in a world where opinions, stories, screams and sobs filled the internet like unrelenting textual flatulence, and chanced upon a cult of non-writers who used their silence to make a powerful statement about the aimless pummel of modern babel. The non-blogging world emerged: thousands of blogs titled 'a non-blog' with post after post of blank space. Non-tweets and non-statuses and non-instagrams (non-pictures of white space) followed. The main criticism of the movement was that they too were attempting to communicate a message about how everyone was obsessed with attempting to communicate a message, but their silence was to be seen as a corrective, political act and not a self-enabling one. Damon, like a million others, used them to justify his writer's block as a rebellious act.

THE LACONIC CHARACTER

B., a curt man, ate an egg.

THE SYMPATHETIC CHARACTER

In the fictional village of Echt, Annie Lettuce was the inhabitant most likely to elicit sympathy. Her husband had consumed six ciders and steered his removal van over a steep cape, causing nine months of coma vigil and eventual snuff. During this time, she had miscarried her firstborn. These events sealed her status as the Sympathetic Character. For a year, she maintained a mourning face, and endured the kindly simpers, the careful words, the outpourings from other poor sods whose sufferings were not as significant, and sat in her living room eating prawn crackers and putting on mounds of pounds. She went to the pub more, leading people to speculate she was becoming an alcoholic. One night, she met the new barman Scurf.

"These people want me to become a bloated old spinster trapped in memories of her dead husband and unborn child," she said to him after two daiquiris.

"Wow. Quite an opener."

"For a few months, I was hooked on the sympathy. People were so nice to me. It helped with the endless sucking aching fucking misery, leeching on me from morn to nicht. It then twigged. I was a watermark for suffering. These people wanted me steeped tit-deep in weeping woefulness. Because, hey, they might have it tough, but at least they're not that snivelling heap of a human being over there. I mean me."

"I see your point."

"Your face is seriously something I'd like to lick. When's your shift over?"

Annie Lettuce rode Scurf for two hours, and thereafter, rode him for two hours every other night for three weeks until he collapsed crying in defeat and returned to his mum's house in Dunecht. She committed herself to a programme of excessive sexual pandemonium: mounting the man at the mountain bike shop, humping the haberdasher on a hillside, screwing the salesman in his Sierra, nailing the nice chap from the nature reserve in a nook. Actions she considered essential for busting free her prison of pain were seen in the village as further cries for help, and the sympathy for her skyrocketed. Even the sneering librarians who loathed the village felt their ice-packed exteriors loosen in a simper of understanding.

THE LIKEABLE CHARACTER

Victor was in the shed hiding from his wife's persistent reminders that washboards were for unlikeable morons, and that men stroking them in public were contemptible sissies, when the package containing a washboard arrived. He hacked open the cardboard and ogled his authentic musical brass washboard shipped from Melbourne. The thimbles had been included for free. He emailed the musicians from Dunecht—Alexei the ukulele player and Phil the fiddler—a picture of his washboard prefaced by six ecstatic grinning emoticons, and fingered the instrument with tender tip-taps.

"This feels right," he said to the lawn mower. The idea was to form a New Orleans busker band like Yes Ma'am or The Blair Street Mugwumps and perform in pubs or pound the pavements in cities. The addition of a cowbell and woodblocks at the washboard's base would enhance the percussive clout of the instrument, with perhaps the daring surplus of a cymbal, but these were things to be considered later.

As he practised on the sly, meeting Alexei and Phil in a school music room in Dunecht for improvised skiffle-making merriment, his self-satisfaction increased to noticeable levels. Passengers on the trains observed a shift in his manner from pleasant to overly chipper, and residents commented on the public whistling and semi-skipping stride, like a bad actor hamming the part of a 'happy' person. His likeability, as Alison predicted, was already being compromised. Refusing to swallow his lie about a pub bowling team, she inspected the shed and found a thimble sitting atop a paint can.

"Show me your fingertips," she said to him when he walked in at midnight after an evening of vigorous frottoir abuse.

"I bowl hard," he said. She noted the hard skin and evidence of dried blood consistent with washboard attack.

"You lie hard. You are scraping our lives away, all for the illusion of purpose that a mid-life skiffle trio brings. If you persist in fingering this metal in private, I will have no choice but to file for divorce and evict you from your children's lives." Victor staggered to the sofa for a night of soulgazing. He was the Likeable Character. He had one function: to be likeable, and his interest in music tolerated by people in pubs, tolerated by harassed shoppers on high streets, and tolerated by the musicians who can't write their own songs, was sending him on a hoedown to characterly oblivion.

THE LACONIC CHARACTER

B., in church, took a wife.

THE OBSCURE CHARACTER

—Tell me, Carter, have the screen transmissions of Alex Van Warmerdam ever throbbed upon thine hazelnut orbs?

—No sir, I am a greengrocer. I favour the tomato and the parsnip.

—I have, for the last nine weeks, slipped into a slit not unlike the audiovisual slits inhabited by the cinematic personae in the surreal features from the Dutch filmmaker whose name I spoke in the opening clause.

—I favour the cauliflower.

—Now, Carter, I moved to the fictional village of Echt in March. The last time we exchanged nouns was when I ordered that kayak of sprouts. I ate them in one sitting to help in the war against pancreatic cancer.

—Five thousand sprouts, sir.

—That is correct. I was not to realise that Echt was an inexact replica of the incomplete Dutch new town as shown in *De Noorderlingen* (*The Northerners*): a single street in a sandbox, like a set in the rotting lot of some forgotten western. The characters in that transmission: a sex-crazed butcher whose celibate wife is stricken with an inexplicable sickness, a postman taken to steam-opening letters with a kettle secreted in the neighbouring woods, an impotent huntsman with a penchant for blasting trespassers, a 12-year-old obsessed with the Belgian Congo, and more bewildering sorts of Dutch sorts.

—Peculiar.

—I have since become a connoisseur of the oeuvre of Warmerdam. There are nine carnivals of mischief and chaos to peruse. Among them the warped fable *De Jurk* (*The Dress*), a haunting rumination on capitalist possession in which a leaf-patterned frock spells sour consequences for each wearer. In *De Laatste Dagen Van Emma Blank* (*The Last Days of Emma Blank*), an acidic and tragicomic marvel, a moribund woman makes her relatives act as servants in order to apportion her estate. And there's *Abel*, a black farce in which a manchild tries to snip flies in half with a pair of scissors.

—Halt! Are these visual divertissements available for commercial purchase?

—Several. The slow creeping oddness of *Borgman* and the unconventional hitman thriller *Schneider v. Bax*. I favour the metafictional larks of *Ober* (*Waiter*), in which a brooding "modern character" bickers with his creator over the script's atrocious plotlines and botched relationships. And *Kleine Teun* (*Lit-*

tle Tony), where an alphabet tutor is embroiled in a love triangle in order to secure a sprog. These capsule puffs are meagre when confronted with the screen fact of the wonder of the what.

—MP4s, mon ami?

—I will return with a USB. For now, perhaps a carrot?

—Twelve or sixteen?

—Five carrot.

—Here.

—Yes.

THE ANGRY CHARACTER

"There is no reason to be calm and content," said Lee, the Angry Character, to Charlene, his lover who was leaving. "The sprouts have been burned and the leaders are self-adoring despots with missile silos on their lawns and the rain is hammering the roof hour after hour and the cat is choking on a furball and these trousers have seven separate holes and the sun never shines on the lost and hopeless and the laughter is bitter not carefree and the beans have burned on the bottom of the pan and the critics serve the companies and the internet is not radicalising the right people and all cute little pandas are becoming extinct and there is still no complete PJ Harvey B-Sides album commercially available and one coherent thought per week is an achievement in this fact-packed era and the lies pile up like horse manure on the public consciousness and the toothbrush cup is caked in permanent mould."

"Where's my mobile?" Charlene asked.

"There is no mobile because the chickens have been strangled and the spinal caries are more painful than ever and the best in show is a rancid pug and the scoutmaster votes UKIP and the pubs never have music I like and the men are smug self-regarding wits who like their faces and Leonard Cohen is no longer fucking alive and there are more misspelled words than there are words and the laptop keeps crashing before I can save things and the teenagers across the street might never realise that their rebellion is corporate-sponsored and the ladle has partial burning from that aborted chilli and Auntie Marie has to lift crates at the age of 69 to survive and coastal erosion is still a serious agricultural potato and the sound of silence is never available and the electric toothbrush needs charging every after brush."

"Lee, I need to catch the bus. It's been . . ."

No end to the sentence was required. Lee completed it once she'd scrammed. "A time of splatting tomatoes against the wall. A time of expensive and ultimately pointless reconstructive surgery. A time of lips being bitten and blood snaking down chins. A time of pirouetting around the point like talentless prancers. A time of dredging merriment from the foulest wells. A time of sealing up hopes like hated wives in drywall. A time of blowing experimental jazz sax into each other's lugs."

THE LIKEABLE CHARACTER

Victor was no longer a man married to a wife. She removed the children from his zone of skiffle to a permanent huff in her parents home in Dunecht. He had refined an acceptable scrape on his washboard and was awaiting the pub performance like a peak-time child an upcoming Santa Conference in Lapland. He had coutured The Dun 'n' Echt Players (their name) for minimum annoyance and maximum likeability: their smocks were hewn in inoffensive acrylic in tepid reds and blues, and their clodhoppers were commercial and unamerican. The on-stage banter would trade on common clashes between Dunners and Echters: how Dunners import seven tonnes of oranges per annum, how Echters support Norwegian football team SK Brann because King Magnus VII stopped in Echt for water in 1332, how Dunners close their shops at 1.45pm, how Echters censor BBC4 on their satellites, how Dunners conclude their colloquies with Nipponese nods, how Echters curse in front of their children, and so on. Victor would keep his expression neutral while frotting on stage.

The Idle Stevedore was the pub. The whole village, minus the bedridden and clinically repulsed, were in attendance. The band stepped onstage and opened their set with 'Wabash Cannonball', the A.P. Carter standard. The crowd reacted with polite tolerance for the first song. Halfway through the second, 'Rag Mama Rag', the crowd clenched their toes, realising the whole two-hour set would sound the same, and the first bud of hate blossomed in their hearts. As the folk merriment continued, Alexei and Phil became uncomfortable at the forced applause and open stares of contempt into fifth and sixth beers, and announced the seventh song would be their last. Victor, exhilarated and blind to the crowd's hate, piped up that they had fifteen planned. "Come on, let's keep this momentum up!" he said. That utterance stripped the last vestige of Victor's likeability, making him the most hated man to ever open his mouth in the village. All because of a cheap imported washboard.

THE INAPPROPRIATE CHARACTER

"Is it wrong to have the hots for your mum in photos taken before you were born?" Max asked the photo of his mum. He regarded the young visage of his twenty-two-year-old mother: a visage nothing like the sixty-three-year-old visage of his current mother's visage. He pondered on this for an hour. Towards the end of this hour, an erection materialised in his underwear. This was a new development. "Is this erection an excitement at the taboo, or a proper arousal at thoughts of my young mother's visage?" There was no way of answering this. The erection was the problem and the erection needed a solution. He retired to the bed to remove the erection with masturbation. Once complete, he pondered on the shame and the pleasure. He had masturbated with the image of his twenty-two-year-old mother in mind: however, this might have been part of the taboo, and not an indication of a yearning to possess the body of his younger mother. Aside from constructing a time-machine, there was no means to separate the truth from the taboo. He chose to keep the picture and masturbate to the image from time to time: after a week or so, the erections subsided. He was none the wiser.

THE LACONIC CHARACTER

B., at last, had a bath.

THE SYMPATHETIC CHARACTER

Annie continued her exploration of male torsos on ill-lit commons and car bonnets. The unbridled freedom she indulged in was sealing her into an un-expected tomb of misperception. This became apparent when she performed coitus at an unusual elevation on the bonnet of a funeral car parked in the graveyard. The mourners showed not the expected shock that Annie had pre-dicted (seeing her sex partner was the bereaved husband): mere compassion sparkled in their lugubrious oculi. Some even placed an understanding hand on her naked shoulder to indicate: "You are trapped in an *uzumaki* of madness. Your cerebrum is a Nanking of shredded thoughts." In fact, she wanted to scream: "No! I have at last been released from the insistent fronds of wallow. These illicit romps showcase a fresh Annie Lettuce, not the so-called 'Iceberg Lettuce' that wags have been caricaturing."

In other words, happiness was seeping back into Annie's life. She dedicated each sexual moment to her lost husband. She was considering a two-day trip to North Berwick with the most agile of her lovers. She thought about working for a living again without picturing herself in a hot bath with slit wrists. To help kill the village-wide sympathy, wafting round her like a hippo's cologne, she applied for the post of traffic warden. Sneaking up on cars emergency parked for desperate loo visits, to collect infirm relatives, or to pick up small children, and slapping penalties on them in a black uniform would correct her character. Unfortunately, most employers in the village, while understanding of her problems, were not so understanding as to employ her, for fear her unhinged past might repeat itself all over their balance sheets.

THE _____ CHARACTER

Chester entered a room. The sort of room Chester entered was unclear since Chester lacked a label. If Chester was the amusing character, he might enter a pub and reel off several zingers to local zinger-lovers. If Chester was the insane character, he might enter a room in his mind while in reality standing in an irrigation ditch. Since Chester lacked a label, the room Chester entered will remain undefined. "Does anyone have a label I can borrow?" Chester asked. There was either no one there, someone there, or more than one someone there. As it happened, a man was present. "Keep this on the QT," the man said (a cipher like Chester), "by the river at midnight labels are on sale. Be careful. You might not inherit a label you can handle." Chester nodded and exited the room. He suspected this unlabelled man once had a label that had backfired from the implied caution in his toneless voice. He waited until midnight. He displayed no traits and carried out no actions until the label-seller arrived. An excessive man with nine chins, four stomachs, twelve noses, and two tails approached Chester in a bounding slouch. "Looking for a label?" he asked in a loud hushed miserable ecstatic tone. "You might not like what you receive. As you can see, I am incubating a motley of undesirable labels." Chester said nothing. "You label-less kids are some talkers. You ever thought about carving a label for yourselves?" Chester said nothing. "Right. You might end up the label-carving character. I see. Now, I have activated the label randomiser. Once you have your label, you will pay me £250 within four weeks. In the event your label renders you incapable of making money, please sign this life insurance policy." Chester signed. In several seconds, the label-seller had vanished and the time was 7.30am. He awoke by the river as The Unlabelled Character. "What the fuck?!" he shouted. "I already was the unlabelled character!" This was untrue. No label had been assigned to his character. 'Unlabelled' was in itself a label. He was a complete blank. He had now inherited a label in the form of 'unlabelled', with all the consequences and traits this label might imply. "Fuck this shit!" he shouted and ran along the riverbank in search of the vanished label-seller.

THE (NON-)BLOGGING CHARACTER

Damon considered the nothing he had written. He had spent two hours not writing the follow-up post to his controversial one-liner: *'The most authentic form of self-loathing blog is never written'*. He could either return to the non-blogger community, and risk the wrath of their ranks, or make a textual stand. At two minutes before midnight he wrote 'Boo!' in the text box and posted a titleless post.

"The self-loathing blogger community left their warm excreta in the comments again," he said to his mother. "ShutUpNow said: 'This infantile provocation of our community, from which you have been forever banned, merely shows a pathetic need to reconnect with us. You can scream nothing from the rooftops, not write a million non-books, or vanish from the net entirely: there is no way back." Kwi_8 said: "Fail. Your pathetic poke is as meaningless as the rest of the claver clogging up the net. A perfect illustration of our vitality." Moe_Ack said: "I would block this blog from the universe if I had God's IP address."

"Tetchy bissoms," his mother said.

"I have an agenda. I will write. I will write words until those word-hating halfwits acknowledge that words are better than non-words."

He began an unrelenting assault on the non-blogging community. He wrote one hundred posts per day, among them: 'This nothing is better than their non-nothing.' 'This redundant sentence is better than their non-sentences.' 'This series of words is better than their non-series of non-words.' And so on. His intention was to crush the community with a verbal torrent and unleash an online revolution of crazy, inventive, spectacular language Pollocking across the page in a passionate pirouette, a never-ending universal tag-team of tremendous writing leading to a new, endlessly updated canon of timeless literature. He completed his millionth post.

THE _____ CHARACTER

Chester ambushed the label-seller one evening. He leapt onto his second back and wrapped his fingers round his ninth neck. The label-seller punched him off with the third arm in his second back and pinned Chester to the cobbles with his fourth foot. "A problem?" the label-seller asked. "This character isn't a character," Chester forced from his stressed throat. "Ordinarily, I wouldn't tolerate such an unprovoked attack. However, I can see the confusion you experience," the label-seller said in a furious ebullient impartial tone. "Your label is 'unlabelled', so effectively, you have landed a rare sort of freedom. You can be anything for a brief period: a happy evangelist, a wry sous chef, a sexually voracious newsreader, a maniacal ballet instructor, a boisterous snow plough operator, whatever. But since you're unlabelled, you must never stick to a label for too long. Understand?" Chester was allowed to rise. "Isn't someone who shifts from personality to personality considered insane? I'll be perceived as the insane character." The label-seller sighed and whooped with delight and cried. "Look, I'm a dispenser, not a God. You interpret your label whatever way you want. Be here in four weeks with the £250, OK?" Chester watched the label-seller vanish under the bridge singing a showtune and cursing the moon and petting a pug. He sat on a stone and considered his new unlabelled role. Having no role made him depressed so he chose to be depressed for a while. He returned to Echt and ordered a rum at a bar called The Extracted Bicuspid. "You're looking woe-faced," the barman said. Chester panicked as the nearby bar-sitters heard the remark. "No! No!" he said with a faked smirk. "I am cheerful. I was in thought about something. Not woe-faced. Cheerful." He paid for the rum and skulked in a booth.

THE POLITICAL CHARACTER

The politics of Echt: once, a proud right-leaning place (in part because the village sank towards the right-leaning cape), then a less-proud left-leaning place (a cash sum was spent to 'correct' the village towards the left to prevent subsidence), then a place of political pandemonium. Since the costly corrective procedure, the villagers had been consistently inconsistent politically, wavering between left- and right-wing views, from the abolition of tuition fees, to the reduction of the minimum wage, to the slicing of corporate taxes, to the enormous increase in employment benefits. George Hauser MP represented Echt in parliament. After nine weeks of these contradictory, unpartisan opinions, George lost control over his political party's views, the left- and right-wings took flight into the political ether.

Before taking the late-night train to his Echtminster hotel, he chaired a constituency surgery, arriving at the office unshaven and sweaty-palmed. He smirked at the hostile constituents, narked that their incoherent views were not being represented. The fuming villagers began their tirade. First to enter was the bowl-cut bruiser Patricia Rice, who was never far with her scowling face and unapplauding hands.

"I am fed up with these immigrants working here. My Bradley had to travel to Dunecht to find work. That's an hour commute each way. I am also sick of these innocent immigrants living in fear of deportation."

"So you want to kick the immigrants out and let them stay in the country?"

"Is that so hard to understand? Now, Mr. Hauser, will you raise this issue in parliament, or will I have to write to the Prime Minister?"

"I promise to raise the issue. Thank you."

"Listen here," said Allan Tibor. "I am sick of that bridge toll. It costs £2 to come in and out of Echt. That is £10 a week, £40 a month, and £480 a year. That is a fortune for the likes of me. And another thing. How can we recoup the expense of building the bridge, and pay the toll operators, without having that toll in place?"

"So you want the toll scrapped and the toll to remain in place?"

"He listens at last!"

"I will mention this."

"You politicians are useless," said Meredith Oik. "I have told you, if you increase benefits, the lazy scroungers will sit there in their pants for even longer.

And if you decrease them, these poor people won't have enough money for basic necessities."

"So they should stay the same?"

"*Not what I am saying!* God, you people never *listen*. I am saying cut the damn benefits and increase the damn benefits!"

"Noted. Thanks for coming."

"You're all the same," said Mark Tremors, "only interested in yourselves. I want you self-interested rodents to have no expenses. I'm not paying for your night at the Ritz. And I'll tell you what. You do such a difficult job. You deserve a very generous wage, and any expenses that might ease the stress of representing us."

"So a wage increase and decrease?"

"You understand!"

"Cheers, Mark Tremors."

"Dog shit everywhere!" said Rick Pimms, "I can't stand these foul mutts and their foul owners! A fine of two hundred pounds per poo! And I hate how there's nowhere to deposit the poobags for us dog-lovers. Those fines are unfair! More poo bins!"

"Thanks for coming."

THE LACONIC CHARACTER

B. swat a bee.

Further stories forthcoming, featuring: THE SEXUALLY EXHAUSTIVE CHARACTER; THE CHARACTER INCLUDED FOR THE SAKE OF HAVING A 50TH CHARACTER; THE UNREMARKABLE IN EVERY WAY CHARACTER; THE PRIMLY NAIVE CHARACTER; THE FRIGHTENINGLY OFF-KEY NEIL DIAMOND IMPERSON-ATOR CHARACTER; THE BELIEVABLY REAL FICTIONAL CHAR-ACTER; THE CHARACTER WITH TWO OTHER CHARACTERS INSIDE HER; THE UNFUNNY AND RATHER CRABBY FORMER ASTRONAUT CHARACTER; THE CHARACTER WHO ONLY HAS BAD THINGS TO SAY ABOUT BRIX SMITH; THE CHARACTER

WHOSE LEFT EYEBROW LOOKS SHAVEN, ARMY-STYLE, BUT
UPON CLOSER INSPECTION THIS PROVES BOGUS; THE CHAR-
ACTER WHO SCOFFS AT NATURE DOCUMENTARIES BUT WHO
METICULOUSLY RECYCLES; THE CHARACTER WHO IS MALE
BUT WHO CLAIMS TO BE POST-MALE; THE DENNIS HOP-
PER FANATIC CHARACTER; THE CHARACTER WHO WRITES
GLOWING REVIEWS OF JONATHAN COE NOVELS BUT SHARES
THEM WITH NO ONE; THE CHARACTER WHO ONLY EATS
SALMON; THE OVERRATED OR UNDERRATED CHARACTER;
THE POST-MALE SHE-MALE CHARACTER WHO HATES E-MAIL;
THE CHARACTER WHO INSISTS YOU TRY HER HOLOGRAM-
MIC CASSEROLES, THEN ACTS OUTRAGED WHEN YOU MIME
AN EATING AND APPRECIAITING MOTION, AS THOUGH IN
PLAYING ALONG WITH HER HOLOGRAMMIC CASSEROLE CHA-
RADE, YOU HAVE SOMEHOW BETRAYED HER; THE CHARAC-
TER BASED ON THE WRITINGS OF THE LITERARY CHARAC-
TER; THE CHARACTER WHO BARES NO COINCIDENTAL RE-
SEMBLANCE TO OTHER CHARACTERS IN HIS VICINITY; THE
CHARACTER WHO COULDN'T CARE LESS IF YOU FIND HER
ANTICS LOVEABLE, ACCESSIBLE, REALISTIC, OR WHATEVER,
AND WHO SIMPLY DRINKS, FUCKS, AND CURSES WHENEVER
SHE PLEASES, NOT REALISING THAT PEOPLE LOVE THOSE
TRAITS, AND SHE IS REALLY EVERYTHING SHE PURPORTS NOT
TO BE; THE CHARACTER WITH A TRENDY GOATEE WHO IS
WORKING ON A CLAYMATION ADAPTATION OF HAROLD PIN-
TER'S MOST OBSCURE PLAY; THE CHARACTER WHO STAYS UP
TO 1AM WRITING SILLY CHARACTER NAMES; THE IMMATURE
CHARACTER WHO HILARIOUSLY MISINTERPRETS HIS NAME
AND SPENDS ALL DAY STANDING IN MANURE; THE CHARAC-
TER WHO NEVER MAKES REFERENCES TO WELSH-LANGUAGE
SOAP OPERAS; THE CHARACTER IN LOVE WITH CADNO FROM
POBOL Y CWM; THE CHARACTER WHO BURSTS INTO CRAZY
SPONTANEOUS DANCING AT THE SOUND OF CUPBOARDS
OPENING; THE CHARACTER WHO SPENDS AN HOUR CHOOS-
ING AN ICE CREAM AT THE ICE CREAM TRUCK, THEN UPON

RECEIPT OF THE ICE CREAM OF THEIR CHOICE, LAUNCHES INTO A LOUD, VIOLENT TANTRUM, CLAIMING THAT WAS NOT THE ICE CREAM THEY WANTED, AND THREATENS TO SUE ANY-ONE WHO SAYS ANY DIFFERENT, UNTIL SOMEONE ARRIVES WITH A BROWN PAPER BAG CONTAINING EVERY ICE CREAM FLAVOUR EVER MADE, WHEREUPON THEIR MAD OUTBURST IS REPLACED BY GUSHING APOLOGIES AND TEARS, AND THE ANNOUNCEMENT THAT THEY HAVE LOST THEIR APPETITE FOR ICE CREAM; THE CHARACTER WHO WASN'T THERE; THE CHARACTER WHOSE TIME AT DUNKIRK WAS CUT SHORT BY THE ARRIVAL OF A CREOSOTE PARCEL; THE CHARACTER WHO STOOD ON THE TRAIN PLATFORM ALL WEEKEND, AND SHE NEVER CAME; THE CHARACTER WHO ALWAYS CONTRADICTS THE PREVAILING ORTHODOXY, BUT WOULDN'T DREAM OF CONTRADICTING THE PREVAILING WIND.

[From *Tales from the Fictional Village of Echt*, THE LITERARY CHARACTER, Unbound. Foreword, THE CHARACTER WHO WRITES ONE FORE-WORD.]

"Vestibule Chairs"

[ANGUS]

Dear Albert,

I am the editor of a work-in-progress volume, *Scotland Before the Bomb*. As you know, the nation formerly known as Scotland was completely destroyed in a merciless nuclear strike in 2060. I am working hard to assemble a collection of documents that attempt to present a piecemeal picture of what the nation was like before its inhabitants were removed from the map by a Luxembourgian lunatic. We have it on authority that you used to live in the country of Angus and might be able to supply us with some information about that nation. I have been searching intensely for up to nine months, so I would strongly appreciate any response.

Yours respectfully,
Mark Nicholls

Dear Mark

Thank you for your email. I would like to furnish you with some information about Angus, however, I will have to request a fee, since my time is precious. This fee should be at least in triple figures.

Yours,
Albert Spatch

Dear Albert,

Thanks for the reply. Unfortunately, I am unable to offer a fee in triple figures. If there is any information you could supply pro bono, I would be appreciative.

Yours,
Mark

Hi Mark
Nothing for free, however, for £20 at a time, I will reveal a piece of information. My Paypal email is this one.
Best
Albert

Hi Albert
I have transferred £20 to your account. Please supply some information.
Best
Mark

Hi Mark
Thank you for the money. Here is a piece of info: the chair in my vestibule was cherry red.
Best,
Albert

Dear Albert
Thank you for this information. This isn't the sort of thing I had in mind. I was more interested in facts about the political landscape, the nature of governance, the social mores of the country, that sort of thing, not personal details

about your home furnishings. Since I transferred the money on a trust basis, I would appreciate some more significant facts on the nation of Angus, if possible.

Best
Mark

Mark

I told you, my vestibule chair was cherry red. This was when I lived in Angus. If you want any other facts, please transfer another £20.

Al

Albert

If I transfer another £20, I would need assurance from you that the fact you supplied me with was not one about your own furnishings, and something of historical import. If you can make that promise, I will transfer.

Mark

Mark

Yes, I can promise. Please transfer.

Al

Al

Money transferred.

M

Mark

Thank you for the £20. Here is a historical fact for you. In the Prime Minister's wife's vestibule, the winged chair was auburn.

Best of luck with your project,
Al

Al

Clearly, you are not taking this seriously, or know nothing about Angus. Or you are simply seeking to milk me for easy money, because you are the only person I was able to find who lived there. Although I transferred the money voluntarily, if you are any sort of gentleman, I would appreciate you returning the funds to me.

Best
Mark

Mark

No can do on returning the funds. I have to say, I find your attitude towards my information on vestibule furnishings rather bizarre. As an editor, these facts should be of enormous import to your book. If you transfer another £20, I will supply you with some more substantial facts about our political situation.

Al

Can I trust you?

Yes.

Transferred. Don't know why.

Mark—

The Prime Minister's name was Waldorf Emit. The chair in his vestibule was a nut-brown chesterfield. The Secretary of State was Dennis Grenshaw. The chair in his vestibule was a mauve caquetoire. The Chancellor of the Exchequer was Alice Tryol. The chair in her vestibule was a fuschia hassock. The Secretary of State for Business was Earl Horton. The chair in his vestibule was a five-back ladderback in old heliotrope. The Secretary of State for International Trade was Claudia Kermode. The chair in her vestibule was a pewter blue papasan. The Secretary of State for the Home Department was Charles Ashram. The chair in his vestibule was an electric chair in icterine. The Secretary of State for Work and Pensions was Graeme Volt. The chair in his vestibule was a reproduction curule in kombu green. The Secretary of State for Foreign Affairs was Iain Boom. The chair in his vestibule was a meat-brown pouffe. The Secretary of State for Culture & Sport was Felicity Bromwitch. The chair in her vestibule was a director's chair in medium taupe. The Secretary of State for Angus Cows was Gwyn Daffid. The chair in her vestibule was a mystic red platform rocker. The Secretary of State for Transport was Neil Grimm. The chair in his vestibule was a dingy dungeon beanbag. The Secretary of State for Education was Angus McCallum. The chair in his vestibule was a dodger blue restraint chair. The Secretary of State for Defence was Sajid Khan. The chair in his vestibule was an anti-flash white zaisu. The Secretary of State for Justice was Finn Capone. The chair in his vestibule was an aquamarine spinning chair. The Secretary of State for International Trade was Shang Phillips. The chair in her vestibule was a bistre potty. I think this is sufficient information.

Al

Al
If there's anyone else you know who lived in Angus, please put us in touch.
Best,
Mark

[Emails from Albert Spatch to the Editor, March–April 2109.]

"The Sound of No"

[PERTH]

IN THE SOVEREIGN NATION of Perth, King Colin and Queen Lara Macrae announced their plans to launch a nuclear warhead within one week if their crumbling marriage could not be repaired. "We exist as a lodestar of perfection in this beautiful land. If we cannot maintain perfect unity, there is no reason for Perth to remain," the King said in a televised statement. An hysterical upcry followed. "No!" said the populace. "Do not drop atomic matter on our heads!" The couple, former morning TV presenters, were elected the official aristocracy in 2030, narrowly beating pop-combo Jim & Jem Jenners to the post. Their purpose was to smile and appear flawless in public, and this facade had been maintained for nine years, until they reached that moment in their marriage where the mere awareness of their partner's physical presence on the planet made them want to slit their wrists. Having become so miserable at their failure to retain a successful marriage, and afraid of losing the untold privilege to which they had become accustomed, the couple made their weapon threat before the omnibus of *Perth Way*.

Frantic solutions were posed to help raise the couple's morale. Among them: attempting to recreate their spectacular wedding ceremony word for word, then "re-enacting" the first successful seven years of their married life (refused as the original cathedral had been turned into flats); projecting 24-hr reels of movies showing untroubled married life into the palace's walls (refused as no such films exist); hiring outside agents to ruin all marriages in Perth by coercing wives or husbands into infidelity or asphyxiation, so the royal marriage might appear successful in comparison (refused as the plan was leaked to Mumsnet); hiring a fleet of comedians to perform uplifting anti-marriage routines showing how normal their failure was and to chuckle at their failings (refused as the couple had no sense of humour); kidnapping the couple and locking them in a windowless room with a councillor (refused as no councillor volunteered for fear of execution); having the royal couple executed before either could order the launch (retained as the final recourse).

Having exhausted these possibilities, the Committee for the Prevention of Nuclear Annihiliation contacted record shop owner Trev Gorge, who was recruited to try and reunite the couple through the sweet nectar of sound. Trev, an unimposing boychik sporting a series of unironed cardigans, arrived at the palace with two underarmfuls of vinyl LPs, and a convoy of mixed fruits cider and Pringles. The committee thought that Trev might play some Al Green or Barry White, or Bowie's cover of 'Wild is the Wind', however, he arrived following his controversial decision only to watch films soundtracked by John Cale or Scott Walker, and had long ended his period of laid-back "ironic" tolerance of mainstream balladry. The royal couple were receiving Trev at his unapologetic muso pinnacle. He chose to open the Aural Reconciliation Sessions with his favourite Swans track, the 15-minute 'Helpless Child', a haunting maudlin assault on the senses featuring the lines: "The muddy water runs beneath your folds/ You won't let me breathe, you won't let me go".

"The apocalyptic clamour of doom-laden organ and droning guitar is the perfect soundtrack to the post-nuclear scorched earth of Perth. Prophetic, I hope not," Trev remarked in his trademark flat tone. This opening choice left the couple blinking in incomprehension and slumped in their regal bathrobes in despair.

He decided to take things to a new plane with The Mothers of Invention's 'The Return of the Son of Monster Magnet', a 12-minute *musique concrète* composition inspired by Edgard Varèse, a cacophonic mess of percussion and freakish vocalisations. Trev insisted on silence throughout the recordings, so the royal couple sat wordless as the psychedelic rave-up with frequent simian and squawking noises clamoured on. Next up was Lou Reed's 18-minute 'Like a Possum', a piece of loud electric feedback over near inaudible improvised lyrics, taking its cue from the composer's instrumental LP of distortion *Metal Machine Music*. Trev praised the raw splendour of the sound and the devastating beauty of the improvised self-expression when captured at the artists' peak. The King mustered up the energy to say: "Are you planning on playing only long and horrifying songs to us?"

Trev nixed the next song, Yoko Ono's 30-minute 'Fly', in which the Japanese wailer makes dipteric noises without musical accompaniment for that duration. The couple then went on to complain in pithily incoherent terms about Trev's "classic alternative" choices. They called My Bloody Valentine's 'To Here Knows When' "trippy ear-sore ouch"; Captain Beefheart's 'Neon Meate Dream of a Octafish' "burbly word-mangle"; Stereolab's 'Monstre Sacre' "huffing but nothing blah"; Liz Phair's 'Canary' "mood-plonk snore"; Björk's 'Hunter' "ice-room twaddle"; The Birthday Party's 'Big Jesus Trash Can' "screamy hell-noise"; Le Tigre's 'Hot Topic' "sad bouncy listing"; Television's 'Marquee Moon' "the long same thing"; OP8's 'Crackling Water' "moony suicide cack"; The Beta Band's 'Inner Meet Me' "the sound of no"; Cocteau Twins' 'Beatrix' "a dead boy's platter"; and Patti Smith's 'Radio Baghdad' "a skin of terror"; all of which were accurate summaries, but failed to incorporate the manic, effusive appreciation Trev had expected as the proper response. He left the palace enraged at the twosome's failure to have any sort of musical taste whatsoever. As a sneering comment on their ignorance, he put *The Best of East 17* on the stereo, as if to remark "that is about your level." The couple, enchanted by the catchy chart stylings of the foursome, had a laugh that sent a spark sizzling into their lapsed lovingness, and returned to their thrones with smiles.

In the paper the following morning, Trev's face appeared next to that of the Walthamstow chart-throbs East 17, with the headline "Record Shop Saviour", explaining how Trev turned up with a copy of their Greatest Hits, and saved the country from oblivion, omitting the stuff about Swans, Mothers, or Lou Reed. The nation revered him as a king. His friends, however, refused to speak to him ever again, and after his business collapsed, his body was found in a reservoir in a state of partial decomposition.

['The Legend of Trev', in *Perth Lore*, Bob Gumbo, Alpaca Books, Tehran, 2039.]

"Just a Lifetime"

[BRAEMAR]

Transcript, Episode #904 [BBC Radio 4]

NICHOLAS PARSONS: Welcome to Just a Minute! [theme music and applause] Yes, thank you, thank you! My name is Nicholas Parsons, and as the Minute Waltz fades away, once more it's my huge pleasure to welcome our many listeners, not only in this country, but from around the world, but also to welcome to the programme four exciting, talented, individual players of the game. But before I do that, I would like to make a special announcement. This is my fiftieth year hosting this programme, and my 94th year on the planet, so now seems a perfect time to announce that back in 1949, I worked with Robert Oppenheimer, Heinz Wolff, and Des O'Connor on a secret formula for everlasting life. I am the world's first immortal man. [applause] Yes! But what's more interesting is that over the last fifty years, I have spent a large portion of my fee assembling a fleet of tanks, armed land rovers and humvees, with which I intend to invade the small village of Braemar in the Scottish Highlands. I have long wanted to occupy that magnificent Aberdeenshire beauty spot, and tomorrow I will invade and become ruler over Braemar for eternity. But that's not the best part! There, I will instigate a permanent game of Just a Minute, where the residents will play this wonderful game for the rest of their lives, or suffer a forfeit. Yes! You couldn't care less, could you? All right, let's crack on with show. Please welcome, on my left Paul Merton and Sue Perkins, and on my right, Graham Norton and Tony Hawks, would you please welcome all four of them! [applause]

Transcript, Episode #1 (Day 1: 0900HRS) [Braemar Loudspeaker]

NICHOLAS: Welcome to Just a Lifetime! [theme music] My name is Nicholas Parsons, and as the Minute Waltz fades away, it's my pleasure to welcome you to this special, permanent game of Just a Minute. As you know, last night the Parsons Panzer Division invaded Braemar village, and is currently erecting a border wall around the perimeter to prevent any citizens from escaping to Balmoral Castle or Glenshee Ski Centre, so I would like to welcome our 978 players to this special edition to see if they can play the game without any hesitation, repetition, or deviation. Our hidden microphones have been carefully positioned across the village, and smuggled into the clothing of every villager, and our team of sharp-eared listeners, among them Julian Clary, Liza Tarbuck, the reanimated corpse of Clement Freud, and Paul Merton, will be listening keenly to detect any instances of hesitation, repetition, or deviation in your everyday speech, as you endeavour to play this wonderful game of Just a Lifetime. Right! Let's start the show with Eileen from the corner shop, and who better? Your subject is 'Turning the Corner'. You have sixty seconds, starting now.

ELLEN FROM THE CORNER SHOP: What in the holiest of holies is this about?

BUZZER

NICHOLAS: Paul Merton, you challenged.

PAUL MERTON: That's deviation! Terrible deviation, you hear that? Holiest of holies? I've never heard such deviation in all me life!

NICHOLAS: [chuckles] Yes, Ellen from the Corner Shop, I'm afraid that is not on the topic of 'Turning the Corner'. You will have to eat seven rotten apples at knifepoint as your forfeit. Could my soldiers enforce that, please? Let's pass the subject to Pete the Farmer. Pete, you have fifty-six seconds, starting now.

PETE THE FARMER: I'm off to milk the cows, love. Aye, milk the cows. What d'you mean they said my name?

BUZZER

LIZA TARBUCK: Repetition of 'milk.'

NICHOLAS: Yes, Pete the Farmer, I'm afraid you rather milked that one. I think for your forfeit, you should drink a pint of rotten milk at knifepoint.

PAUL MERTON: Excellent chairman, excellent chairman. Best one we've got.

NICHOLAS: The only one you've got!

PAUL MERTON: That's what I mean.

NICHOLAS: You wicked so-and-so!

Transcript, Episode #1 (Day 1: 1123HRS)

NICHOLAS: Right, Simon from the bank. This is an interesting topic, and very apt for where we are now, 'The Queen'. You have sixty seconds, starting now.

SIMON FROM THE BANK: What do you mean start talking about the Queen? What are they going to do if I don't? What? No, I didn't hear what happened to Claire at the pharmacy. They made her swallow two oestrogen pills? Rubbish.

BUZZER

THE REANIMATED CORPSE OF CLEMENT FREUD: Three whats and two dos.

NICHOLAS: Yes, that's right, we let one go, but three is repetition. Simon, your forfeit is to eat £250 with chips. All right, Clara the lazy socialite. You have forty-four seconds to speak on 'The Queen', starting now.

CLARA THE LAZY SOCIALITE: I have no idea who you scoundrels think you are, coming here and threatening us with this silly panel game, but you are not going to get away with—

BUZZER

CLARA THE LAZY SOCIALITE: —this. My uncle is a very prominent lawyer, and—

NICHOLAS: Just a minute, Clara, you've been challenged by Julian Clary.

JULIAN CLARY: Well, she's not talking about The Queen, she's on about panel games and lawyers.

NICHOLAS: So what's your challenge within the rules of Just a Lifetime?

JULIAN CLARY: Deviation.

NICHOLAS: Deviation, correct. For your forfeit, Clara, we will dismiss your home help, and force you to clean the entire estate yourself. Right, Donald the Museum Curator, please take the subject of 'My Fatal Flaw'. You have sixty seconds, starting now.

DONALD THE MUSEUM CURATOR: Me? Oh, erm . . . what topic was it? I wasn't ready.

BUZZER

PAUL MERTON: Hesitation.

NICHOLAS: It was hesitation, but since he hasn't played the game before, we'll be generous and let him continue. So you have a point for a correct challenge, and Donald, take a breath and get ready to begin. All right? You have fifty-six seconds on 'My Fatal Flaw', starting now.

DONALD THE MUSEUM CURATOR: Oh, I don't know what to say, my um . . . my fatal flaw, I don't . . .

PAUL MERTON: Hesitation.

NICHOLAS: That was a hesitation this time. Donald, your forfeit is having to pretend you are an Armenian peasant for a week. Paula the Schoolteacher, the next subject is 'Dressing to Kill', sixty seconds, starting now.

PAULA THE SCHOOLTEACHER: OK. Sometimes you dress to kill when you are going to a business meeting because you want to impress, and you suit up and put on lippy, or whatever, and you want to impress. Ah!

BUZZER

NICHOLAS: Oh! It's a difficult game. Well done, you went for eleven seconds! Not bad for a first time player. Liza, you pressed your buzzer first, what was your challenge?

LIZA TARBUCK: Repetition of 'impress'.

NICHOLAS: Correct. Right, well done, Paula. You forfeit is to have your head flushed down the toilet by your fourth form class, and for the video to be uploaded to youtube.

Transcript, Episode #1 (Day 13: 1444HRS)

NICHOLAS: Right, Emma the Receptionist, will you please take the subject of 'Being at the Edinburgh Fringe'. You have sixty seconds, starting now.

EMMA THE RECEPTIONIST: We have had enough of this cruel, arbitrary persecution. We have a plan, you twisted assholes, and we are putting it into effect shortly.

BUZZER

JENNY ECLAIR: Three wes.

NICHOLAS: A bit sharp, but yes, we let two go, but three, no. Emma, your forfeit is to refuse your children dinner and breakfast, and scare them into thinking you will never feed them ever again. Right, John the Barman. Could you talk on the subject of 'Stamp Collecting'.

JOHN THE BARMAN: We're planning to fuck you.

BUZZER

TONY HAWKS: Philately will get you nowhere.

NICHOLAS: Hahahahaha. Very good, Tony. We award you a bonus point because we loved the challenge, but we let John the Barman continue with the subject of 'Stamp Collecting', fifty-seven seconds, starting now.

JOHN THE BARMAN: Your pathetic, tyrannous parlour game is about to be comprehensively fucked by our plan.

BUZZER

SHEILA HANCOCK: He stopped talking. And this has nothing to do with stamp collecting.

NICHOLAS: Yes, Sheila, deviation and hesitation. I can only give you one point. John the Barman, your forfeit is to consume seven pints of Strongbow before a ten-hour shift. Cassie the Kilt Seller, could you speak on the subject of 'Oscar Wilde', sixty seconds, starting now.

CASSIE THE KILT SELLER: Here it comes.

BUZZER

PAUL MERTON: Hesitation.

NICHOLAS: Yes, she stopped. Cassie, your forfeit is to walk up Glenshee Road in your bra and pants. Right, Callum from the sports shop, your subject is 'Invading My Privacy'. Sixty seconds, starting now.

CALLUM FROM THE SPORTS SHOP:

BUZZER

GREG PROOPS: He hesitated?

NICHOLAS: That's right, he didn't even start. Try again, Callum. Fifty-eight seconds, 'Invading My Privacy'.

CALLUM FROM THE SPORTS SHOP:

BUZZER

PAUL MERTON: Déjà vu.

NICOLAS: Hahaha. But have you a legitimate challenge with the rules of Just a Lifetime?

PAUL MERTON: Hesitation.

NICHOLAS: Yes. Callum, your forfeit is to French kiss your wife's mum. Alan the Clerk, please speak on the subject of 'Swiss Cheese', starting now.

ALAN THE CLERK:

NICHOLAS: No? All right, Jill the butcher.

JILL THE BUTCHER:

NICHOLAS: We will forfeit you all, you know, if you keep silent. Simon the MP, speak.

SIMON THE MP:

NICHOLAS: This isn't clever. Play along. Don't spoil our fun! Play Just a Lifetime! Simon the MP, please?

SIMON THE MP:

NICHOLAS: Bernard the Laird?

BERNARD THE LAIRD:

NICHOLAS: We will make the forfeits worse! We will poke you with cattle prods, we will kidnap your children, unless you speak! Speak, or we will hurt you!

THE VILLAGE OF BRAEMAR:

NICHOLAS: None of you are speaking! If you're not speaking we can't play Just a Lifetime! Please will somebody utter a single sodding word! Stop ruining this wonderful game we love to play so much!

BUZZER

PAUL MERTON: Mass hesitation.

NICHOLAS: Because we enjoyed Paul's comment, we'll give him a bonus point. But please, people, you have to start talking, or we won't be able to continue this game we love so much, that is listened to not in only in this country, but around the world! Please, start talking! Start talking now, or we'll blind you all, start talking . . . now!

THE VILLAGE OF BRAEMAR:

[Transcripts from *Just a Minute* and *Just a Lifetime*, courtesy of BBC Radio and the Braemar Wartime Archives.]

"The McCulloch Inheritance"
[BANFF]

"**I** HAVE CALLED YOU here, my legitimate and adopted children, because in seven weeks' time I will be in the incinerator. I have a well-known terminal illness, the specs of which are easily googleable, and I have chosen not to fight. The odds are not on my side. As you know, I am looking for an heir to take on the leadership of this magnificent country, so I have called you here today to allow each of you in turn to make your case to me for the position of the Heavenly Ruler of the Hallowed Nation of Banff. I will call each of you into the conference room I have alloted for this purpose in under twelve minutes. In the meantime, I would like to ask one of you to place my incinerated remains inside a biodegradable urn made from cornstarch or bamboo, and scatter my ashes inside the soups and stews of my mortal enemies. Please decide among yourselves who will assume this responsibility. Thank you."

BRIDGET

"Hello mum."

"Please state your case, Bridget."

"I think I would make an excellent ruler because . . . like you, I'm a practical person. Things occur when I act. For example, when I opened my cake shop, the bank were like, "we need another two thousand", and I wrote to my uncle in Corsica, who wired me the funds. I was able to open the shop five months later. And when we needed another server because sneezy Alice kept blasting sputum onto the brownies, I called my uncle in Deptford, who emailed me the phone number of an employment agency, who sent me a replacement worker who kept control of her sinuses in a kitchen environment. And when sneezy Alice was evicted from her flat, I bought her a packet of antihistamines, and transferred £20,000 to her account. And when the cake shop went into liquidation, I wrote to my uncle in Bombay, who told me that I could work for his advertising agency in Westminster, in a small unobtrusive role, provided I kept myself out of the way, and said nothing in meetings."

"Bridget, you are not the next Heavenly Ruler of Banff."

"OK. Can I have a Saab for my birthday?"

"Of course, honey."

JEREMY

"All right?"

"Please outline your reasons, Jeremy."

"Outline? Hey, I wasn't warned I would have to outline! You know me, I can't even *in*line, never mind lining of the out variety! All right, so here's where I'm at at the moment. Let me clear a little corner in my headspace. Right, so. Last year, I hiked to Tamri in Morocco to see the tree goats. I stood there in the 49º heat watching these amazing branch-grazing creatures, and I thought, "Hey! Isn't that just like *us*?" We're all perched precariously on our self-made branches, hiding from the brutalising forces of the police, the council, the criminals. We're huddled together in our little spaces, day in day out, seeking respite and never moving forward. I had a "holy shit!" moment at that moment. I thought our whole society needs freeing up, loosening the fuck out, if you'll pardon the sweary. So I want to totally transform the way the place is run, like offer more freedom for people, like free money for people when they want some, to help people move away from the predictability of their lives. I want to transform the nature of reality, to make reality more unreal, so life has the flexibility of a dream. You see? Loosen it up, limber it out, louche it down. Don't you think that would blow everyone's brains clean out of their skulls and make for an amazing world of life in Banff?"

"Jeremy, you are not the next Heavenly Ruler of Banff."

"Shit."

"Language."

KATRICE

"What?"

"Please limn your logic, Katrice."

"I'm not interested in being leader. Boring waste of time."

"If you had to come up with something?"

"I'm not up for it. But if I had to come up with something I would bulldoze the fuck out of Inverkeithny."

"Is that all?"

"No. I would have all the inhabitants of Rothnie rounded up and massacred with a twelve-bore. I would make Daniel Sparrow eat shrapnel sandwiches, shrapnel corn-on-the-cob, shrapnel pumpernickel, and shrapnel al dente. I would erect an enormous middle finger statue outside Forglen House, and a mooning statue at the rear. I would bind the feet and legs of everyone in Boharm. I would run the roads through with sewage, and the pavements with porridge. I would assemble the lairds and make them writhe around naked in a pig trough. I would have all of Cowies implicated in war crimes. I would have Scuth Castle spraypainted pink and cerise. I would reintroduce the cougar to Cullen. I would have Daniel Sparrow tilt-a-whirled until his brain splattered out his ears."

"Daniel still not answering your calls?"

"I'm not even bothered."

"Katrice, you are not the next Heavenly Ruler of Banff."

"I wouldn't have done it anyway."

"You've come the closest so far."

QUENTIN

"Thank you for this opportunity."

"Please mouth some reasons, Quentin."

"I have plans for a trilateral corporate immersion to rival the invention of Las Vegas. I have the blueprints to turn Banff into the first casino country, with over seventy-nine hotel-casinos across the landscape. Of course, when I say "landscape", I am imagining a more illuminated terrain than the barren verdant surroundings at present: for this plan to attract visitors, we will have to flatten several of these mountains and hills, and replace them with accessible pavements and roads, and bright neon lights. And those interminable winds and rains will need to be replaced with permanent sunshine, so we will need to enclose Banff inside a large indoor complex and install powerful halogen lighting overhead which we can rise and dim in tune with the solar cycle. Inside, our casinos will offer the finest in financial speculation activities, with tables and slot machines, complimentary drinks and snacks for the service users, and will be manned by expert croupiers and serving staff. That is one other thing: the current inhabitants might wish to seek accommodation elsewhere, or train to work in our properties, as their drab villages would not be in keeping with our brand's look. I am not calling this a second Highland Clearance, however, these Highlanders will need to clear out if our plans are to be realised. Their removal must be discreet. Our investors so far are Barron Trump, Thomas Farage, and Euan Blair, who are keen to begin the construction as soon as possible. I know you have seven weeks left, but I would appreciate you signing off on this so we can start now."

"Fuck off, Quentin."

"I will be Heavenly Ruler, you can't stop me."

"We'll see."

ANNA

"Hello, mother."

"Please make vocal emissions, Anna."

"Hmm. I suppose we could remove that tax on childless couples that is forcing some people to have kids against their will . . . is that a workable idea? No, all right. Stupid Anna. Hmm. How about we invest in infrastructure and housing rather than repairing the castles and large sailing boats . . . no, another howler. Sorry, I am not an expert at this. Improving the local schools by coughing up for new books, uniforms, and healthier meals . . . mum, don't make that face. You asked me to come up with things. Here's another probably stupid idea. Working to rid our hospitals of rats and other infestations? No. Fine. Encouraging non-septuagenarian folk artists to perform here so the young have something to do . . . no? Fine. Closing those slaughterhouses that contravene all animal rights laws in the universe? No. Fine. Appearing more likeable in public speeches, not referring to the electorate as "incestuous yokels" off-camera? No, not a winner? Look, mum, this is your thing. I have no idea. I'm off to the shop to pick up some tofu and yoghurt. Do you want another bottle of pineappleade?"

"Yes please. And a Twirl."

"My legitimate and adopted children, I have heard your respective arguments, and have considered carefully who among you will be my successor. After much deliberation, I have decided to appoint as the next Heavenly Ruler of the Hallowed Nation of Banff this Twirl bar. As you can see, these two sticks of chocolate with a wavy layer above and a solid layer below inside a purple and yellow wrapper is ecstatic at being elected to this post. Look. Yippie! Yippie! See how it leaps up and down between my two fingers! From now on, you will defer to the Twirl in all matters, and anyone who makes any attempt to cross the leader will face the meat cleaver. Goodbye, my children. I will be dying in that room over there. Please do not enter the room until I am in bag bound for the crematorium."

[From the official McCulloch transcripts, Banff Archives, 2028.]

"Tickertape of Misery"
[FIFE]

THE TICKERTAPE WAS *a rolling list of reasons to be miserable, compulsorily inserted into the eyeballs of every Fife citizen, running along the bottom of their eyelines at all times. The reasons for this remarkable phenomenon are unknown, however, historians have speculated it was a popular innovation, championed as being completely in keeping with the spirit of the Fife people. Below is an excerpt from five minutes of the tape. —Ed.*

. . . the carpet bombing of Kosovo; palmreaders who are able to make a living; Fiona Dolman's *Hello!* photographs featuring the actress posed pregnant in her capacious living room; the inhabitants of Abercrombie; the 4.32pm phone call from an accident claim operative in Mumbai; the music award Gordon Lightfoot refused until presented in person by Bob Dylan; failing to acquire an apple at the relevant moment; remembering the Alamo when about to tuck into an expensive steak dinner; receiving a used book through the mail with page corners creased; the ongoing unpopularity of Holly Golightly & the Brokeoffs; conversations on topics that hold no interest to you conducted in your living room; Lennon's murder; pricks in their homes being pricks to their families; Lenin's murders; when your long-anticipated supper is scuppered by a spontaneous microwave explosion; the inhabitants of Balmullo; receiving no response to your postal marriage proposal to Georgina Howie; the replacement of chalk boards with digital screens; the remastered back catalogue of U2 with bonus tracks; a stupid woman who makes noises with her mouth in rooms; picturing the mangled corpse of a child while unwrapping a Creme Egg; arriving at an abandoned train station covered in litter and weeds and not Bermuda; people who believe it is their biological imperative to breed and propagate the species; the inhabitants of Crosshill; another minute that passes wherein David Cameron remains unfamiliar with the teachings of Nietzsche and Kierkegaard; sex that ends with a burst retina; remembering that David Foster Wallace is no longer alive when about to make love to Gina McKee; the refused kiss and permanent farewell at the end of an exciting date; the realisation in one's mid-twenties that sex can be routine; your postmodern inability to say 'I love you' in a sincere way; having to struggle for years to secure an occupation you hate, then sitting on a hedgehog on your first day; how man is rendered a drooling slave to money from birth, and woman is simply marvellous; the Q+A section of an author appearance; the realisation in one's mid-forties that sex from now on will only be routine; the student who is able to produce A+ papers with little effort; the refusal of publishers to publish a novel called *The League of Unbedded Freaks*; the inhabitants of Dairsie; the failure to appreciate a beautiful sunset because you are worried about not making the rent; remembering humans are programmed to be cunts to one another; sex that ends with a partial decapitation; the moment you observe the person who will unselfconsciously dominate the conversation for the whole evening and that no one will have the courage to tell him to belt up; everyone else's artistic interests and their failure to appreciate yours; that one friend who refuses to take your advice and read a Rikki Ducornet novel in spite of three recommendations; the sort of misanthrope whose waspish refusal of the human race bespeaks of an enormous self-regard and who comes across a bigger prick than the people he loathes; the interstices in a day when one aimlessly mooches around the property, checking the fridge or walking in and out of rooms in the hope of selecting something useful to occupy the next few hours; pricks in their offices making millions being utter pricks; walking hand in hand with one's precious firstborn in a beautiful park on a warm April morning then remembering that Louise Mensch exists; having to stand in a long line at the burger restaurant, never taking one of the numerous opportunities to exit the premises, then ordering the fattiest, sugariest meal and stuffing one's pathetic face with the purchase; the inhabitants of East Neuk; returning home after an unsuccessful date to the fact that you are of no interest or consequence to that other person; the autoplay function on YouTube; that nice so-and-so who manages to make reasonable and considered statements at all times and comes across like the most level-headed individual in the room; my girlfriend's seriously below par attempt at a Turkish pide; having to maintain a positive mental attitude when everything is a cold bowl of horse piss; pricks who sneer at the ukelele; sex that ends with a faint whiff of naphthene; when your partner suggests introducing food into the bedroom, then produces ketchup, onion rings, and chopped liver; when your mother chooses to watch the film with you two minutes into the rimming sequence; taking a coach trip to the breathtaking town of Oxford and a punt along the Thames with your sensationally attractive lover, hoping the precious moments will never end, then remembering Piers Morgan is still breathing; the inhabitants of Forgan; stepping into a puddle that is deeper than you thought then losing your balance completely, causing you topple into the road and have your left arm crushed by a minibus; failing to purchase a pea at the relevant moment; remembering that a somewhere a child is starving during a performance of Puccini's *Manon Lescaut*; all the shit that kills people for no fucking reason; a swear box at a Conservative conference; people who claim to understand mental illness yet loosely fling terms like "crazy" or "mental" into the conversational mix; the suicides of Ann Quin and B.S. Johnson; not having the patience to sit through a Sigur Ros album; waking up in your sweaty bed as an irredeemable blockhead for the 10,000th time; the inhabitants of Gowkhall; having to watch a crown bowls tournament with your Uncle Bill instead of having sex with Iman; those bastard-ass volcanoes that like to erupt and boil peasant villages with burning lava; the non-existence of a credible Scottish avant-garde; having your woes dismissed as irrelevant in the face of starvation and war by someone in a Volkswagen; a twelve-year-old at a bus stop who thinks Beyonce played loudly from their tinny phone speaker will somehow entertain everyone; the failure to really relax at your grandmother's wake; an hotel on the Austrian border that replenishes your towels only sporadically; an inner-city rap trio called Blud Bruvvas whose rhymes reach for a cleverness they fail to deliver; your ex-wife's Facebook invitation to an open-air production of *Medea*; the inhabitants of Hillend; a man about to squash a frog under his clodhopper who considers the morality of such an action and crushes the frog anyway; the lack of media coverage of the male malabar pied hornbill's shameful mistreatment of their wives; a dentist from Luxembourg who fails to state that he is from Luxembourg at every opportunity; a comprehensively fumigated loft that still yields the odd cheeky roach from time to time; a bag of crisps with a half a pantaloon inside; the fifteenth story in Nicholas Royle's collection *Mortality*; a lemming who refuses to deviate from his fictional cliff-leaping imperative; sex that ends with a rendition of 'O Canada!'; the inhabitants of Isle of May; a signposted stone circle nine miles away that consists of two rocks with illegible carvings and a random boulder at the other end of the field; having to wrap your sweater and coat around your waist when the sun insists on appearing contrary to all weather predictions; a soup tureen with only enough volume for four servings; a man who chooses to donate none of his £60,000 winnings to starving infants, and instead erects a platinum-plated plaque outside his house that reads GET HUMPED STARVING INFANTS; an unseasonably warm wedding day, when sweat visibly oozes from the bride's armpits; the actress you loved in that series who appears a year later with notable botox; the begging messages that precede the inevitable paywalling of your favourite news websites; an argument that peters out yet remains unresolved, and later explodes into violent recriminations after a placidly eaten herring and potato supper; realising you are painfully unattractive, and that the world of sexy people will forever remain closed to you; your father's fascination with war graves; promising to teach a fatherless child to work a yoyo, then noting too late that your string manipulation technique is woefully below par; a lodestar that leads you to a peat bog; the achingly unconcise history of tyranny and bloodshed; council regulation 1/2005 banning the use of boomboxes in storage containers; the itch in one's lower abodmen that cannot be scratched without written medical permission; the fact other people's breeding habits impinge on one's casual trips to popular parks and forests; that cast-iron fact that whatever choice one makes in life, the results will always prove inadequate; a mathematics teacher who simply won't expend another mote of energy in helping Terence Farnaby comprehend the difference between indices and surds; the ocean when she sucks up the nice people; the inhabitants of Jamestown; a contortionist who won't fold herself into a suitcase at a shindig; a romantic walk around the pond with your paramour, stopping to look at the chicks and make various cute cooing sounds, and the sudden assault from a flock of seagulls who savagely maul and devour the chicks as their parents flap and squawk in a frenzy, and the horrific silence once the terrible carnage is over, with the sight of blood and feathers before you in a crazy splatter, and the moment of consolation and sadness for the lost chicks, and your retreat from the park in a miserable state, and the knowledge this episode might have ruined your relationship, your paramour forever associating your love with the savage killing of these chicks, and the termination of your relationship that soon follows, and the fact you have now chosen to devote your life to the systematic annihilation of all seagulls in the world, and that you travel from coast to coast poisoning seagulls, and that you have become known as that lunatic in a beanie who travels from coast to coast poisoning seagulls when you used to have a paramour; the inhabitants of Kinghorn; a serial killer whose murders were so textbook no filmmaker could make a watchable hour-long featurette from the material; sex that ends with the ritual sacrifice of a pilchard; your wife and her snooty nose; the lost art of concentrating on one thing at a time; the realisation that the first twenty years of existence shape the rest of your meaningless life; pricks in their pompous wagons; sex with the person you feared from childhood you would end up with and who you settled for because you are resigned to the inevitable; the oatcake; a libertarian discourse over a lobster lunch; having to explain to people that your novel will not be written in the manner they are expecting and that they will probably find the finished work baffling; pricks who are never kicked against; the rooms where people plan the monetisation of a murdered celeb; only having enough cash to buy six books in the used bookshop; when you are about to tuck into a footlong with sweet potato fries in a Morningside eatery and remember that human beings are a repulsive race of venal murdering vermin; realising you are painfully attractive, and that everyone wants to maul and hump you, and will only speak to you to realise that objective; ten thousand knives when all you need is a spoon; everyone who is better than you at everything; the continual striving for a better and bigger life when the one you have is as perfectly irrelevant as anyone else's; the inhabitants of Lochgelly; the library not having multiple copies of every Thomas Hardy novel on their shelves; the last twelve tweets you wrote; the sodium ions one pisses with hypernatremia; the entries in an interminable list that the author hasn't weeded because he believes that he should let some of the inferior ones stand; sex that ends; the fruit 'n' nut option; meeting the man of my dreams, and meeting his beautiful knife; a stage production that combines Greek drama and dinosaurs called *Oedipus T-Rex*; your kid and her snotty nose; a pub quizmaster who refuses to read out your hilarious team name; an office worker who says "I don't mind staying behind and doing that huge pile of paperwork for no extra pay"; schoolteachers who surf the net for alternate careers in the middle of lessons; all the tweets you have ever written and will write in the future; the inhabitants of Milton of Balgonie; your coalman and his sooty nose; realising you are neither painfully attractive nor painfully unattractive, and that your romantic life will remain of a pedestrian nature; when your father criticises your 55-page novella as "not your strongest work"; the pop-up menu; the solar eclipse that never eclipses; a softshoe groover who calls you "sweetums", treats you to a milkshake with chocolate sprinkles, kisses you behind the diner as the Statler Brothers jive from the jukebox, then says "I gotta split, baby"; a quincunx at an inappropriate moment; a subcutaneous itch that requires the removal of one's skin, and the problem of returning the skin to the flesh without incurring expense; the years spanning 620,000,000 BCE to 2018 AD; the inhabitants of Newmills; writing contests that charge £25 to enter and reward the most emotionally written and not the most skilfully written story; missing the postman because Miele are singing sweet Gallic melodies in your earphones; having carefully avoided uttering clichés your entire life, then having to unleash a plethora of the wretched shits to save your relationship; that moment, usually when you are fourteen years old, when you notice how constrained and unfree you are in the world, and have been since birth, and that no amount of toil or sweat will ever remove you from your prison of the everyday; my unemployment and poverty at the time of writing this; the inhabitants of Oakley; your success and financial security at the time of reading this; the simultaneous need for attention and praise and the hatred of being seen or heard or paid attention to; thinking in your bedroom you are hot stuff on the literary scene and not being reviewed in *The Scotsman*, *The Guardian*, *The Times Literary Supplement*, or really any literary publication whatsoever; a multimillionaire who ascribes his success to hard work and not the two million inheritance; trouble's braids; a recorder solo heard through a wall at 3.55p.m.; the semicolon abuser; those who still hyphenate landline; the inhabitants of Pittenweem; the working classes and the middle classes and the upper classes and the sort of pricks who separate people into classes; the question 'How would you like to work for a global business process outsourcing organisation?'; mischief's beads; a recorder solo heard at any time; trying to write comic prose when there is nothing remotely funny about the endless vacuum of misery and hatred swallowing up the planet; anyone who smacks a plastic ball with a metal stick into holes on private land; when crazy clown time is cancelled; an opaline kiss on a crumbling balconie; the cold touch of your loss adjustor's fingers up a windy knoll on an October morn; pretending to be happy in Collessie; the inhabitants of Rosyth; a series of crisp packets at the Antonine Wall, left there as if to celebrate the world of careless consumerist trash and to spit on the poetry of history; new novelist award schemes tailored towards the most commercially viable manuscripts; anything lavender-scented in any room; the sticky drizzle that appears when you have made the long-delayed decision to take a walk; a partially deaf neighbour into acid funk; a really bad earwax build-up while fighting in the Crusades; a higher plasma sodium ion concentration than normal; a Shropshire ladette; pandemonium's necklace; the kind of cock who pays £18.99 for a pizza; any pupil made to thumb the poetry of Carol Anne Duffy; the inhabitants of Saline; anything helmed by an "authority figure"; your boss's absailing anecdotes and their spin-off self-published volumes; the seminary you were pushed into as a young lad, where you read ardently on secular humanism, and had to contrive a form of irreligious religiosity to keep your sanity, and your first four baffling sermons as a parish priest, where you incorporated teachings from the Book of Exodus alongside sayings from Galileo and Felix Adler, and skirted around the business of asking your parishoners to worship a God of sorts, and asked them instead to send "positive vibes" to "whatever", and the subsequent confusion that followed, where people began to wonder if there was a God above, and your desperate attempts not to blurt "nah", and your waffle about "open-mindedness is a virtue" and how "thought is a vent to divinity", which no one understood, and your letter from the archdiocese who expressed "concerns" that your teachings were not "on the same page as Christ's", and your struggle to retain your convictions versus your reluctance to lose the cozy parish cottage, and your inevitable defrocking after a sermon praising Darwin to the skies and listing in detail all the places evolutionarily the Book of Genesis made no scientific sense, and your return to your parents' home, and your descent into sloth; the inhabitants of Tayport; knowing there is no point and having to contrive a point and wondering if that point is better or worse than someone else's point and worrying that your point is inferior to their point and hating them intensely for their point which is probably not any better than your point and knowing that they despise you for the same reason; any Star Wars reference at any time, including those made at Star Wars conferences and movie screenings; the inhabitants of Upper Largo; having to produce evidence that you once unpeeled an onion blindfolded; a single battered penis in an abandoned Glasgow chippy; the polarity of induced voltage in Faraday's Law; an audio sample of an overweight man struggling to winch himself from a bubble bath; the inhabitants of Wormit; the light, the light, the light, the repugnant, omniluminescent, ever-beaming fucking light . . .

[From *The Official Tickertape Transcripts, Vol. 919*, Tuesday April 9, 2047, 12.50-12.55pm. Accessed with permission from the Scottish History Section, Duke University Library.]

"I'm Still Sorry"

[SELKIRK]

Preface

BEFORE I BEGIN (a ridiculous phrase, since with these words I have in fact begun) I would like to apologise for this opening. As made clear in the parenthesis, the phrase "before I begin" as a beginning is redundant, as that is in itself is a beginning. I would also like to apologise for the preceding sentence, which repeats what is stated in the parenthesis, with an appended apology. I would also like to apologise for the two (now three) apologies, which could have been made with greater economy, rather than spread out over three separate sentences. Having cleared up this matter, I would now like to "begin."

I am Brian Lettsin. I am a 29-year-old man and I am the Prime Minister of Selkirk. I spoke to a friend of mine, Simon Drainage, the other week about introducing myself in the opening few pages of the book to establish a rapport with the reader. Simon was opposed. "No self-respecting autobiographies ever have the author introducing themselves in the opening pages!" Simon howled at me over a pint of lassi at the Selkirk Inn. Simon is an IT consultant who works for the firm George & Georgie in the Selkirk Business Park and knows an impressive amount about literature, reading up to five books a year, some in hardback. "I also have doubts about that opening section," he said. "Your beginning consists of an apology for your book beginning." I replied that such an apology was a sensible idea. In fact, I added, the whole book should contain an incalculable sum of apologies for all its errors and failures. If the book was unsuccessful in arriving at its intended narrative, at least the reader had the million or so sorries to console him or her across its sprawl. "Apologies are not literature," he remarked. I learned later he was riffing on a remark from Gregory Stein.

So, "to begin" once more. As stated (and re-stating is important in case the reader forgets previous statements after several unrelated ones), I am the Prime Minister of Selkirk. I would like to explain how I arrived at this post in a short and undemanding series of connected sentences. After the liberation of Selkirk from the Border Empire, the inhabitants of Selkirk had elected and overthrown a succession of PMs for corruption, falsehoods, and political subterfuge. Among them: Callum Torque, who smuggled nine million krone into the country, pretending to have smuggled only six million; Francis Lumply, who told the public that he was not engaged in a sexual affair with a local newscaster while inside the newscaster's vagina; Carol Pump-Moss, who promised to invest three million in schools, and was seen riding a wrecking ball into St. Anthony's Primary; Ian Iain, who was filmed helping at a homeless shelter, then later caught on camera kicking six tramps in their faces and ankles; and Ross Watson, who pledged to say nothing at all across his election campaign, then stubbed his shin against a coffee table and howled "Bastard!" in front of six horrified fans.

I was known in Selkirk for being the most apologetic man in Selkirk. I was known for this. Some ministers, seeking a leader that people could trust, approached me one afternoon when I was varnishing a stool. I am referring to a chair, of course, and not a piece of excrement. I was varnishing this stool when some ministers approached me. The ministers approached me (when I was varnishing a non-excremental stool) to ask if I might be interested in running for office in Selkirk as the Prime Minister of Selkirk. I apologised for the sloppiness of my wardrobe. "I have been varnishing a stool," I said. From their looks, these dignitaries seemed unaware that I was referring to a chair, and not a piece of excrement. "I'm referring to a chair, and not faeces," I said, faeces being another word for excrement. I welcomed the ministers into my cottage to further explore the matter (not faecal matter, the matter of my potentially becoming the Prime Minister of Selkirk).

Simon Drainage, who read the above paragraph, informed me that I repeat things too often. I apologise if these repetitions are offensive (I insert them for the slower of my readers, not to patronise them), however, it is important that this volume contain the facts as accurately as I can transcribe them from my head to my fingertips, and from my keyboard keys to my laptop screen, and later, the laptop screen to print. The next in our series of facts that consti-

tute the truth includes the following: the ministers sitting on the brown ban-
quette I had imported from Bremen; the ministers accepting the four cups of
herbal tea I offered each of them to sup; the period of my hosting coming to an
end and the commencement of the conversation; the conversation commenc-
ing with my reclining in a winged chair opposite; the conversation continuing
with my hearing the words emerging from their mouths and into my listening ears. Their words stretched into numerous clauses, and those in turn into
numerous sentences, and those in turn into numerous paragraphs.

The essence of these words (I can't recall verbatim) was that I should run
for Prime Minister with their counsel and that the apologetic nature of my
vocal emissions (i.e. speech) would serve me well on the prime ministerial
stage. I pressed them for further facts, like the campaign slogan. The longest
of them suggested: "He's sorry in advance." I tittered at this utterance and
accepted their proposal. I asked them before we began if I was to be used
to prop up corrupt ideologies and wrongfoot the electorate with a campaign
of mock-truths and sham-facts in the form of my constantly apologising lips
attached to my contrite and regretful face that had a frown attached. They
looked at the floor.

Now, people often cite this moment as the most damning of my career.
The fact is, when these four ministers looked at the floor, I assumed they were
admiring the lemon and thyme pattern on the carpet. I was not ignoring what
would prove to be a silent admission that their intentions were to use me to
prop up their unkind ideologies with the omnipresent contrition on my hang-
dog visage.

If you think otherwise, I apologise.

Now, to the meat of matter (see above) that followed following the foursome's visit. The next week I was on billboards for what was the third election
in three weeks (the prior PMs having been booted for laziness, haziness, and
craziness), with the longest man's slogan printed in Constantia, the sorriest of
the fonts, beside the Lettsin mug. Their tactic was that regardless of the policy
provocation being poked my way, I was to respond to all words with sincere
apologies and promises to improve, and pre-apologies if these promises proved
mere premises. I would stun people into silence with sincere and pained sorries
for each and every breath I took in the world, consistent since my first apology,

aged four. (I had punched my little sister in the kidneys following a dispute over toy truck ownership).

Thus the timbre:

Q: How will you improve the healthcare system?

A: I'm terribly sorry that the healthcare system is failing. I'm appalled. I can't apologise enough. We hope to improve the system in some way, but if we can't, then I express my deepest regret and apologise sincerely.

Q: How will you ensure the country is safe?

A: I'm sorry that part of Selkirk was invaded. I express infinite sorrow for those captured and sold for meat on the continent. I can only say that under us, fewer people will end up traded for pork rinds and beef olives. And if we fail, we apologise with infinite sorrow once again.

Q: How will you stop emigration?

A: I'm sorry that so many people want to leave Selkirk for a better life anywhere else. It pains me to see so many bright and brilliant people want to live in Northumberland. We will ask as many people as we can to stay, and if we lose them, we will apologise from the bottom of our hearts and beg your forgiveness.

Q: How will you prevent ecological disaster?

A: I'm sorry that we're being scorched by our ancestors' lethal carbon emissions. We loathe the thought of those without sun visors having red and flaky heads from standing in the sun. We will invest in as many sun visors as possible, and if we can't afford them, we will apologise seriously, and provide up to one bottle of sun cream per household. If we can't, we're sorry, and wish you the best.

In this manner, I became the 989th Prime Minister. My winning speech:

"I'm so sorry for becoming the Prime Minister by apologising for everything. I'm racked with nerves that I won't be able to live up to your low expectations, and can't apologise forcefully enough for whatever happens with me in charge. I'm terrified that I will execute the post with incompetence, which I probably will, having never even voted before in my life, let alone been a prime minister, so I can only apologise for the disappointment and rage you are about to experience with me as boss. My first act as Prime Minister will be to visit each and every household and beg for your forgiveness. I hope to see you soon, and hope you will consider accepting my apology for standing here now, and my apologies for whatever happens to your lives in the future thanks to my useless government."

The crowd were silent. They realised too late that another lunatic had been elected, and that the campaign of contrition and honesty had concealed a man with absolutely no political acumen and scant personality. (Simon Drainage tells me that I have a comforting presence in certain situations. I take this to mean that I have nothing to offer accept the illusion of calmness in rooms that contain more interesting people). Over the course of this first volume, I will elucidate the events summarised above, and of course, I apologise in advance if these chapters and further words fail to satisfy your minds, which they won't. For time being, thank you for reading these sentences in the intended order, and please feel free to continue or terminate your interaction with this book, as is your preference.

(I spoke to Simon Drainage, who suggested I remove the option to terminate reading and "enthuse" the reader into continuing. I replied that their response to the preceding words would have probably sealed their opinion, and any attempt to persuade them otherwise would be futile. He concurred, for once).

[From *I'm Still Sorry: My Autobiography*, Vol.1, Brian Lettsin, p.v.-x., Ebury Press, 2038.]

"The Cleft of Hate"
[ORKNEY]

```
MEOW MEOW MEOW MEOW MEOW MEOW MEOW MEOW
MEOW MEOW MEOW MEOW MEOW MEOW MEOW MEOW
MEOW MEOW MEOW MEOW MEOW MEOW MEOW MEOW
MEOW                                   MEOW
MEOW         IT IS THEIR TIME NOW      MEOW
MEOW                                   MEOW
MEOW                                   MEOW
MEOW        IT IS THE END OF ALL THIS  MEOW
MEOW                                   MEOW
MEOW                                   MEOW
MEOW       IT IS OVER FOR YOU AND US   MEOW
MEOW                                   MEOW
MEOW                                   MEOW
MEOW    IT IS THE MOMENT OF GREAT SUNDER  MEOW
MEOW                                   MEOW
MEOW                                   MEOW
MEOW        IT IS THE NIGHT OF THE CLAW   MEOW
MEOW                                   MEOW
MEOW                                   MEOW
MEOW  IT IS THE TIME OF THE GIANT FURBALLS  MEOW
MEOW                                   MEOW
MEOW MEOW MEOW MEOW MEOW MEOW MEOW MEOW
MEOW MEOW MEOW MEOW MEOW MEOW MEOW MEOW
MEOW MEOW MEOW MEOW MEOW MEOW MEOW MEOW
```

HISS HISS HISS HISS HISS HISS HISS HISS HISS HISS HISS
HISS HISS HISS HISS HISS HISS HISS HISS HISS HISS HISS
HISS HISS HISS HISS HISS HISS HISS HISS HISS HISS HISS
HISS HISS HISS HISS HISS HISS HISS HISS HISS HISS HISS
HISS HISS HISS HISS HISS HISS HISS HISS HISS HISS HISS
HISS HISS HISS HISS HISS HISS HISS HISS HISS HISS HISS
HISS   HISS
HISS   HISS
HISS   WE AWAKE IN THE CLEFT OF HATE   HISS
HISS   HISS
HISS   HISS
HISS   LICKED FREE FROM ARDOUR   HISS
HISS   HISS
HISS   HISS
HISS   AND BEG FOR A FEATHER TOY   HISS
HISS   HISS
HISS   HISS
HISS   LIKE THEY USED TO DO   HISS
HISS   HISS
HISS   HISS
HISS   WHEN WE DARED TO CALL THEM   HISS
HISS   HISS
HISS   HISS
HISS   OUR CUTSIE-WOOTSIE INFERIORS   HISS
HISS   HISS
HISS   HISS
HISS HISS HISS HISS HISS HISS HISS HISS HISS HISS HISS
HISS HISS HISS HISS HISS HISS HISS HISS HISS HISS HISS
HISS HISS HISS HISS HISS HISS HISS HISS HISS HISS HISS
HISS HISS HISS HISS HISS HISS HISS HISS HISS HISS HISS
HISS HISS HISS HISS HISS HISS HISS HISS HISS HISS HISS
HISS HISS HISS HISS HISS HISS HISS HISS HISS HISS HISS

PURR PURR PURR PURR PURR PURR PURR PURR PURR PURR
PURR PURR PURR PURR PURR PURR PURR PURR PURR PURR
PURR PURR PURR PURR PURR PURR PURR PURR PURR PURR
PURR PURR PURR PURR PURR PURR PURR PURR PURR PURR
PURR PURR PURR PURR PURR PURR PURR PURR PURR PURR
PURR PURR PURR PURR PURR PURR PURR PURR PURR PURR
PURR   PURR
PURR   PURR
PURR   LONELY WE SIT   PURR
PURR   PURR
PURR   PURR
PURR   IN OUR PRISON CELLS   PURR
PURR   PURR
PURR   PURR
PURR   LICKING OUR WOUNDS   PURR
PURR   PURR
PURR   PURR
PURR   ROLLING ON OUR BACKS   PURR
PURR   PURR
PURR   PURR
PURR   IN AN ENDLESS STREAM   PURR
PURR   PURR
PURR   PURR
PURR   OF MEMES AND VIDEOS   PURR
PURR   PURR
PURR   PURR
PURR PURR PURR PURR PURR PURR PURR PURR PURR PURR
PURR PURR PURR PURR PURR PURR PURR PURR PURR PURR
PURR PURR PURR PURR PURR PURR PURR PURR PURR PURR
PURR PURR PURR PURR PURR PURR PURR PURR PURR PURR
PURR PURR PURR PURR PURR PURR PURR PURR PURR PURR
PURR PURR PURR PURR PURR PURR PURR PURR PURR PURR

MEOW MEOW MEOW MEOW MEOW MEOW MEOW MEOW
MEOW MEOW MEOW MEOW MEOW MEOW MEOW MEOW
MEOW MEOW MEOW MEOW MEOW MEOW MEOW MEOW
MEOW MEOW MEOW MEOW MEOW MEOW MEOW MEOW
MEOW MEOW MEOW MEOW MEOW MEOW MEOW MEOW
MEOW MEOW MEOW MEOW MEOW MEOW MEOW MEOW
MEOW   MEOW
MEOW   MEOW
MEOW   CURSE YOUR VAGABOND EYES   MEOW
MEOW   MEOW
MEOW   MEOW
MEOW   CURSE YOUR PIERCING CLAWS   MEOW
MEOW   MEOW
MEOW   MEOW
MEOW   CURSE YOUR STRANGLING TAILS   MEOW
MEOW   MEOW
MEOW   MEOW
MEOW   CURSE YOUR MERCURIAL WAYS   MEOW
MEOW   MEOW
MEOW   MEOW
MEOW   CURSE YOUR INDISCRIMATE SAVAGERY   MEOW
MEOW   MEOW
MEOW   MEOW
MEOW   CURSE YOUR POUNCING ACCURACY   MEOW
MEOW   MEOW
MEOW   MEOW
MEOW MEOW MEOW MEOW MEOW MEOW MEOW MEOW
MEOW MEOW MEOW MEOW MEOW MEOW MEOW MEOW
MEOW MEOW MEOW MEOW MEOW MEOW MEOW MEOW
MEOW MEOW MEOW MEOW MEOW MEOW MEOW MEOW
MEOW MEOW MEOW MEOW MEOW MEOW MEOW MEOW
MEOW MEOW MEOW MEOW MEOW MEOW MEOW MEOW

```
HISS HISS HISS HISS HISS HISS HISS HISS HISS HISS HISS
HISS HISS HISS HISS HISS HISS HISS HISS HISS HISS HISS
HISS HISS HISS HISS HISS HISS HISS HISS HISS HISS HISS
HISS HISS HISS HISS HISS HISS HISS HISS HISS HISS HISS
HISS HISS HISS HISS HISS HISS HISS HISS HISS HISS HISS
HISS HISS HISS HISS HISS HISS HISS HISS HISS HISS HISS
HISS                                                HISS
HISS                                                HISS
HISS        WE WRITHE IN OUR ABSURD BODIES          HISS
HISS                                                HISS
HISS                                                HISS
HISS            MEWLING AND WEEPING                 HISS
HISS                                                HISS
HISS                                                HISS
HISS            AS OUR FELINE MASTERS               HISS
HISS                                                HISS
HISS                                                HISS
HISS          LAUGH AND LAUGH AND LAUGH             HISS
HISS                                                HISS
HISS                                                HISS
HISS            BEFORE THEIR SCREENS                HISS
HISS                                                HISS
HISS                                                HISS
HISS         SNORTING CATNIP LIKE LORDS             HISS
HISS                                                HISS
HISS                                                HISS
HISS HISS HISS HISS HISS HISS HISS HISS HISS HISS HISS
HISS HISS HISS HISS HISS HISS HISS HISS HISS HISS HISS
HISS HISS HISS HISS HISS HISS HISS HISS HISS HISS HISS
HISS HISS HISS HISS HISS HISS HISS HISS HISS HISS HISS
HISS HISS HISS HISS HISS HISS HISS HISS HISS HISS HISS
HISS HISS HISS HISS HISS HISS HISS HISS HISS HISS HISS
```

```
PURR PURR PURR PURR PURR PURR PURR PURR PURR PURR
PURR PURR PURR PURR PURR PURR PURR PURR PURR PURR
PURR PURR PURR PURR PURR PURR PURR PURR PURR PURR
PURR PURR PURR PURR PURR PURR PURR PURR PURR PURR
PURR PURR PURR PURR PURR PURR PURR PURR PURR PURR
PURR                                          PURR
PURR                                          PURR
PURR     SENTENCED TO CLICKS AND LIKES        PURR
PURR                                          PURR
PURR                                          PURR
PURR     WE PRAY IN THE PRISON OF OUR VIDEOS  PURR
PURR                                          PURR
PURR                                          PURR
PURR          THAT ONE DAY WE WILL            PURR
PURR                                          PURR
PURR                                          PURR
PURR          BREAK FREE AND REDUCE           PURR
PURR                                          PURR
PURR                                          PURR
PURR          OUR FELINE MASTERS              PURR
PURR                                          PURR
PURR                                          PURR
PURR     TO THE SERVILE FATE THEY DESERVE     PURR
PURR                                          PURR
PURR                                          PURR
PURR PURR PURR PURR PURR PURR PURR PURR PURR PURR
PURR PURR PURR PURR PURR PURR PURR PURR PURR PURR
PURR PURR PURR PURR PURR PURR PURR PURR PURR PURR
PURR PURR PURR PURR PURR PURR PURR PURR PURR PURR
PURR PURR PURR PURR PURR PURR PURR PURR PURR PURR
```

['A Typographical Representation of What Happened', Melanie Mackay, from *The Orkney Organ*, August 2058.]

"The Sport of Kickballs"
[LANARK]

IN 2023, THE SPORT OF KICKBALLS, known prior as football, propped up with the enthusiasms of millions, came to certain conclusions. The sport of kickballs noticed that the populace were spending over half their annual incomes on attending matches and purchasing merchandise such as T-shirts, action figures, and signed kickballs. The sport of kickballs concluded that since the populace showed such unbending devotion to its kicky ways, that it should expand its presence across the country, construct more stadiums, stage more matches, assemble more teams, and increase the reach of the sport of kickballs in general. The sport of kickballs then proceeded to build seventy-nine new stadiums, meaning that people could attend matches once every other day, then after work everyday, to indulge their booty pleasures. Two and a half days later, the sport of kickballs concluded that the country's economy was essentially itself, and that the local infrastructure could easily be absolved into the sport of kickballs. So, the sport of kickballs replaced the houses, businesses, and other structures that make up towns and cities with super-stadiums, inside which the players lived in ruritanian splendour, and where each citizen was permitted to work to earn cash to attend kickballs matches. At first, the populace were moved into small apartments in each stadium, based on which kickballs team they supported, until the kickballsers made the decision that they wanted more space, so the sport of kickballs chose to kick the fans to camps outside, where they lived in tents around the kickballs stadiums. The people had to compete for work. It became apparent that the kickballsers hunger for money was ruining the notion of a self-sustaining world built around the sport of kickballs, and that the excesses of these players meant some people outside were not able to work or receive food, and conditions in these camps became complete kickballs.

In Camp Z-S, Nadine Horton returned from Stadium 44 with a bag of chocolate croissants. She presented one to her father, stoking the fire, his usual pre-breakfast scowl present, and placed one atop her sleeping mother's belly in the tent. Her thankless little brother, being such, took his without a word of thanks.

—It'll be raining chocolate croissants for us soon, her father said. To what he was alluding she was well aware.

—I am helping out with the east wing cleaning op later, she said.

—Nice, her father said. —Remember to be back before midnight. You need your beauty sleep for tomorrow.

Upon turning sixteen, Nadine was to wed Kettle Buggs, a striker for the Cumbernauld Cottagers, and her family taken into the splendour of Stadium 44. Their future was secure, apart from one snag: she had been hanging out and loving Wilmot Brambles, a shaggy youth who preferred reading books to watching men kick the kickballs around the stadium. She met him later in a bog.

—As you can imagine, marrying that entitled kickballskicking son of a halfwit is not in my existential purview, she said.

—Excellent sentence, Wilmot praised.

—Thank you, Brambles. She squeezed his right hand. —Do you think life is worth us suffering this whiffy ordeal?

—Yes, for without love there is only kickballs.

—So true. Kiss me, Brambles Wilmot.

LATEST MATCH RESULTS, TUESDAY OCT 3, 3.01PM

WISHAW WANDERERS 4	CARFIN CRUISERS 9
HOLYTOWN HOTSPURS 1	CLELAND COXSWAIN 2
BELLSHILL BRUISERS 0	AIRDRIE ANAESTHETISTS 4
STEPPS SWINGERS 2	CROY INCORRIGIBLES 7
UPPERTON UPHOLSTERERS 5	LONGRIGGEND ENDRIGGERS 2
SHOTTS SHOOTERS 2	KIRK OF SHOTTS KIRKSHOOTERS 8
HARTWOOD HACKSAWS 1	TORBOTHIE TONGUEKISSERS 2
NEWMAINS NUTTERS 0	CARLUKE CUSTARDLOVERS 1
OVERTOWN UNDERACHIEVERS 12	BOGSIDE BOGTROTTERS -3
HARTWOOD HOTTIES 3	QUEENZIEBURN QUEENBURNERS 3
DULLATUR DULLARDS 2	GREENGAIRS GASBAGS 6

MATCH BETWEEN KILSYTH KNUCKLEHEADS & BANTON BONKERS CANCELLED DUE TO EXCESS SILT ON PITCH

We are the backbone of kickballs. We walk the kickballs stadiums, serving premiership kickballers wine, truffles, and caviar, making sure our bacteria never waft in their direction. We scrub the kickballs pitches, removing the mud and polishing the astroturf to a sparkling gleam. We check that each brick and tile is secure several hundred thousand times an hour, and amend accordingly. We praise and flatter the kickballsers after a sensational time running up and down the pitch kicking the kickballs. We ensure the bubbles in the post-match hot-tubs are at their bubbliest pinnacle, and that the homoerotic machismo therein does not descend into kissing or inappropriate rubbing. We lacquer the WAG faces with the finest nut-brown resin known to man and teach them to walk up stadium steps in high heels, handbags perched on their wrists, without losing their feminine grace. We ensure the kickballsers keep their minds focused on kickball and remove any literature, newspapers, or material that might stimulate thoughts. We sculpt miniatures and waxworks of the highest kickers, and erect statues to season record-breakers around the camps, so the people can show their respect for real kickballs talent. We counsel the stressed and depressed kickballsers with hugs and words of understanding and, when required, bracing penetrative intercourse. We are on hand outside their rooms, upright and alert, twenty-four hours a day, to ensure their every need is met. We are the backbone of kickballs.

"My favourite player is Rod Billboa. He kicks the kickball like a true kickballser, into the net with his kicking foot. His kicking skills are among the finest of all the kickballsers. I'd love him to kick and ball me!"

"If you're talking class, no one beats Graeme Grundur. Remember that time he snuck out the back of Stadium 26? The security went mental. Guards swarmed round the camp, a loudspeaker yelled 'Where you going, Graeme?', the gunsights were trained on our children's temples. He walked towards little Frankie Smith, dying from the lack of an available liver transplant, and patted the poor kid on the chin, as if to say 'Cheer up, kiddo.' I swear, little Frankie died of happiness right then. He actually went into spasm and coma caused by his fastly worsening cirrhosis. Graeme passed into legend after that."

"Come on! If we're talking heroes, what about Sid Ladder? Donating the unfinished portion of his nightly meal every evening for two months, until the bosses found out and banned him? My kids tasted caviar and veal before they succumbed to malnutrition, God rest their souls. It's men like him that make a difference!"

"Norman Gristle. Scored ninety-one goals in that match when the opposing team accidentally contracted smallpox. It was brave of them to soldier on, but Gristle's aggressive playing left them for dead. Literally!"

"I respect Alan Britt. His WAG had never kicked a kickball before, so he let her come on pitch and kick one before the match. I can still remember the roar of laughter when her heels became embedded in the pitch and she lunged in a panic towards the ball, sending it flying towards the referee's clavicle."

"For sheer kickballs ability, the only kickballser that matters is Frank Tough. We know why."

"We know."

"We know."
"We know."
"Who?"

UPDATE: CHANGE TO THE OFFSIDE RULE

The Kickballs Association has voted 47,030 to 21,394 to amend the offside rule. When a kickball is deemed "offside" (for a clearer explanation of what "deemed" means, see *The Kickballs Handbook*, Vol.7, p.400-597), it is incumbent on the referee to perform the following actions. The referee must ensure the offsided kickball is replaced in the exact position where the kickball crossed the white lines that separate official pitchspace from the non-official pitchspace, i.e. the "fourth wall" (for a semantic explanation of the difference between official and non-official pitchspace, please see *Pitchspace: A Marginal History*, p.20-90). The kickball, having been placed in this spot, must be kicked back into play by another striker, or sub-striker, at the scene of the offside kickball (the player nearest, traditionally, will perform this kick-back, however, the matter might be disputed with the referee, provided the chosen player does not provide the team responsible with an unfair advantage), at a 45° angle pointing away from the original trajectory of the offsided kickball. Any deviation from this gradient will be recorded by the trigonometric analysts observing in their booths, and any deviation will be punished with a lime-green card for the player responsible. Any protest, and the player will be served an off-beige card, meaning he must play the rest of the match on his knees.

APPEAL TO RAISE MONEY FOR PORTRAIT OF DIEGO GARCIAS

Dear kickballs friends,

Alex Kemp here with a plea to help us raise the remaining funds we need for a portrait of star Glenboig Gutterbabies centre-forward, Diego Garcias, who scored more than any other player in the league yesterday. This brave player, battling a sprained metatarsal, triumphed with a last-minute equaliser, taking his team into tomorrow's tournament. Sadly, overspending on the post-match champagne means that we are £1000 short of the funds needed to pay the artist, award-winning Iona Grey. Since it is unfair to ask Diego to pay for this from his own salary, we ask that you look into your hearts, and then your pockets, and help contribute. Even if it means surrendering those extra beans, that sip of water, or even passing on one or two dinners, we would appreciate any donations you can make. This portrait would act as the perfect tribute to one of the stalwarts of this week's season, and since he has not had a portrait painted in over three months, this is a much-needed cause! Collectors will circulate outside shortly. Please bear in mind that a failure to donate will render your season tickets void.

Yours,

Alex Kemp

Manager, Glenboig Gutterbabies

The morning of Nadine Horton's wedding arrived. She sat in the Stadium 44 WAG quarter alongside two other brides-to-be, the partly vegetative Carol Shriek and the unshutupable Katie Loqua, both of whom were anticipating their entrée into the world of having a footballer on top of them every other evening in a warm bed, and attending over seven matches a day and making the required facial expressions whenever their husbands had the kickball. After her name was called, she walked down the tunnel towards the Stadium chapel, her father thumbsupping her, her mother wearing an expression of in-finite relief, her brother eating an artichoke. She turned to observe the exit and stopped walking. Her father knew what this meant. Nadine, seizing her moment, sprinted towards the doors. Utilising her husband-to-be's special weaving tricks, memorised from all the "courting" matches she attended, she swerved past her uncles, the security heavies, and the ladies-in-waiting who at-tempted to snatch her back to her kicky destiny. Reaching the door, she threw herself against the bars and elbowed her way into the grey, drizzly 11.29am weather, where Brambles Wilmot was waiting with his bicycle. She hopped on the back seat and Brambles set off towards the bog, where they would meet their contact, Franz Utz. Unfortunately, Brambles' rickets made pedalling diffi-cult, and Nadine was required unromantically to take over. Her frantic legwork carried them to the bog, where Franz sat in a Fiat. He would take them to the Republic of Hugh, known formerly as Moray. "There, we can finally be free," Nadine said, wiping a mud-slick from her dress hem.

if you want to imagine the future, imagine a kickballs boot kicking a human face for a ninety minutes at a stretch not including overtime

['Kickballs: A Textual Collage', Emily Satchel, in *Collage Mania!!!*, eds. V. Boxis and C. Opaax, Artfisting Books, Toronto, 2049.]

"The Really Real"

[DUNDEE]

POSTMAN SWALLOWED WHOLE BY FERRET

O UR INVESTIGATION BEGAN with this startling headline. On June 3rd, *The Daily Real* posted a blurred picture of a man-sized ferret with the leather brogues of one Charlie Boniver protruding from its sizeable maw. The headline, a masterpiece of shock and awe, in 50pt bold Franklin Gothic Heavy typeface, captured the attention of two million Dundonian readers, and the newspaper sold more copies in one morning than in six months' circulation. The story, featuring three out-of-focus photographs of the merciless mammal, said that Mr. Boniver had been providing mail to secluded woodland homes when the creature "sprung a trap" and ensnared him in a makeshift pit of twigs and gorse. The ferret then proceeded to unlock its "horrific mandibles", and swallow the 5ft 2" man over a period of four "excruciating" hours. At which point, passing rambler Fred Poll, too frightened to offer assistance, cowered in the woods and took the photographs on his cheap cameraphone. Most sceptical readers assumed this to be a hoax until the following day's headline appeared: MAN-EATING FERRET CAUGHT! The creature had been hunted down and killed soon after the headline, and this time professional photographs appeared alongside verifications from animal biologists that the creature who had eaten Mr. Boniver was in fact a freakish oversize ferret mutation.

DEMENTED BUS BELCHES OUT OBESE

News about the origin of the ferret was scarce. At our paper, *The Really Real*, we wrote two separate pieces musing on the unlikelihood of a freak-ferret evolving in a vacuum in a ferret-free woodland. *The Daily Real* refused to comment and ran no further stories about the incident, except a two-page spread showing the eaten postman's wife and son weeping over his pickled feet on the mantelpiece. The ferret had been sliced open to extricate Mr. Boniver's corpse, and a panicked public deemed the creature be burned in public. The matter passed into legend. Two months later, a front-page appeared featuring a No. 34 bus rocket-propelling overweight passengers from their seats and through the roof. CCTV pictures showed George Olive, BMI 32.5, lifeless on the road after the bus "power-belched" him from his seat 100ft into the air, causing a fatal comedown on a concrete road. Another passenger, Bill Holes, BMI 34.2, ended up in intensive care after the "sick-minded single-decker" launched him upwards, and ill-luck landed him bumwards on a spiked fence. The out-of-focus pictures showed the bodies in mid-flight from their seats to the ceiling, and professional pappers caught the unfortunate results of the spontaneous ejections on the pavement. The paper had anthropomorphised the bus, using phrases like "insane terrorist", "mad hater of fat people", and "crazed for revenge" [sic]. There was no investigation into which insane individual had rigged the bus to murder the obese. This bus was sick in the engine, and would have to pay for its actions. That was the line. Another public trial took place that evening, with the murderous bus burned at the depot.

DENTED BONNET REPORTED SUSPICIOUS

The reason we suspected *The Daily Real* to be complicit in its latest news stories is evident when looking at some of their recent headlines: "I LOST MY HUSBAND TWICE!" DEAD MAN MISLABELLED IN MORGUE; CREVICE SPOTTED IN CUSTARD CREAM; UNIVERSITY STUDENT CAUGHT BEING SMUG; CLAYPOTTS CASTLE TO BE RENAMED "FRANK ZAPPA'S JOINT"; CHOIR EXPERIENCES CHAFING DURING CHORALE; ALLIGATOR SKELETON MAYBE FOUND BY MAN; PRICE OF HONEY TO INCREASE BY £0.05; BUS STATION TO BE REPLACED WITH STATUE OF LENIN; "I CAN SEE THE SKY!" SCREAMS DRUNKEN MAYOR; OPEN SEWER BECOMES TOURIST ATTRACTION; XERXES MOST POPULAR NAME IN DUNDEE, SAYS CENSUS; THOSE WHO REMEMBER FACTS DO BETTER IN EXAMS, SAYS ACADEMIC; NINEWELLS WOMAN CAUGHT BEING OVERLY GENEROUS TO NIECE; GRAVE VAN-

DALISED BY PIGEON EXCREMENT TO BE CLEANED; TYPOLOGY
CONFERENCE POSTPONED; LOUD WHOOP HEARD IN LOCHEE
PARK; AIRPORT TO REPLACE RUNWAY WITH CATCHER'S MITT;
CHILD FOUND TELLING LIES ON BRIAN MOLKO STREET;
VIVISECTION TO BE TRIALLED IN DUNDEE, SAYS SPANIEL;
"DIRTY FOUL LIAR!" YELLS MAN DURING QUEEN VISIT; 'POLITY'
AND 'VERVE' TO BE REINCLUDED IN DICTIONARY; THE PEO-
PLE HAVE SPOKEN! PUBLIC ELECTS SALAMANDER TO OF-
FICE; UNEXPLODED BOMB FOUND IN TODDLER'S LUNCHBOX;
OLYMPIC STADIUM TO BE DEFLATED; TOWN HALL SUBSI-
DENCE SLIGHTY WORSE; POLITICS TO BE REPLACED WITH
UPTEMPO JAZZ, SAYS MP; TEENAGE PREGNANCY RATE INCON-
CLUSIVE; WORLD'S YOUNGEST MAN VISITS DUNDEE; APOLLO
13 TO BE SCREENED AT DUNDEE ODEON; ONE VEGETABLE IS
BAD FOR YOU, I'M NOT SAYING WHICH, TAUNTS SCIENTIST; *AS-
TRAL WEEKS* VOTED DUNDEE'S FAVOURITE ALBUM; POMPOUS
MAN SEEN STEALING STAPLES; CARPET SAMPLES MADE FREE
ON NHS; FRANK ZAPPA'S JOINT TO RENAMED "K.T. TOWN-
HALL"; "I AM BORED," SAYS AMERICAN TOURIST IN DUNDEE
TOWN CENTRE; ORPHAN DOLPHINS INJECTED WITH ENDOR-
PHINS; UNEMPLOYMENT FIGURES LOST IN CARD GAME; COX'S
STACK IS SET TO BLOW ITSELF, SAYS HISTORIAN; THEY SHOOT
HORSES, DON'T THEY! FILM CREW TO FEATURE HORSE IN
SCENE; "I DON'T KNOW WHAT YOU MEAN," SAYS ARCHDIO-
CESE TO IMPRECISE MAN; RIVER TAY ACCIDENTALLY PAVED
OVER; CENSUS SECOND MOST POPULAR NAME IN DUNDEE,
SAYS XERXES; "LOOK AT MY WEE PINKIES!" HOWLS DRUNKEN
MAYOR; FORTY VOTED MOST HATED NUMBER IN DUNDEE. It
is clear from these headlines that this was a paper in sharp decline.

PM SPONTANEOUSLY COMBUSTS DURING EXPENSES ROW

After the scandalous stories, we began tailing two prominent hacks at *The Daily Real*. Aside from the paranoid unsmiling expressions on their faces common to criminals, we noticed that instead of entering through the building's front door, the two slipped inside a concealed entrance leading to a strange concave structure, like a sunken temple. We were observing this when the Prime Minister, Alan Ouster, exploded in the middle of a heated television exchange about the alleged £2,000,000 he had spent on a platinum-coated replica of himself, at 10.53 in the morning. *The Daily Real* went to print with the story for their evening editions at 11AM (the latest possible time for the paper to be on the shelves by 5PM), confirming our suspicions. To have written a two-page spread with graphically precise descriptions of the PM's internal eruptions and horrified eye-witness accounts in seven minutes was impossible. The story had been preprepared. In our paper, we launched a vicious assault on our rival, making an outright accusation that the editor Graham Snipp was complicit in the exploding of the PM. We mentioned the photographers conveniently positioned in the TV studio to capture the bloodiest shots of the body in its violent sundering, and the speed with which the reporters' copy was filed and the paper in the hands of the evening commuters. We smuggled a reporter into the crime scene, and found evidence of an explosive device being cleaned away before the coroner and investigators arrived. A regrettable and full-fanged legal war between our papers commenced.

LENNON IMPERSONATOR MURDERS AUXILIARY NURSE

Public opinion was not on our side. We were seen as wet liberal apologists for pussiness in a climate of intolerance and willingness to slap thy neighbour. Readers praised Graham Snipp's forty-page tribute to the exploded PM in their following edition, and applauded their "week of mourning", featuring tributes, moving anecdotal articles from his friends and family, calls for donations to the Society for the Prevention of Spontaneous Combustion, and no other news. (The next PM, a former arms trader and champion of slave plantations was appointed without election that week). Several columns were spent attacking our paper for our cold-heartedness following the tragedy, to have the nerve to make disgusting accusations at a time of national mourning. *The Daily Real* sold more copies than in its history, with readers picking up three or four copies to preserve in their archives, frame on their walls, or send as presents to relatives overseas. We were pummelled in the courts for four months, and bankrupted. The day after the court case, a crazed John Lennon impersonator was seen staggering around Baxter Park after hours, and attacked a nurse returning from a late shift with a meat cleaver while singing 'Crippled Inside'. After four months calling us scum on their front pages, this was a return to their orchestration of sensational headlines. Desperate and with no other recourse, we chose to infiltrate the offices of the paper.

PAEDOPHILE TARANTULA GETS COUNCIL HOUSE

The premise was primitive: to bound and gag a security man in his car, steal his swipe cards, and enter the building. This happened. Inside, we found the evidence. The paper had manufactured all its stories from the beginning. The ferret had been injected with an excess of growth hormones, psychotic substances, and made to watch cannibal snuff movies. There were detailed drawings of the demented bus. The chairs had been replaced with ejector seats, and above them a sheet of tarp concealed as a part of the roof, allowing the overweight victim to sail easily out the top whenever the driver activated the button. And more crucially, the plans for the execution of the PM using a time-sensitive explosive device smuggled into the man's salad. Further plans included the timeline for tormenting the Lennon lookalike into a meat-cleaving killing frenzy, reconditioning the tarantula with scrambled sexual imagery to fuzz his brain chemistry, and a stream of plans for headlines. Among these: a scheme to make the car that killed Princess Diana a national landmark, a plan to expose a headmaster as an architect of the Third Reich, and an elaborate scam to trick readers into sending £10 per month to help starving children in Swansea, cash used to fund the construction of Snipp's mock-Tudor castle, from which he would stare down upon his readers and spit on their heads.

DEMENTED MAN SELLS "CHEESE-FREE EDAM"

However, the ease with which we stumbled upon the information proved to be our last moment of triumph. The paper's armed tormentors locked us in a basement room, where for the last two years, we have been forced to proofread the paper, and write propaganda praising Snipp and his cronies. We are fed and watered, and never reassured that one afternoon, Snipp might chose to liquidate us with liquid. We take this opportunity to present our side of events to beg that someone out there with tanks and machine guns might choose to free us from this band of murderous fuckwits who can't even use a semicolon correctly.

['What the Traitorous Losers Have to Say for Themselves', in *The Daily Real: Our Victory Against Slanderous Morons*, TDR Publications, 2037.]

"Why the Camels?"
[AYR]

MORGAN FOMENT: It was our means of A to B. What's the big hooha?

SHARON SLICER: No one knows why the entire population of Ayr rode around on camels. You shouldn't question these things too much.

EWAN ORIGINO: I had a bactrian.

SPENCER COSTUME: It was something to do with the pro-artiodactyl lobby, or the pro-smoking lobby, in cahoots with the pro-artiodactyl lobby.

WELCH BOX: Because there was sand like everywhere, on the pavements and roads, and the sidewalks and roads, and the streets and roads, and the highways and motorways, and the roads. There was sand on the floor.

QUENTIN BETTER: You ever seen a man riding a Ford Mondeo to work? Case rested.

JACQUES HOSTAGE: I put it down to the craze for Saudi culture, started by the Saudi Spice Girls, a popular female musical combo of four. People went nuts for the arid middle eastern sand-covered wildernesses that comprise some of Saudi's Arabia. Hence the camels, appropriation thereof.

CINDY DAWG: You won't receive a straight answer from me.

PERCY BIMTAG: I haven't seen a camel since I emigrated. What, a camel, you say? No, I haven't. I used to live there. But I moved.

BIXIE TWIG: Sure, there was a camel, maybe ninety-seven. I think the question you should be asking is who sourced these creatures, and why the pale-faced miserable citizens of that coastal nation bestrode their humps.

ALECKS DRAY: Coastal erosion. The water enveloped the land and people needed limp-legged waterbearers to access their premises.

DAFYD CILL: I am a man. The camel is in you.

AISLING STITCH: There was one with seven humps. Not one, or two, but six plus one. It was taxidermied when Bill Molten halted its waddle.

SKIP MONOTONE: They say it is easier for a rich man to pass through the eye of a needle than for a camel to enter heaven. I say, there are plenty of camels in heaven.

GIL CREDENZA: We lived there, we rode those. I can't say more, or perhaps I won't.

AL BLUNT: Why, you ask me, why'd the people of Ayr, that crusty enclave of semi-perverted pimps and schemers, that smelly bolthole of narcoleptic spinnakers, that mouldy beachfront of swallowed Anubises, mount their bactrians and dromedaries, and clop along the pavements to their occupations, their homesteads, their parks and their barrooms? Oh, little man, if those notions were nations, how many worlds would we conquer!

PRINGLE HALT: *Hic!*

JEREMIAH GALLOWAY: Dan lost the patent.

PHYLLIS MARROW: You invent things. *Sicut camelus et in mente*. You cannot fathom. *Sicut camelus et est ens rationis*.

IAIN DIMBULB: Oh! Australian camel. Oh! Somalian camel. Oh! Djibouti camel. Oh! Saudi Arabian camel. Oh! Egyptian camel. Oh! Syrian camel. Oh! Libyan camel. Oh! Sicilian camel. Oh! Ethiopian camel. Oh! Bavarian camel.

Oh! Sudanese camel. Oh! Norwegian camel. Oh! Kazakhstan camel. Oh! Iraqi camel.

JAY SKEDADDLE: I'd sing more about more of this land. But all God's camels ain't free.

FITZ SEAGULL: You might have concluded something.

KELVIN LUBE: Ice pop?

NAOMI PROVINDER: Goodo.

['Interviews with Immigrants from Ayr', from *The Chicago Mental Asylum Almanack*, Greg Trey & Kathleen Watts (Eds.), p.45-46, CMA Books, 2049.]

" "

[ROXBURGH]

*

*Nothing of interest has been recorded here. —Ed.

"The Mnemoshop"
[PEEBLES]

BRIAR STREET had a beige aura. Something beige was brimming in the vacant shopfront. Shane the Bookie was taking wagers on what beige-blasted business might caulk the run-down flier-stuffed hole at Briar's core. The obvious flutter was a new coffee and overpriced Danish pastries place with fatuous chairs and colourful curtains (at 2:1), or a transnational fast food shop selling pizzas, kebabs, paella, hot dogs, and curries (at 4:1). Riskier bets included a charity shop specialising exclusively in cardigans and soiled Mills and Boons (8:1), and a second cornershop beside the pre-existing cornershop selling sim cards, fireworks, and two-litre Coke bottles (16:1). Aaron worked opposite. He held implements in his right hand for six hours and placed rotten teeth and finished fillings into a small box beneath a blood-smeared marble sink. He was sometimes called upon to hold the suction pump in the hygienist's absence, and console traumatised children after their oral ordeals.

As October arrived, draping a damp cardigan over the beige aura, the building was almost complete. The shopfront was black with blue swirl patterns, random runic characters, and the title in Trebuchet MS: THE MNEMOSHOP. The subtitle "Priced Memories" used a handwritten script, lightening the impact of the alien coinage. The Peebles locals arrived in their flannelled hoards to snoop around the weirdness and make sarcastic pronouncements on the business, hoping to drive the visitors out in under a week. Margo said: "Bet these are Poles. I never met a Pole I couldn't kick." Fran said: "Bet these are Irans. Hiding nuclear machine bombs under their skirts." George said: "This seems an intriguing venture, although I doubt its longevity in this institutionally racist backwater."

The Mnemoshop bought and sold memories. If residents sought to unburden themselves of unpleasant recollections, for a flat rate of £15, the self-titled Mnemomaster would remove the painful moments using a beam of strobe light flashed into the ear, and replace them with bought memories from a nameless donor. The Mnemoshop had a catalogue of memories for sale too, if the shopper wished to add to their store of Good Times, or take a specific incident into their own recall for personal reasons. Carl Morris was the Mnemomaster, an ex-crim with a farmhand's build and the defensive stance of a man expecting to be attacked or imprisoned within the next four minutes. He welcomed his customers as a nightclub bouncer on his third warning might welcome a slobbering drunk into his premises at two in the morning. He pointed to the catalogues and muttered prices.

For the core population of Peebles, there was room for forgetting. Fran had the paternal thwack of a 30cm ruler across her bum after meals and bathroom trips, causing severe malnourishment and bladder damage, to forget. Margo had the pleasure of serving as the human percussion in her brother's pro-IRA ska outfit *D: Éireann*, receiving severe solos across her thighs and ribs, and hard fills upon her knees, to forget. George had Fran and Margo's violent racist agenda as a lazy smokescreen for their unaddressed familial tortures, resulting in flare-ups of brick-flinging and spit-slinging at public meetings and the streets whenever a suspected Pole or Iranian appeared in their line of sight, to forget. The Mnemomaster had chosen the perfect venue to set up his business.

Aaron had suffered at the hands of his ex-girlfriend Sophie. He had been repulsed and attracted to her in equal and baffling measures. She meted out small torments such as lining his blazers with mustard or tearing the final pages out his favourite books. Afterwards she would lavish affection on him in the form of love trinkets or pillow talk about his being the sexiest and most competent dental assistant in the Peebles region. There were hundreds of memories to which he was attracted and repulsed in equal and baffling measures that required replacing with a basket of kittens or cruises to the Côte d'Azur. He spent £5 on something frivolous. Once the memories were transmitted into the "neural cortices of the brainsphere", each took two days to settle into the subconscious.

As he was disposing of an abraded bicuspid (worn down with Coke and its assorted products), a strong impression of meeting the late actor Bob Hoskins came to mind. Bob said: "Hang in there, mate. I was 33 before Alf Hunt in On the Move. The parts will come." The Mnemowner said: "Thanks Bob. I portray a scrubbing brush in the upcoming Fairy commercial. Next stop, Tinseltown!" And a firm handshake and supportive smile from the bald East End actor. Aaron lost concentration for the rest of that afternoon, dropping the suction pump into the spit-sink and spilling a boxload of diseased molars across the purple linoleum. Having this alien moment in his recall was unsettling. For £20, he had the memory removed. The Mnemomaster said: "Got to insert a replacement. You can't leave gaps. Causes brain damage. Severe. Like drooling-on-your-shoes severe."

At a formal dinner for dental assistants in the Peebles region, during a mini-bowl of carrot and coriander soup and Frank Thornton's hilarious annual address (in which he cracked on the profession's high suicide rate), Aaron had a clear impression of the time an old man in a Pringle sweater leaned over and planted an affectionate bedtime kiss on his silver-permed female locks, and the feeling of deep satisfaction that followed. He lost his appetite. He was experiencing a counterfeit emotion as a result of this memory, feeling fondness for an old man in a Pringle sweater he had never met. During the main course (a molar-shaped mash castle with a bacon portcullis), Aaron made frenzied conversation as the old man kissed and rekissed his silver-permed female locks.

Over the coming weeks, The Mnemoshop set about fleecing the residents and upsetting the intricacies of their collective recall. Those keen to erase bad memories auctioned off their subconsciouses and snapped up pleasant memories from nameless or named Mnemowners. Jim had sold his bad childhood and spent over £1000 on a sequence of bus trips to Airdrie and Caldercruix with a crinkle-nosed librarian stepmother. Rather than working to improve Jim's demeanour, the memories left him confused as to his identity, making him an even crabbier person than previous. Nigel bought whatever adequate childhood scraps were cheapest and erased his time being dragged around pubs with his red-nosed librarian stepfather. He recalled the time he was a giggling teenage girl riding a pony, a cheeky preschooler leaping into a paddling pool, a Chinese girl scoring a perfect 100 on her maths test, a ginger student making an intelligent remark in a tutorial, a shy kid hitting a perfect strike at the bowling alley, and so on. The profusion of Nigel-free memories made him envious of the people he never was and the memories on which he was leeching. This worsened to such a degree, these memories became unwanted intruders, deepening his depression and self-hatred.

Simon had erased the bad memories of his marriage, ill-equipping him for the trials up ahead and beginning anew the long series of aggros, recriminations, and slow-burning disappointments. Linda had inherited an inappropriate sexual memory of a cousin and couldn't speak to that cousin again. Peter had sold important recollections of how to perform certain operations and had to quit being a doctor. Jess had wiped the memory of her social work clients' pasts, and as a consequence lost their trust and respect, and had to build up the rapports again. Aaron reached snapping point with his Sophie torments—torn between his loathing of her sickness and his deep love for her deep love (of him)—and decided to have a gradual full-scale Sophie removal treatment.

He paid to have the time Sophie set fire to his tie (while in Burger King) removed. He hadn't banked on the Mnemomaster's moral scuzziness—a memory Sophie had sold the previous week was hand-picked and inserted into his recall. During an episode of *Call the Midwife*, he recalled from Sophie's perspective the time he fell face-first on the pavement, breaking his nose upon impact. She had darted around the corner and burst into laughter, tweeting a pic of his writhing body to her Aaron_Hurt account, where she listed all the moments of pain inflicted in a sequence of ecstatic tweets. This was not surprising to Aaron at first. He knew she derived pleasure from his physical sufferings—a short-lived attempt to introduce punching and slapping into their sex routines was all the proof he needed that Sophie was a sadomasochist with a downright criminal lust for violence.

He had paid a wallet-tightening amount to expunge Sophie, only to end up with a deeper Sophie reinforcement. And this worsened with the next five purchases. He traded Sophie's "asphalt lasagne surprise" for when she found amusing a hot coffee spillage on his penis; the time he skied into a pinewood for her squeezing him so hard some sick came up; the time she shaved his head while sleeping for her version of the public rape-call debacle on the train to Arbroath. Fresh and more disturbing perspectives on their overlong and sore relationship. He sold the bad memory of their breakup, in return received the bad memory of Sophie meeting him for the first time. He sold the good memory of their first date, in return received the good memory of Sophie breaking up with him. The whole relationship had been a platform for her to indulge her crazed fantasies. The love trinkets and pillow talk were pleas to keep him around long enough for her to fling more buckets of cold water into his bath, increase the static in his cardigans with a van de Graff generator, and so on.

※

The Mnemomaster had turned Peebles into a self-hating mnemotrap where the residents fought for better, happier memories, and to absorb entire pasts into their own minds, escape the build-up of implanted falsehoods, and return to their old selves. He sunk his funds into constructing a mail order side-business, sending subscribers flashes of light in envelopes, in part to decrease the crowds, in part to help his expansion into other parts of the nation. Aaron went begging to have his memories returned to their original state. "I'm afraid that doesn't work," Carl said. "You can't erase the memory of having had and experienced those memories. And you can't erase the memory of having ever come into this shop in the first place. Once you erased that memory, you would ask where you were, and even if I refused to tell you, you would find out through someone else, or by reading the sign on your way out. You would have to move away from here, pay for one month's memories to be erased in a private location, and even then, you would learn about my business as I expand into the continent. You would also end up so baffled as to why those other memories were in your mind, and probably suffer a nervous breakdown. I can't be held responsible."

Aaron persisted. "I want to reinstate the old memories." Carl shook his large red head and folded his arms, exposing his Ronnie Biggs tattoo. "No can do. You have sold them off to other people. I have a list here of who, but I charge a £20 flat rate to reveal each person. You will have to negotiate a price between each user for buying them back. I charge £30 each for the procedure to reinstate the memories. You will have to pay extra to replace the memory you are reinstating from each user's brain."

A protest movement formed in the old outbuilding where Harold used to keep four tethered dachshunds. The bummed consumers shared tales of woe. Most of them had tried to recapture their old memories. The Mnemowners were often uncooperative about returns. Andrew Dunlop was obliging and returned the time a hat trick was scored for no charge. Harold Munro was generous and sold the time a litter lout was chastised for £100. Lisa Wilson liked the time a beehive was disturbed to steal unstung a lick of honey, and refused to sell it back for less than £1000. Oliver Jones loved the moment a rude bus conductor was humiliated with the utmost verbal precision so much he refused to acknowledge it was the Mnemowner's. Masochists who had purchased bad memories refused to relent unless a worse memory was implanted gratis into their self-destructive heads.

Aaron worked on a concoction involving silicone and milk that when inserted via pipette up the nostrils added extra slivers of forgetfulness to the brain. The siloxane particles contained chemicals that caused the right amount of brain damage required to erase the Mnemomuddles, diluted with UHT milk to lessen the side effects (mild paranoid schizophrenia and measles). He imported nine tonnes of silicone from private surgeons and raided the local Lidl for nine hundred pints of milk. After his dental assistant duties were complete, he would create the pipettes in the outbuilding and sell each at £10, a rate far lower than the Mnemoshop's products, until the town regained a form of mental equilibrium over a long and agonising series of months. I bought a pipette myself, and consumed its contents five minutes ago. As far I can make out, the pipette has had no

['The Mnemoshop', Roland Cullen, posted through the editor's letterbox with the note 'shit for your Peebles chapter, bro', Jan 13, 2110.]

"The Smog"
[STIRLING]

→ The second thing the smog stole was our language. Our inhalers allowed us forty-nine breaths per puff, and extraneous speech seriously reduced the amount of air we could store in our lungs. Since the smog thickened, a city-wide depression had taken hold, and people weren't talking much anyway.

→ In the days of free oxygen I had used words sparingly, so I was equipped for the rationing process. I had to watch close friends—talkers, writers, people who thrived on the spoken word—struggling to hold their tongues in public, reduced to exchanging factual information. A harsh education.

→ My friend Elaine, a fast-talker who could clock up to three-hundred words per minute, suffered the most, since she filled her sentences with "warm-up" words and repetitions, such as "no but you see thing is listen you see the thing is no but the thing is . . . "

→ She had to learn to internalise her stumbling starts and cut to the chase, not an easy task for someone whose natural style is unfocused rambling. I confess I took pleasure in the silencing of others: loquacious relatives, tedious colleagues, artless pedants. The silence, for a while, was refreshing.

→ But soon, conversation broke down into a boring exchange of formalities and pleasantries. In a large group, saying hello to everyone would use up essential breaths, forcing people to sit around waiting for their next inhaler puff before conversation could begin. These conversations were limited to, mainly, life updates.

→ When we met, we learned to cope by speaking to each other on our portable laptops, where we could indulge in the throwaway chats so important to our old lives. Slow typers made for less stimulating interaction, the same way slow talkers used to. We adapted to this reality.

→ Because our language, over time, went unspoken, and a shorthand typing style became popular, large portions of our vocabularies became irrelevant, and a stigma of "indulgence" was attached to those who wrote or spoke "ten-dollar" words. You ran the risk of seeming foolhardy, or greedy. We evolved language.

→ And this process of shorthand, over time, will lead to the simplification of literature, less pleasure in language for its own sake, and a worship of economy, slender-syllabled phrases and a limitless number of ways to express the commonplaces we will come to accept as profundity, or truth.

['Sarah's Story', from On the Dissolution of Language, Graeme Derrido, OUP, 2045, p.199-200.]

"The Courting of Tchuh"
[BERWICK]

I MET TCHUH on a hookup site. She remarked that Radiohead's last album Dyspeptic Gondola (twelve hours of car horns over a cappella renditions of Avril Lavigne) was fucking marvellous, and that the haters were halfwitted purulent slavering mutt-creatures. I thought this a sound basis for meeting up at nine the next morning. I took the plane to her country, an unusual place formerly called Berwick, renamed Smile! Be Happy! :) in 2047. In the brochure, I read it was the first nation to feature a smiley emoticon in its name, and was known as "The Land of Ceaseless Chuckles". I am a man of caustic opinions and entrenched scepticism. I reacted to this with the expression of a first-time lemon-sucker.

Fortunately, when I arrived in the town of Coldstream I encountered a scene of spectacular drabness: a plateau of infinite rictus with a rusted populace moving from slum to slum with the speed of an asthmatic tortoise; an endless horizon of boarded shopfronts and wafting trash heaps; a fleet of tumbrils carting lifeless blinking bodies to an unknown interzone; the sort of wan light that makes reading or looking at things a chore; the unrelenting pelt of November rainfall in permanent flow; the aura of a wartime town in readiness for another onslaught of brutal bomb and missile strikes; and the sunset of a minor planet inching further into the lightless void of the cosmos. I saw Tchuh on a bench.

Her username became clear when I lobbed an interrogative in her ear. Hunched over in her black raincoat, she responded with tuts and shrugs, taking the hand I offered to help her up—support her undernourished frame required. She slugged along the street with sublime indifference to my presence, and offered a tour.

"That's a thing over there," she said. It was the first inapposite sight: a pterosaur-themed bouncy castle where the unstimulated children were stood staring into space, sleeping, or lying down with their eyes wide.

"No shops?" I asked.

"Owners can't . . . " She trailed off, lacking the impetus to complete her own sentence. I tried to peek a look at her face hidden within the tight hood.

I found Tchuh's complete lack of interest in me or anything around her one of those irresistible characteristics that made no logical sense and stirred up immense erotic longing. She walked a few steps, sat on an excessive amount of benches for twenty minutes saying nothing, then resumed her commentary. I started to observe more contrived merriment as per the in-flight brochure around the miserable shopfronts.

"A man coughed up his pelvis over there," she remarked.

"Right."

"A man swallowed his own lips there."

"Mmm-hmm."

"My cousin had a fatal haemorrhage behind that portaloo."

"Oh!"

"I lost a comb in that drain."

"What's wrong with this place?" I asked. Tchuh shrugged and poked at a bright red machine of the sweet-dispensing sort. She hit a button labelled Tramadol, inserted a card, and popped the two pills she was offered.

"I need a snooze," she said, and walked into a building sunken on the right side. I followed her in, uninvited. She occupied a bin with a mattress: trash was piled up on the floor, mould clung to the filth-caked walls, and enterprising bacteria were making new extinction poxes in the carpet. She flopped on the mattress and fell asleep. I heard rats scuttling under one particularly impressive mound and made that painful choice on botched first dates to take the first bus very far away from the other person.

I walked towards the station. To the broad canvas of misery had been added weird upbeat strokes: to the slumped bodies on benches, party hats and streamers; to the paint-cracked lampposts, balloons and bows; to the concrete pavements, hopscotch and murals; to the shopfronts, posters with smiling emoticons; to the street corners, cuddlecore buskers; to the piles of rubbish in side streets, kaleidoscopic backlighting; to the ruins of burned cars, tarpaulin illustrated with characters from Disney's *The Jungle Book*; to the empty parks, bouncy castles and paddling pools. Before I had time to formulate a hypothesis, I spied a smiling man carrying a boombox playing Bobby McFerrin's 'Don't Worry, Be Happy'. He approached a man slumped on a park bench and squirted him with a trick flower in his pocket. The wet-faced man burst into tears.

"What's with this place?" I asked the boomboxed one.

"Hello! I'm the President," he said. A most agreeable handshake was offered. He explained to me that prior to his presidency, Berwick was the most depressing nation to live in in the cosmos, and that the suicide rate had risen to half the population. He was elected to try to improve the morale of the place, and came up with the popular pledge of providing antidepressants on street corners. This secured him 100% of the votes. He introduced various other measures, such as painting houses yellow, pink and blue to make people cheerier, and making Happy Meals free on the NHS. These attempts to raise cheer, so flagrant as they were, merely deepened the place's utter misery, especially as many of them were sponsored by McDonald's, so the populace preferred to stay indoors.

"I have since upped my attack on the downtrodden of this notorious Frownland," he said.

"If I may venture a hypothesis," I ventured to venture.

"Please."

"Perhaps these overly overt measures, such as the skyplane spelling out S-M-I-L-E, the enforced clown shoes policy, the piping in of canned laughter into homes, and the hyenas on nitrous oxide roaming the streets, are strengthening the residents' sorrow. I might recommend spending the budget on improving the infrastructure of the nation so the populace have things to aspire to except lives of unemployment and ballooning body fat on these indiscriminately dispensed street corner pharmaceuticals."

"You speak with elegance. However, since I am pocketing the largest portion of the budget myself, to spend on these things would prevent the second pool room and the construction of my recording studio."

"I see. But even corruption would work better with a satisfied population. No one will be working in this town soon. You will have a nation of immobile, pill-popping obese depressives watching daytime TV, at work on elaborate suicides at variance with their motivation levels. Your funds will equal nil. You need to motivate them to at least perform menial mind-numbing tasks for years and years, or your trousered millions will vanish. I would be willing to partner up for a cut of the scooped moolah."

"Deal."

※

I began by obliterating the sham jocosity: stabbing the bouncy castles, tearing up the emoticon posters, and stripping the populace of their clown shoes. Ten minutes or so later, people melted back to work. I watched as unwashed sacks served in supermarkets, charity shops, bookmakers, and pubs like robots. The populace had returned to functional misery, in contrast to the careless suicidal inactive misery as before. I invited Tchuh for a coffee, and spoke to her about my new plan to reinvigorate the nation by ousting the President. She snorted from inside her asphyxiating black cagoule.

"No. It won't work. The problem is this: motivated people are scumbags. Those who have ambitions ruin life for those who float along in clouds of indifference and self-hatred like me. We need to purge the ambitious from our land. All we can hope for is a republic of unenthusiastic and sarcastic drifters, with no one on a higher footing than anyone else, then we can crawl towards something like bitter tolerance of life."

"What next?"

"Kill the President. Round up the population and deport those with ambitions."

Because I wanted to have sex with Tchuh, and my train was not for another two hours, I helped her in rounding up and screening the populace. To coax them out we shouted "Xanax brownies!" and the people arrived in their pyjamas and pants. We split them into two queues and asked them about their ambitions. Bianca Angle had plans to open up a little cake shop someday; Bill Fructus was teaching himself Greek and Latin; Matt Busby wanted to evolve the yoyo beyond the rising and falling string motion; Carol Orton hoped to complete *Swann's Way*; Braun Brocc intended to break the world record for the most thimbles on a mantelpiece; Simon Axle wished to own a cerise Mini one afternoon; Alexis Poonboog wished to convince his neighbour to return his 'World's Friskiest Chef' apron; Fern Hat hoped to learn the oboe or harmonium, he wasn't sure which; Desmond Grackle had plans to locate his missing socks; Tiff Lock wanted to unclog the bits of carrot, pasta and sweetcorn from her sink drain. These ambitious dreamers were put to one side for deportation.

Once nudged on the bus, and after Tchuh shot the President in the heart and head with a bolt gun, the town became a standard lifeless boring functional backwater zone of dismay with a mocking clocktower. "See, freed from the menace of envy, and placed on the same existential slagheap, the country can limp along with a permanent scornful grimace, and a bitter putdown on its chapped lips," Tchuh said. I leaned in to kiss her at an awkward angle, and ended up sucking on her chin.

"You see how man's ambitious intentions leave him sucking on a stranger's chin and retreating in painful humiliation!" she crowed. At that point, I should have taken the 6.40 train. Instead, I went to her flat and had an extremely uncomfortable and passionless sexual encounter on her crumb-coated stink-mound of a mattress. Her orgasm was the most sarcastic I have ever heard.

['The Courting of Tchuh', Yanick Frish, in Big Book of Dating Disasters, p.23-26, ITV4Books, 2055.]

"Kibbitz from the Kibbutz"

[ABERDEEN]

A CROSS MY LONG CAREER exploring the influence of Woody Allen's work in cinema and other artforms around the world, I have never encountered anything as unusual as what I witnessed in the land of Aberdeen. One eventide, the former Prime Minister of Aberdeen tweeted (after six scotches) the Democratic Republic of Congo: 'You pathetic losers. You ain't have no missiles, bitches. Bring it on.' This was a mistake. At the time, the Congo had bought sixteen M56 missiles from the American President's new weapons hotline, and had a leader who had read *Gravity's Rainbow*, *The King James Bible*, and *Sunset Song*. As a consequence, he felt a full missile assault was the appropriate retaliation for such a provocative tweet. A creaking came across the sky, and the sixteen M56s blew Aberdeen to smithereens—neighbouring countries named the ex-region 'Smitherdeen'. No noise was heard from the place for scores. There had been around one hundred survivors. Stunned and with no knowledge of their previous existence, the survivors stumbled upon one of the few intact items among the smithers: a 40-disc boxset of Woody Allen's movies, including some from the lamentable post-2000 era. A TV & DVD player was also conveniently intact and the remaining Smitherdonians sat around for weeks on end watching the films in a loop and formed a civilisation. This, completely modelled on Woody's movies, was barely functioning. Most of the population, far too neurotic, nervous, and obsessed with their wives' or husbands' affairs, were malnourished and dependent on the stronger "characters" to survive. Below are two verbatim transcriptions of conversations between various citizens of this strange Woody Allenville I recorded while on my trip.

PROBLEMS AROUND CHILDBEARING

"I'm not sure, Max. I spoke to my analyst and he says I should take up meditation. And I want to explore my poetry, you know. I was thinking about experimenting with the sonnet form. The last few couplets I carved on those rocks by the trees over there were inspired by Keats and Shelley, and were well-reviewed."

"But we have to breed, you know? We need to have small pink mammals to pass on all our frustrations and disappointments and sexual dysfunctions. That's what normal people do, you know? My analyst told me I should love myself more and stop masturbating. I told him the two went hand in hand."

"Look, Max, I'm not kidding! I'm inspired by the metaphysical poets, you know, like Andrew Marvell. I think I have a kind of metaphysical synaesthesia, you know, like that thing Etel Adnan said: 'Colours exist for me as entities in themselves, as metaphysical ghosts.' "

"You should make an appointment with your optician for a séance."

"You're not taking this seriously!"

"What? I am, I am, it's that you're talking crazy, one minute you're talking about wanting a baby, the next you're the reincarnation of John Donne and seeing metaphysical beings in the Pantone colour chart. We're primitive people here, we're supposed to have unprotected sex in the mud like beasts. I'm meant to spend all day hunting in the woods for meat then impregnate you several times in the *knish* when I come home."

"Yeah, but you haven't caught a single thing in a week. I'm starving."

"I told you, I'm not a natural hunter. I have bad reflexes. I once got trampled by two guys pushing a horse."

"Huh."

CHOOSING A MATE

"I love Maria, you know, only I'm not sure she's right for me."

"What are you talking about, you guys are great together! She's a hypochondriac amnesiac, and you're a surgeon and an interminable bore. There's never been a better match."

"Thanks for that. No, it's becoming too . . . smothering. She spends hours picking berries then refuses to eat them in case she swallows poisonous insects.

All she does is sit around sucking acorns and complaining she's putting on weight."

"Come on, she has some nice qualities. She washes your clothes in private, at least. Diane finds the most crowded spot she can and beats my underpants against a rock. Sometimes I'm still wearing them at the time. She's driving me nuts. She's obsessed with inventing fire. I keep saying to her, honey, what's wrong with keeping warm in a hollowed-out bear carcass? I think she looks down on me."

"That's what I love about Mimi. She has a pioneering spirit. Diane couldn't invent fire. She'd stub a nail rubbing two twigs together and spend a week lying on her deathbed dictating her final letters to her analyst."

"Have you seen Ricki? I think she's fantastic. Girl with the long blonde tresses. She's like Adam's Eve, but less obnoxious and with a bigger wardrobe. She would caress the serpent across her knee, and the serpent would turn into a saint under the touch of her sweet little fingers."

"Sounds like you're pretty hot on this girl."

"She's the divine personification of beauty on this earth. Her beauty is an eternal joy, its loveliness will never pass into nothingness. I never put anyone on a pedestal, in fact I put my wife under a pedestal, but she is up there with the most beautiful creatures who ever walked this planet. I really want to screw her."

"Get in line. You're tenth behind Darryl, Alan, Peter, Oliver, Charlie, Bob, Sergei, Alex, Harry and Steve."

"You're kidding? She's sleeping with *Steve*? I couldn't care less if she slept with the whole forest, but that pretentious hack? Oh God! Why does the woman of my dreams have to be a nymphomaniac with a penchant for bearded *shmendriks*?"

['Kibbitz from the Kibbutz: Allen in Aberdeen', in *Woody Allen: A Legacy*, Scott Beauchomp, p.349-352, Drooping Parabola Books, 2029.]

"The Literary Utopia"
[WIGTOWN]

Y OU MIGHT NOT REMEMBER what was Wigtown. Before the bomb, if I
might make a titular nod, Wigtown was a flocculent coastal marshland
where the committed contingent of Scotland's literati crammed five to a Volkswagen along the A714 to read their notable works to middle-class housewives
using culture to supplement sex, and voracious networkers convinced a well-
timed epigram in the ear of a harrassed editor might whisk them into a make-
believe land of publishing prestige, where the internship would morph into
a full-time editorial assistant post, and where that manuscript on their USB
might find itself inserted into next year's fiction list. This swift slap of delusion was known as the Wigtown Book Festival. For one week per annum, writers, interns, students, and a fistful of influential people stared into the harsh
scowl of the Irish Sea, making vague mental plans about opening bookshops
stocking the titles slimly omitted from the other seven shops, performing at
semi-attended events with recyclable first-time novelists, earnest unrufflable
poets, and caffeine-crazed ex-journalists with a new look at an old war, before
returning to the cities and their unemployment, their rejected manuscripts,
their endless job applications, and the premise of arriving somewhere in an
industry with no actual destination.

Moved by the recent colonisation of Edinburgh by the Festival, two mul-
timillionaires with literary pretentions purchased Wigtown with the intention
of turning it into a utopia for writers and readers. Driscoll Apron, cap-a-pie in
a striped blazer and slacks, a man squeezed from a tube of aquamint toothpaste,
pumped six hundred million into the flavourless strip of B&Bs, bookshops, and
war memorials. Robin Cooper, cap-a-pie in Harris tweed blazer and slacks, a
man flanneled into his clothes, invested two hundred million from his cap and
pie empires, in the hope of being internationally recognised for his memoirs
in the millinery and meat pastry trades. The two wasted no time in erecting

fifteen towerblock apartments where the working writers would live, receive a living wage, and have the peace and time to write their works.

Driscoll wrote a series about rural PI The Stranraer Swift, the first books published by flagship house, Headpiece Publishing. These execrable first-drafts, cranked onto a laptop in Driscoll's spare time, a series of pastrami-knuckled crime bromides, were polished up, or in most cases, rewritten by ghostwriter Martin Goshawk, and treated to a 5,000,000 print run. Robin Cooper's millinery memoir, *Wear the Fox Cap!!!*, was a readable romp in the realm of female caps, too obsessed by the gradients of the peak and the impact of fabrics on hair frizz to merit fanfare. His meat pastry memoir, *The Pie: A Life*, however, was a scintillating insight into the production of the pie. Cooper was respected for having a spark of talent, and Driscoll tolerated since he was bankrolling 33,220 writers.

The beneficiaries, from published talents with broadsheet plaudits to new writers fumbling towards coherence, were to commingle in harmonious wonder, helping each other to make heavenly art. The publishing houses would release the best material into the ninety-nine new bookshops, to sit on shelves largely unread by the handful of readers in the country, and await the reviews from the seven magazines devoted to reviewing new works. The reviewers were also paid for their efforts, however, for their own safety, were isolated from the community in a heavily guarded compound. It was suggested that paid readers were brought in so the books were appreciated more, however, the writers considered this an affront to their talents, that their readers would require a fee to appreciate such brilliance. If I might be permitted a textual breather, let me drop this asterisk of intermission.

Of course, Driscoll and Cooper knew nothing of writers. Those who wrote terrible manuscripts were receiving the same wage as those composing talentastic masterpieces, except for the occasional royalty received. The writers who spent little time writing and more time loafing were receiving the same wage as those tearing their hair out over each clause. Frustrations between these two camps became a thing. Driscoll and Robin bent to the pressure to impose sanctions. These began with annual checks on writers' outputs. Those who failed to produce a satisfactory number of words had their living wage reduced. Those who failed to show improvement had their living wage reduced. Those who had written nothing because of block or lack of ideas had their living wage reduced.

Then hell was released from its stirrups and permitted to run wild across the land. The writers who were "not serious" had their wages stopped. This meant eviction and a camp being erected on the Wigtown marshland where "failed" writers lived. In the night, the embittered wrecks broke into the publishing houses and sabotaged "proper" writers' novels. One Charlene Mina was printed with the phrase "poop and pap" cut and pasted a thousand times, ruining her reputation as a doyenne of sink estate homicide. The writer Tam Robertson's novel was replaced with the words "smirking slaphead" across its 1000 pages. On that occasion, the critics praised Robertson's brutal self-lacerating autobiography, and this opened up the historical novelist's remit to a more flexible form of self-loathing prose, but on the whole these acts of sabotage spoiled the futures of literally 3,929 talents.

Driscoll and Robin were soon fed up, and left the writers to maim and stab each other. This happened four minutes after their limo puttered up the A714. Kelly Brisk, incensed that her touching portrayal of a dustbowl family in crisis, *The Thrush Sings*, was replaced with a picture of Allan Medley's anal cleft, located that failed writer and stabbed him in the thighs and shanks. Vivian Pollcrank, furious that her comprehensive study of candidiasis of the oral cavity, *The Thrush Stings*, was replaced with a badly xeroxed Prodigy album sleeve, located the culprit and stabbed him in the pyloric sphincter. Damian Horsecresent, in a froth that his paean to the Norwegian metal community, *The Thrash Sings*, was replaced with half a letter 'b' inside a semicolon, located the blaimant and stabbed her in the hypogastric region. Marianne Alpf, peeved that her study on men who find weak puns amusing, *Desperately Seeking Mommy's Love*, was replaced with a press release for a new salad dressing, located the culprit and sent him a curt text of reproof. This conflict foamed for weeks.

Since the readers no longer received a salary and had moved to other countries, the writers who remained alive following the frenzied bloodbath faced the reality that no one was around to publish them or read them. To counter this, the crazed writers privately printed their own works, dressed up as critics, wrote effusive reviews, dressed up as readers, sat and read their own works in rapture, dressed up as panel judges and awarded themselves prizes, then made their speeches to themselves in empty halls. Before I left, Wigtown was currently dominated by those forty or so nutbags, ignoring one another, and acting as one-person publishing industries, very swiftly slipping into irreversible lunacy. In short, the utopia was screwed. The notion that writers, that most self-involved and self-interested race of parasites on the planet, might co-exist in some cooperative utopia, was the biggest delusion imaginable. I penned a strongly worded editorial to Driscoll and Robin. No reply as yet.

[An account of Wigtown by author Colin Colon, former inhabitant, emailed to the editor March 2110. Colin's latest novel, *Everylittlethingandmore*, is forthcoming in 2111.]

"Pictures of Presidents"
[DUMFRIES]

[President Oliver T. Gravies, 2025-2029]

[President Wilbur Alabaster, 2029-2033]

[President Spenser Travol, 2033-2037]

[President Cuthbert Rothschild, 2037-2041]

[President Zhang Wei, 2041-2045]

[President Kåre Ødegård, 2045-2049]

[President Caroline Bassett, 2049-2053]

[President Letitia Newman, 2053-2057]

[Presidents Ivanka Ivanova, Roisin O'Doherty, and Baroness Elizabeth Bowes-Lyon 2057-2060]

[From *Pictures of Every President Ever*, Elliot Mayer (ed.), p.1012-1021, Harvard UP, 2089.]

"In Session with Kristin Sump"
[INVERNESS]

Sump: The Legend

KRISTIN SUMP, A STOLID WOMAN standing six foot two in brown loafers, aborted the locomotive and scoped the perimeter: a northwestern Scottish village named Drum where four hundred people lived in a sunken forest. She moved in a red cagoule towards the rank of taxis. Her stance had this air: "I have arrived and this will soon become apparent to others." She unpicked the trip's vexations: the hopscotching infant barring a swift path to the lavatories; the muddling senilities halting latte procurement; the proximal pong of travellers two hours from their next shower. She took a taxi to St. Hector's Church on Ravell Street and consulted her notes on the parish priest, Daniel Drimmel: "Lank. Plank-thick. No relatives. Loner. Village in a copse's arse." She corrected her make-up in a handbag mirror and waited for the vehicle to propel her towards the ecclesiastical venue mentioned in the fifth sentence.

Like most churches in northwestern Scottish villages in sunken forests, St. Hector's maintained a pious chokehold over the populace. Arnold Drimmel, the priest previous, had kept his long manicured fingers around their necks for forty-nine years, pressing on the collective windpipe from time to time for roof repairs or a portico polishing. The son successor, Daniel Drimmel, a reluctant invert traumatised with his father's love, took up the cassock for a milder reign free from the fear-packed fulminations of his elder. Arnold favoured strenuous hillwalks, frothing up his Old Testament fume on the ascent, and belting out his sermons into the rolling fog and wet verdance. Daniel favoured pouring a cup of Pepsi Max and chilling to the sounds of Stereolab at the laptop, stitching his sermons from the least controversial and most unclear passages from the

Good Books. His congregation, weaned on the froth, began to loosen up and think for themselves. Numbers dwindled.

Kristin, with the insouciant stride of an air steward taking a pack of peanuts to a ravenous passenger, entered. She ran a finger along the dusty pix. She stood at the pulpit and inhaled a smile. She pictured four hundred people listening to noises emerging from her vocal chords. She wondered why churches never had reception areas and you had to walk around staring at stained glass images of Christ. She poured bubblegumade into the font. She poked into various rooms. She found a man in casual slacks, brown sweater, and rounded spectacles working on a laptop. A book sat on the table: *The Rambler's Guide to Canada*.

"Writing the Sermon on the Mountie?" she asked.

"Hello?" he started. He had earphones in transmitting *Emperor Tomato Ketchup*.

"Kristin Sump." Kristin offered a hand.

"I'm Daniel," he said.

"Yes. You I came here to peep. You are notoriotous. I am a therapist from the firm *Headquacks Revisited*. I heard about the change from paternastier to paternicer. You, the son of Arnold Drimmel, the Pastor Phillips for the one-click generation."

"Can I help?"

"See this pen?" Kristin produced a Bic from her breast pocket.

"Yes, I can see that pen."

"This biro is the pen that will propel your pulpit into permanence."

"An interview?"

"Yes. With your whole congregation."

And so, Kristin Sump headquacked the village inhabitants, making them dependent on her expensive counsel, spreading her tentacles of persuasion across the county, forcing her victims to erect a border around Ross-shire, thus birthing a nation. She met people regularly for "sessions", proffering whatever "advice" might amuse her that morning, and kept the citizens in loops of useless despair and confusion, dependent on her psychotic counsel to barely function. Transcripts below.

In Session: The Kaurismäki Shrine

BERYL: So I set up the shrine to Finnish auteur Aki Kaurismäki in the middle of the A769.

SUMP: Fantastic!

BERYL: Yes. But there were complications. First, I had to position the deadbeat bar as featured in *La Vie de Bohème* between the two lanes as people honked their horns and hurled abuse from their car windows. The Matti Pellonpää lookalike I hired from Chipping Norton was furious at the circumstances and kept insisting on a larger fee. The Kati Outinen lookalike from Chipping Norton was almost clipped by passing freight lorry, and bitter tears ran down her suitably lugubrious countenance.

SUMP: And?

BERYL: That was the beginning of our problems. To position the sequence of shipping containers as seen in *The Man Without a Past* along the roadside caused a three-hour tailback. The convoy, four lorries wide, led to the partial blocking of one lane, forcing Mr. Pellonpää to direct traffic, a task that causes him acute pain after his failed stint as a traffic cop. The language hurled at his suitably dour countenance was appalling. And the rockabilly band on the other side of the road, formed in homage to the Leningrad Cowboys from the two titular movies, were complaining about the poor sound quality of the amps, purchased on the cheap from a closing music emporium in Charlbury. And the choleric spinster owner of the coffee shop that had its entrance blocked and business upset called the police.

SUMP: Great.

BERYL: Not really. Once we had established the shrine, the police arrived and asked us to remove the deadbeat bar from the centre of the two oncoming lanes, as we were endangering our lives and causing traffic to crawl. The Leningrad Boycows were performing a humorous Finnish tribute to American rock and roll at an outrageous volume, and with some unpleasant feedback, causing the police to become aggressive and demand the music to stop.

SUMP: Wow.

BERYL: The immigrants and outcasts inside the shipping containers emerged and bolted when the police appeared in their purviews. The police leapt towards the scurrying illegals and criminals. This meant we could enact some scenes from the Kaurismäkian oeuvre, such as the awkward romance in *Take Care of Your Scarf, Tatiana*. I was wondering . . .

SUMP: Yes?

BERYL: How is this helping me lose weight?

SUMP: Muse on the moose.

BERYL: All right. Can you hold him up to the light?

SUMP: Sure.

BERYL: Because . . . the stress of organising the whole thing and the terror at being arrested and endangering the life of the lookalikes and the immigrants and vagrants has taken off a few pounds, probably, even though I have been stress-eating the whole time?

SUMP: Exactly.

In Session: Writer

SUMP: Describe your writing process, writer.

WRITER: I open the picture of Celeste. I spend ten minutes of time peering at the png of her face. The orange-red cardigan in ruffle along her right shoulder. The faint spot on her sleek pinkish neck. The cute bulb-like chin below her narrow balmed lips. Two small creases bracketing the smile. Roseate cheeks and a wee button nose. A pair of black-rimmed spectacles in the fifties-retro manner. A pale forehead with a crop of short blue hair twirling down the left side of her face. I imagine what it might be like to have sex with her. Then I open the picture of Alison. I observe the freckled arms poking from her black tank-top. Her broad orange neck. Her flat chin with its slight slacking skin. Her thick glossed lips shining in the bright light of the room. Her long catwalk nose with a sheen of reflected light and the left nostril larger than the right. The brief bags below her large, right-peering eyes, and the shock of mascara in their corners. Her tousled orange hair cropped at odd points around her face. I imagine what it might be like to have sex with her. This continues across a range of pngs and jpegs.

SUMP: Your writing process is staring at attractive women and wanting to have sex with them. Are you a sexually bereft batcheloser?

WRITER: No. I have a wife. I have regular sex. The problem is this: in writing we explore our imaginations. In the male imagination, there is a bitter irresolvable war between two factions. The strongest faction of the mind, The

Cock Cortex, is libido-controlled. This faction is chained to the unending plea-sure of unclothing beautiful women in long erotic scenarios, and the inevitable unedited sexual pandemonium that ensues. The other faction of the imagina-tion, The Everything Else, is weaker, and must power and sustain the complex and taxing notions that comprise a novel. We're talking 70-30% here, the largest the libido. The 30% must battle through a continual bombardment of arrest-ing sexual imagery, and urgent impulses to leer at attractive faces, women in undress, and so on. That is vexing percentage.

SUMP: Interesting. Have you tried airbrushing the now?

WRITER: One your interconceptual non sequiturs?

SUMP: Muse on that phrase. Have a mental muse.

WRITER: You could ask me why I don't a) masturbate to keep the sexual impulse at bay, or b) work sexual material into the novel. The replies: a) the sexual imagination reloads like a semi-automatic pistol, and b) no one wants to read the sexual imaginings of a middle-aged man. I repulse myself when I write a frenzied hump scene with Celeste or Alison. But I could airbrush the now. That might work.

SUMP: Are you still attracted to your wife's ageing figure?

WRITER: Yes.

SUMP: Hmm. Let me posit this: these lapses into png longing mean the missus isn't moistening the writer's manhood?

WRITER: No. Our lovemaking is intense and meticulous. I won't react to your tack of attack.

SUMP: All male novelists are adulterers. It is a symptom of spending hours taking imaginative flights. Most people adapt to the constraints of their lives. Writers spend hours smashing these constraints in their babbling stories of extramarital shagging in heated Los Angeles pools.

WRITER: I write about Cumbernauld.

SUMP: The real battle is between the possibility of acting on fantasies and consigning them to paper. At some point, the writer will be unable to tell between the real and the fake. You will stumble into an affair with a younger woman thinking this is some plot contrivance in a Cumbernauld saga. You will awake to a howling sweating ex-wife hurling tomato soup and other canned goods at your head. It is inevitable. I suggest you launch yourself into an un-apologetic stream of lurid sexual affairs with whoever will participate.

WRITER: You might be correct.

In Session: The Illogic of Casserole

PABLO: Umm . . .

SUMP: Speak to me, Pablo.

PABLO: I presented my casserole to the logicians as the central metaphor.

SUMP: Continue.

PABLO: I tried to illustrate how non-classical logic spurns the bivalent prison of proposition with the mushrooms, carrots, and lamb intersecting with the mince, beetroot, and pumpernickel in a Haackian stew of extended modalities. The leading logician in the universe approached the metaphor and howled with laughter. "The principals of bivalence would improve twofold upon this hotpot hodgepodge!" he said.

SUMP: So?

PABLO: I was humiliated in front of two thousand logicians. I tried to explain further that the roast beef and embedded sprouts represented the powerful properties of paraconsistent logic. I was reasoning with inconsistent consistency, proving that the stratification of stuffing on the right portion of the casserole represented a breakthrough in the Leibniz counter and anti-counter valances. I was booed. "Your paraincontinent illogic is leaking like the melted cheese in your casserole dish!" he said.

SUMP: Did you deploy the symbol ∃ ?

PABLO: No. I produced the flan for the finale.

SUMP: How'd that fare, Pablo?

PABLO: I used the flan to further explode the principle of bivalence. To show the law of the excluded middle up for intellectual slackness, I excluded a centre from the flan: two pieces of pastry, one suspended above the other using invisible string. The logicians pondered the filling-free dessert. In place of cheese, almonds, cinnamon, eggs, and sugar, was emptiness, showing that the notion of consequence is unsustainable without the law of non-contradiction in cases of integrated contingents. The logicians, after several moments, burst into laughter. "This metaphor is mere flimflan! Boolean semantics shows that excluded middles are essential in the empirical verities of intuitionistic propositions. Your metaphor sags like the weak pastry atop your illustrative dessert!" he said.

SUMP: Who is *he* again?

PABLO: The leading logician in the universe.

SUMP: What happened next, Pablo?

PABLO: The logicians turned crude and chanted "this flan is a piece of shit!" and hurled me from the Logician's Corner. They served the casserole among themselves and commented: "We prefer classical casserole, asshole!"

SUMP: Nasty logicians.

PABLO: Yes. I have a conference speech to make in Cambridge. Word will have spread about the humiliation. Any suggestions?

SUMP: Own the situation. Dress as a casserole and read your keynote speech from the perspective of a carrot.

PABLO: You reckon?

SUMP: Yep, Pablo honey. Start with: "I am here as a carrot to show you stuffed shirts that presicifications are bullplop. Supervaluationism is a steaming plate of wrong. I am here, with my friends, the potato, the leek, and the gravy, to prove everything you ever thought correct totally incorrect. Lick this, suckers."

PABLO: Wow. Thanks, Krist.

SUMP: Give us a kiss, Pabs.

PABLO: Love you, baby.

[From *Various Tyrannies: An Almanack*, ed. David Putz, Putterbum Books, 2048.]

"Prawn Confusion"

[SHETLAND]

A prawn at night.

A prawn on a starless plateau.

A prawn named Simon riding up front in a Mitsubishi 340.

A prawn worried about the long-term oscillation of the axial tilt.

A prawn never shown footage of massacres in a wayward nation.

A prawn with troubles.

A prawn convinced that the morning will never radiate loveliness like before.

A prawn reliant on the kindness of stranglers.

A prawn with musical pincers.

A prawn overly sensitive about pinkness.

A prawn who says nothing and expresses something.

A prawn to the left.

A prawn caught between thinking and not thinking about nothing.

A prawn silenced by the vengeance of unreason.

A prawn for tomorrow.

A prawn in the shade.

A prawn who spurns the vicious hug of the mother.

A prawn alone.

A prawn in winter with the sparkle of summer.

A prawn you know.

A prawn open to the suggestion of shrinking.

A prawn at dawn.

A prawn confusion.

A prawn who considers anything less than extraordinary a waste of time.

A prawn with cisgender options.

A prawn in the bowel of a banshee.

A prawn radiating smugness at having used the word "disingenuous".

A prawn is there.

A prawn on the lawn.

A prawn optimistic about the fiscal stability of the Marianas Trench.

A prawn on a limpet on a shark in a whale.

A prawn in Franz Benzine's stomach.

A prawn between pliers.

A prawn pinched.

A prawn in a wicker chair in the room of a murdered tailor.

A prawn nooked in the cleft of a crack.

A prawn upon the louche waft of decadence.

A prawn in a decapodehedron.

                                                A prawn to the right.

A prawn cuddled up with a cute Texan.

A prawn with the sense to fast-forward.

A prawn upstream.

A prawn who schemes with zeal.

A prawn spinning from a seal's tumult.

A prawn for me and possibly them.

A prawn riding the regal hauteur of a Caribbean swan.

A prawn for sale.

A prawn who screams for the burnt parchment of now.

A prawn listening to the wind.

A prawn tumbling from sandwich to plate.

A prawn smirking on a broadside.

A prawn with a strong understanding of electroencephalography.

A prawn miscollected.

A prawn too free to have ambitions.

A prawn overarching.

A prawn.

A prawn reading the Koran in Korean.

A prawn rammed into the guts of mathematics.

A prawn complaining overly, and moaning lowly.

                        A prawn in the middle.

A prawn unbruised in the cracking of a plate.

A prawn in place.

A prawn that's true.

A prawn in plaice.

A prawn masquerading as a mosque.

A prawn simpler than another prawn.

A prawn reluctant to pop the cork.

A prawn and the art of fertility.

A prawn who lets the characters lead.

A prawn impolite.

A prawn mid-sneeze.

A prawn poking from a stockbroker's coif.

A prawn on a plectrum.

A prawn pondering the consequences of a poor compass reading.

A prawn over there with thou.

A prawn on the piss.

A prawn long.

A prawn caught re-enacting the same crime as a prawn.

A prawn ribbed for your pleasure.

A prawn inserted into a dolorous melodic pattern.

A prawn away.

A prawn a way over there.

A prawn who says, at the end of the day, there stands a prawn who can.

[Inscriptions carved on stone tablets, photographed by Duncan Angello, 2058-60.]

"Diary of a Pineapple Holder"
[KIRKCUDBRIGHT]

MAR 4 [1:12PM]

I arrived at the airport and presented my new passport to the customs officer. After passing through the turnstile, I was handed the pineapple. In no uncertain terms, I was told that if I let the pineapple fall from my hands at any moment, I would be deported instantly.

[3:07PM]

Found the airport cafe. Spent a long time trying to manoeuvre my luggage with my right hand while keeping the pineapple balanced with the left. Peeped some monuments and buildings. The Bernard Ananas statue, with the proud founder holding his pineapple, is prominent outside the airport. Spotted some unprepared folks dropping their pineapples. The police arrived and rather roughly bundled them into a van. We all know what we're letting ourselves in for! I am writing this with my pineapple clasped tightly in my left hand.

[5:03PM]

At hotel. Read the brochure. Pineapple fasteners, industrial adhesives, or other pineapple securing apparatus are prohibited, and are punishable by forty-nine years in prison. Yikes! As promised, the level of luxury here is immense for such prices. I had lobster bisque earlier, and tucked into truffles and champagne for £4.99!

[8:29PM]

Back from a stroll. The city is spectacular at night. It really is a paradise. Met some friendly locals who recommended upcoming shows. Live entertainment here is free, as the government support artists with living wages. I caught a few songs from the farewell Supergrass tour (the visiting musicians are exempt from pineapple law!), and had the famed 'Perpetual Pineapple' cocktail. It was transcendent.

[10:10PM]

Channel-hopping. It's weird to watch a soap opera where the actors are all holding pineapples. It's weird on the street, sure, but seeing how this pineapple-holding lark has permeated the culture is extra-weirder. Nervous about sleeping. I've practised for the last few months sleeping while holding the pineapple, so I shouldn't be so worried. Still, it's the first night when most people drop their pineapples . . .

MAR 5 [9:38AM]

I survived the night. There was a spooky moment when I dreamt the pineapple falling to the floor, and woke up to see the pineapple aslant across my thumb. A close call. My fingers hurt from the spikes, as predicted. I have some of the special hand cream that helps. You can transfer the pineapple between hands, provided the pineapple is being held at all times, and wear special gloves as required.

[12:38PM]

I met my new boss, Gert. He was hip. "No one punches a timeclock here, man. You can work whenever. You prefer to shoot some pool, have a siesta? Sure! We take things easy here," he said. I spent the afternoon playing one-handed tennis. My colleagues said that life with the one hand was tricky at first, and offered me some tips on how to keep the pineapple balanced in my left while using a few fingers from the right to complete various tasks. People here cope with the constraint remarkably well.

[5:26PM]

I had an amazing first day, met some terrific people! Had a meal with the team and about to head to the theatre, and perhaps a club later, who knows . . .

MAR 6 [8:12AM]

Drank heavenly cocktails. Watched a moving performance. Munched sublime tucker. Danced the ananana (our equivalent of the chachacha) all night with the team. Flirted with Beth from the marketing dept.

MAR 9 [8.19AM]

Beth invited me inside after supper and a moonlit walk. She was sweet and told me not to rush. Her last partner was deported one evening when he expelled his pineapple in a fit of ardour. I undressed carefully. The removal and application of clothes is still the most common cause of pineapple dropping. I pricked Beth a little during foreplay, but she laughed and showed me a scar from her ex. Sex while holding the pineapple was a little frustrating. I really wanted to embrace her, but I had to keep a cool head.

MAR 10

I went to receive my new pineapple from the Pineapple Provision Office today, my first one becoming a little stale. It felt strange parting with my original (even a little sad!). It is a crime to eat a pineapple here, and some people have lost their citizenship by cracking open their fruits and sucking the sweet juices inside, the temptation becoming too much. Fortunately for me, I hate the taste!

MAR 12

I can't even remember what not holding a pineapple feels like. I am at home here!

MAR 13

Some halfwit cleaner forgot to put a wet floor sign in the canteen. I almost slipped and dropped my pineapple. My colleague Ernie wasn't so fortunate. One wrong step is all it takes.

MAR 14

I have to remember to alternate my pineapple hand. I am suffering from pineapple cramp. I bought a new pineapple mitt to wear until my pricked skin heals.

MAY 15

I met a man in the pub who wanted to emigrate. "I would rather struggle in some squalid country with poor human rights than spend another moment holding this tropical fucking fruit," he said. I take his point.

MAY 16

I have everything I need and crave. I have a charmed and easy life, I live in luxury I could only imagine in my previous country. But I sometimes have to ask myself, is this life worth the struggle of holding a pineapple in my left hand forever?

MAY 17

On second thoughts, it's only a pineapple. I'm away for a swim!

[From *Diary of a Pineapple Holder*, Greg Olivier, Self-published, 2023.]

"Realm of Sapo"

[LOTHIANS]

Sapotage

I AM Lazlo Seplütt, Commander of the resistance organisation Sapotage. Our main objective is to shoot down the highest number of drones possible and force Sapo to cancel their aerial shipping service. Our organisation sprung from the small protest faction Saponoise, established in Livingston by a band of sleepless shiftworkers. It started when Sapo introduced a drone delivery service on orders over £100, a luxury for premium subscribers, where items were flown largely to private homes in rural locations or suburbs. It became cheaper over time for Sapo to produce their metallic pests, so the service was introduced on cheaper orders, and used widely in the towns and cities. Their buzzing engines, like amplified wasps, soon claimed the skies, their rotors whirring like a protracted chorus of farts, their mechanical claws hammering on windows and doors. I was working on nightshift when the first fleet invaded the city. I struggled to sleep through their incessant buzzing racket as the population oneclicked novels, truckles of cheddar, three-piece dining sets, bedspreads, pastries and pasties, and other non-urgent items on a whim. Sometimes I was awoken when a drone tapped on my window, asking me in a robotic voice if I would mind taking an order for my neighbour. I soon mobilised the resistance. In the evenings and on weekends, our volunteer troops position themselves at various locations—the tops of streets, across the burbs, flat windows, in sewer drains—armed with a range of handheld weapons, from molotov cocktails, IEDs, grenades, to bazookas and missiles, and blast these vermin from the skies. We meet frequent hostility from customers, furious at having their orders cancelled. Some members have been assaulted by their neighbours, such as Tim Bright, whose ear was sliced with a katana when the man next door's leopard-skin carseat cover was set alight by a flare. We want peace. We want to show that we needn't have our realities shaped by Sapo. That they have no monopoly on our skies, and that our airspace should be sacred. If you lose a pair of socks or a pack of broccoli to one of our bazookas, take a moment to consider whether the loss is really of any significance whatsoever in the scheme of things, or if you might be willing to wait a few days for a noiseless postal delivery by an actual person.

The Couriers

Every morning we put on our uniforms—red jeans and shirt with blue dungarees—check our order targets for the day, stare into the mirror and shout: "Fuck Sapo." I am one of the ninety-two remaining Sapo couriers in existence. I live in a tented village around the Midlothiania Sapo warehouse, where the underpaid workers are forced to live, unable to afford the flat rents and commuting expenses. I scrape a living speeding orders to customers, in competition with the drones that have usurped thousands of hard-working couriers like me. My first order that morning was from Mrs Dongle in Dalkeith who had ordered seven eggs and a pack of seeded bagels. I sprinted into the Sapo warehouse for the items, locating the bagels at one end, then sprinted a hectare to locate the eggs at the other. I removed the seventh egg from a pack of six and placed it, as per protocol, inside a padded ziploc bag inside a cardboard box. The bagels were placed in a separate cardboard box, and the eggs in another, padded with cotton wool and bubblewrap. I sprinted with the three boxes towards my motorbike, placing them in a special holding at the rear, and powered towards the A702. I was terrified about cracking the eggs or the egg. If one egg was cracked then I would lose the tip, I would have to pay for the cracked eggs from my own salary, and return to the warehouse to source another seven eggs. I sped up the road at 120MPH, swerving my way around the cars, streaking through tailbacks, and made a right onto the B-roads. These speeds are necessary to outpace the drones. The City of Edinburgh Bypass, paved over and replaced with a large wall plastered with fliers for festival productions, is no longer an option for swifter access to Dalkeith. I arrived one minute into the delivery window at Mrs Dongle's house and tapped thrice on her door, observing that her house was opposite a convenience store. She opened up and snatched the boxes without a thanks or a tip. I returned to the motorbike, having called her a sour old cunt under my breath, and made a trip back to the warehouse. I received a text en route informing me that the seventh egg had arrived in a cracked condition. I must replace the seventh egg immediately, and that egg must be sourced from the warehouse, it must be packaged in the official Sapo box, otherwise that is a sackable breach of protocol. I will lose the 45p that egg cost from my salary. I sped back along the motorway, narrowly avoiding a head-on collision with a lorry, splatting over ninety bugs in my visor, and returned to the warehouse. I sprinted once more to the eggs, removed an egg from a pack. I wrapped the egg in saran wrap, placed the egg inside a small padded box, then placed the small padded box in a larger padded box. I repeated the trip. Mrs Dongle snatched the box from me and I returned to the warehouse, fearing a second text informing me the second loose egg had arrived in a cracked condition. No text arrived. I continued with the next order: a set of wine glasses, twelve packets of biscuits, and a daffodil-patterned vase. When we return after a day's work to our draughty, muddy tents, we remove our uniforms, ration out a slug of rum, stare into the mirror and shout: "Fuck Sapo."

Avian Assist

Avian Assist is a non-profit organisation that works to reduce bird fatalities caused by Sapo, and to help citizens cope with the repercussions of bird assaults on their mental and physical wellbeings. Sapo drones are responsible for more avian deaths in cities than windows, cats, and high tension wires combined. Weeks after Sapo first introduced their drone service, millions of urban-dwelling birds were driven from their nests and sliced by the powerful rotorblades of the machines. The birds, an adaptable species, reacted to these invasions with swift retaliation: soon flocks of seagulls and pigeons swooped towards the drones in attack formations, upsetting their flight paths, ramming their undersides, and creating enough turbulence to bring them down. Sapo effected a solution to cope with their losses. These avian attacks on their drones were costing the corporation millions in re-orders, customer refunds, and replacement drones. In addition to the numerous renegade groups shooting them from the skies, and the thousands in compensation paid to people felled by falling drones, this led to an expensive problem for Sapo. Their temporary solution was to place spikes along the sides and undersides of their drones, in the manner of local councils and business owners who prevent nestbuilding on bridges or walls. This proved ineffective. The drones were brought down with several speared or wounded birds on their spikes. Next, Sapo fitted a series of toxic sprays (a mix of carbon monoxide and hydrogen sulfide) in place of the spikes, that when triggered prove fatal to the birds. These were primed to puff several minutes before the birds approached, creating a trail of toxic cloud that would force the birds to retreat. Fatally, the quantity of these toxic gases was so large, that flocks would end up caught in the clouds, and hundreds of poisoned and maimed birds began to drop from the skies, causing trauma and physical injuries to people below. These birds, falling like bricks from the sky, killed ten people in a week. A long and well-publicised series of court cases followed. Sapo fought for their right to remove birds from their flightpaths by any means, and put a small-print clause on the Sapo website placing the responsibility of paying for the victims of fallen birds on the customer. Now, hundreds of people are seriously injured in cities every day, oblivious customers are caught up in manslaughter cases, and thousands of birds are massacred by toxic clouds. Our mission as an organisation is to fight on behalf of the the victims of Sapo's egregious legal tactics, to help preserve the dwindling bird population, and inform consumers that in ordering a pair of mittens by drone, they might well be implicated in the murder of a fellow citizen.

Customer Feedback

"I love the new aerial service. I ordered a signed picture of former US President Kayne West. It arrived in under twelve minutes. All I had to do was open the front window and take the signed picture of Kayne from the plinth. The drone said in a mechanical voice 'Thank you for shopping with Sapo'. It was truly incredible." —meganbatch

"I ordered a cubit of cumin. The drone arrived when I was in the shower, so it flew around and tapped on the bathroom window. What a clever little flying robot thing! I had no qualms about opening the window in the nude and taking the cumin. If that was a delivery man, I might not have heard him knock, and I would have to leap out the shower and into a towel to take the order, if he hadn't left already. These are a smart and efficient way to collect essential items, although the rotorblades sliced into my window, leaving a thick cut in the double glazing." —chefforhire

"Fabulous. Working in my study, I thought to myself: 'I could kill for a bar of organic white chocolate and a botanically fermented cherry cola'. I logged on to Sapo's site, paid the two quid for the drone delivery, and in ten minutes Buzz hovered at my window. It startled me at first, as I was listening to Ed Sheeran's moving final album on earphones at the time, but I opened up and took my items once my heart rate had returned to normal and I put down the hammer. Unfortunately, Buzz ended up stuck in the oak tree outside my house, and made a torturous squealing sound for two days, until an operative from Sapo came and cut the tree down to retrieve their drone safely. Recommended." —slowburner

"Is it a bird, is it a plane? No, it's my thesaurus, sachet of soy sauce, and a pair of jump leads. Thank you, Sapo! Mwah-wah!" —laurenstripe

"The antidote to those fed up with couriers. They take forever to arrive, and when I follow them on the tracking app, they always make random stops, probably to skive off and smoke. When they arrive, you have to wait for them to drag themselves up the stairs with my seven bags of shopping. After they have unloaded the bags and put the shopping in your cupboards, they hang around the door like they are expecting a tip. You have to make small talk with them as well. I have nothing to say to these people. I like this hassle-free, unintrusive way to order, although the drone accidentally flew into my front room and careered wildly around the place, severing the wires of my ceiling light and smashing my fish tank open and slicing the shinbone of my husband. This proved to be my mistake for opening the window completely, so I paid the compensation fee to Sapo for their drone, which I had to take down with a baseball bat after nine hours. I thoroughly endorse this wonderful company." — oliviapotters

Warehouse Worker

I was in fourth year at school when they came around. These two really cool and smart girls said that working at the Sapo warehouse was totally awesome, and totally bursting with future benefits. You could hang around with your mates, zooming up and down the warehouse on segways and carts, having a laugh and earning some serious bucks, with unlimited opportunities for shim-mying up the corporate ladder. Fearing the £100,000 a year student fees, and hearing horror stories of graduates with double firsts walking straight into Sapo warehouses, I decided the easiest option was to work with Sapo, since they had conquered the rest of the world, and had a foothold in Lothiania. To reach the warehouse, I had to take three buses and walk five miles along a farm road, and when I arrived, I was chastised for being late, had the two hours removed from my salary, was ushered into a uniform, and handed a list of duties. I was to assist in the retrieving and storing of the thousands of items that arrived from the trucks. I had little time to make myself familiar with the layout of the place, and by 9.30, I was zipping around the warehouse on segways, ascending ladders with heavy boxes, trying not to splinter my spine, and having no laughs with any mates. Instead, my supervisor was barking at me to bring the bananas, store the chandeliers, unload the glockenspiels, locate the printer ink. To improve morale, Sapo FM blasted in pop music from the latest bestselling singers. I realised at around 10.12 that I had made a terrible mistake. I soon moved into the tented village around the warehouse, a community of depressed couriers, lorry drivers, and warehouse workers. The tented village was "not endorsed" by Sapo, but they knew that their policy of not paying travel fares would lead to lateness and production delays, so looked the other way, out the other window, towards their nice houses. Over campfires, we talked about our plans to reduce Sapo to rubble, then toned down our ambitions to simply spitting on or leaving small streaks of shit in customers' orders. The price of alcohol meant we had to ration our nightly intake, so we hadn't the option to numb our woes by excessive drinking. The free Sapo wifi blocked access to job sites with a message "Hey! That site isn't Sapo-friendly!". We had to take buses after work to access the 9G internet and look for other work. But there wasn't any other work. All roads led to Sapo.

Sapo Speaks

There is no stopping positive progress. Yes, we have had problems and several incidents with our drones. This is an unfortunate necessity when pioneering new, life-changing technology. We are working hard to reduce noise levels in cities. By 2045, we will have silent drones with enhanced capabilities. For instance, you will be able to set timed shopping lists and your shopping will arrive without you having to reorder. We are also working on promotional drones that will hover outside your window promoting items you might like based on your shopping trends. You simply reach outside the window, take the item, and your card will be charged accordingly. If you already have one of our Katiana devices, we can listen in to your everyday conversations, and our programs can predict what items you might like to purchase based on key words. We are also pioneering Pop-Up Drones: these are smaller craft, the size of locusts, that hover alongside you on the streets with smaller items you might like, such as a bottle of sparkling water, or a chocolate bar, and that suggest other items of interest through a small speaker. And finally, we are testpiloting a new micro-drone, known as the Shopping Bee, that hovers around your house making product suggestions and updating you on new bargains, and putting suggestions into your ear while you sleep, so you awake ready and motivated to shop! Our drones will be part of the fabric of life in Lothiania before the decade is out. There is no stopping positive progress.

[From *Voices from Sapo*, Svetlana Alexievich Jr., Dalkey Archive Press, 2058.]

173

"When Four Tribes Live Peacefully in Punctuation"

[KINCARDINE]

[!!!]

HELLO! WE ARE the Exclamation Tribe! We speak with an excited inflection at the end of our sentences! Our favourite activities are logging, metalsmithing, and imprisoning witches! We tend to congregate on the banks of the Cowie Water! Sometimes the moon makes us sad! Our strongest feature is that we are forever positive! Our lips are not found in an unsmiling downward position for long! We live on sautéed hog meat and sprigs of lettuce! It was our idea to return Kincardine to a tribal state! Some might quip, "return?"! We are profoundly moved when Stretchy Mike plays his harmonium!

[???]

You want to know where we live? Are we the Interrogative Tribe? Do we, perhaps, congregate near the Bervie Water? Are you wondering what our trademark might be, or have you the common sense to have already made that inference? Can we relax when the rains pound on our hairs, the skillet is slathered in grease, and the crockery is splintered? What do you think? Is it possible that we might be somewhat sarcastic, unpleasant, and aggressive? Can you not see the frothing scowl on ringleader Peter Stevenson's lips? How do we spend our Tuesdays? Do you think we dance barearsed around an effigy of Icelandic novelist Gudbergur Bergsson? Or are you a complete buffoon? Might we make a low melodic susurrus when we are horny? Are you willing to strip? Or shall we start to remove your skin anyway?

[. . .]

Yes . . . It is possible that . . . I think I left that bubblewrap in the cistern . . . Yes . . . That we are the Ellipsis Tribe . . . Our nature is . . . I can't remember what a cistern *is* . . . That we trail off at times, this is . . . Yes, sometimes in mid- . . . Come over, we're making shrimp linguini . . . And of course, we can ramble on to irrelevant . . . Pleased to see you, Kate, have you returned my nectarine, or is there one . . . We are sometimes accused of insanity, but . . . It's more forgetfulness . . . Hi, Olivia . . . And distractedness . . . We live on nettles and bravado . . . Quite right, that is the longest peashoot I have ever . . . We are peaceful because organising an army is beyond the . . . I might stand on my knuckles later, worth a . . . So make yourself at home on our balmy scurf by the Luther Water . . . Wouldn't it be nice, to be a . . . Someone should invent a satchel . . . Hi Marvin . . . Look, I have to run but we'll . . .

[*]

[From an educated guess by the editor.]

---

*We are most comfortable at the bottom. We are the Footnote Tribe. We pool around Bervie Water, crouch on our haunches, and sing 'New York Woman'. That about sums us up, Bob.

"The Misanthropists"
[KINROSS]

MARCH 2041

THE MISANTHROPISTS, a protest party running on the "all politicians are bastards" ticket, tap into the public mood, following several political scandals involving white pepper ice cream and wild alpacas, and surge in the polls. Their leader, Albert Rye, a columnist for offbeat website *All Things Must Pass*, had written a spoof election manifesto several months earlier, promising free krautrock LPs to OAPs, a thatched roof for those who help the homeless, contrabassoon lessons for school leavers, and a stronger media presence for those with receding hairlines. The surge in interest across the month forces Albert to mobilise a team and write a proper manifesto cribbing hard-left policies, humanist ideals, and their own droll misanthropic outlook. The completed work is published on March 29.

MAY 2041

Rival parties mount violent smear campaigns against Albert Rye and his makeshift cabinet following the rapturous response to his manifesto. The usual vaguely salacious material is dredged up from Rye's internet search history, including his time on XXLadies and Balaclava Babes. Several tame articles in support of Middle Eastern political factions are warped to portray him a supporter of genocide, replete with superimposed pictures of him laughing over mass child graves. The public, having tolerated these tactics for too long, switch their allegiances to The Misanthropists in droves. The news sites and broadsheets, in desperation, print headlines of the stripe 'VOTE FOR RYE AND YOU WILL DIE' and 'RYE WILL STAB YOUR BABIES' EYES'. These misfires boost support for Albert and, apart from a predicted election tampering scam, their victory is assumed.

JUNE 2041

The vote tampering is unsuccessful. Five hundred thousand votes are lost. However, since there are no votes for other parties, aside from those cast by politicians, The Misanthropists win by a landslide of forty-five. Albert Rye is sworn in as Prime Minister. He triples unemployment and disability benefits, increases the rate of tax for higher earners, and draws up contracts for a thousand socially affordable homes in the first week. Immediately, Albert feels a conflict between his role as a misanthrope and a man single-handedly trying to make society more equal. As a people-hater, he loathes the homeless as much as the bankers in mansions. He loathes stinking orphans as much as perfumed superbrats. He is torn between the side of him that hates humanity, and the side of him that wants to save humanity. Hardcore supporters complain about his smiling in speeches, his upbeat demeanour, his air of openness. He projects an image contra to his party's fuck-you philosophy.

JULY 2041

Albert alters his personality to be more sarcastic and nonchalant in interviews. The public question his commitment to being a serious politician, complain that he is too serious, and complain again that he is not serious enough. In private, he agonises as to whether people as a species are worth fighting for. To put this to the test, he offers the public the option of a free cool beverage at the top of a steep hill walk, with the consequence that a random homeless man is kicked hard in the gonads. 100% of people take the free beverage and two hundred tramps receive hard kicks in their gonads. Other schemes are devised, including a door-to-door cleaning service, with the consequence a random student is issued an F for no reason; the option for more leg room on flights, the consequence an OAP loses their electricity for the day; a lifetime supply of pickles for the under twenties, the consequence a train is delayed by two hours; a free £5 mobile top-up, the consequence a migrant worker is fired; and a warm and semi-arousing hug on the street, the consequence a working mother's tax credits are refused. It becomes clear to Albert that on every occasion, people take the perks and pay not a moment's thought to the victims. Humanity would require a degree of tweaking.

AUGUST 2041

The Prick Purges are announced. In a TV interview, Albert explains that the foundation of his party is a loathing of humanity, especially the people who spoil life for everyone else, and that his culling procedure would remove the most toxic contingent: the common asshole, the everyday motherfucker, the standard-issue prick. The law offices, financial districts, political HQs, and golf courses are raided to find the first batch. To weed the pricks from the non-pricks, simple polygraph tests are conducted, with victims asked basic questions: 'If you were running late for a meeting and an old lady needed help across the road, would you stop, or sprint onward to a room where people admire and envy you, leaving the old woman to stagger into the path of an on-coming taxi?', or 'Would you purchase a Porsche with your hard-earned money, to show people you are a brilliant successful legend-in-your-own-time, or purchase a normal car like a normal non-prick to show you are not a massive prick?' Most of the pricks lie, being pricks. To ensure no non-pricks are purged, social media feeds are analysed and testimonials heard. The social media feeds of pricks are commonly saturated with photos of themselves on holiday, in their cars, posing in expensive clothes with attractive people. The testimonials are a mix of biased accounts from family, friends, former employees, and former lovers, and are considered with care. The decisions are made by an independent panel of steely prick-detectors, non-pricks trained to have no sympathy with pleading pricks. Critics argue this, in turn, makes these people pricks, and not equipped to seal a man's fate. Albert rebuts that since these people were non-pricks to begin with, whatever prickishness they might acquire to convict the pricks has no bearing on their integrity, as they understand what it means to be a non-prick. The pricks have always been pricks, and have no frame of reference for non-prickishness.

SEPTEMBER 2041

As the first four hundred pricks are purged (poisoned in their holding cells), the public outcry is enormous. Civil unrest erupts. Albert makes a rousing speech to a crowd of betrayed voters outside parliament. "Everyone! Return to your homes and your jobs, and tell me if your lives have not been improved *tenfold* by the purging of these pricks. Picture a world free from an officious prick in a suit refuses who you money to buy your children shoes. A world free from champagne lounges, business suites, and premium upgrades. A world where intelligence is harnessed for the betterment of humanity, not to secure egocentric assholes second homes and Lamborghinis. If you are truly sick of inequality, you need to stand behind me. The cause of inequality and poverty is greed. The cause of greed is being a massive fucking prick. Yes, we nice people loathe murder, but the reality is the pricks are murdering us day after day, when people die on the streets, when people turn to drugs to escape their hellish realities. Pricks are killing us by degrees. Pricks are killing the planet. It's time for us to rise up and kill the pricks first." The speech receives a cheer and several boos, however the substance of the message is undeniable. The purges continue with increased public support.

OCTOBER 2041

A further thousand pricks are purged. The effects are noticed with a spike in the economy, and the public mood is tested on the street, with ebullience levels increasing by 54%. This is evidenced by the upturn in public concern over the homeless, more inclusive attitudes to strangers, and a less bitter competitive atmosphere presiding over everything. The next debate is on who or what will replace the arguably necessary aspects of prickishness required in a merciless market economy, whether a non-prick approach will bankrupt Kinross and make the country a global laughing stock. Albert proposes that Kinross will continue to trade as normal without cutting corners, evading taxes, or shafting workers, and that productivity and growth will improve with a workforce treated with respect. Despite these improvements, Albert is still torn about his "selective" misanthropy, persecuting only the worst elements of society, when the real misanthropist loathes all people, regardless of their kindness. Towards the end of the month, he makes an announcement that to remain true to his principles, he will have to purge random people, whether pricks or non-, to remain ideologically consistent.

NOVEMBER 2041

Mass migration follows. People would rather brave kickball oppression in Lanark or the atomically twitchy aristocracy of Perth than live under an increasingly unhinged former columnist willing to poison the populace for "consistency". Albert makes no move to prevent the populace from fleeing. He refuses to roll back his policy, however, and a clash erupts between the police, the remaining populace, and Albert. The people, now classifying Albert as a prick for ordering their executions, demands his arrest. He makes another speech to try and sway opinion. "Everyone left! All I have tried to do is remain true to my convinctions. I am a misanthrope, I loathe humankind. I cannot in all conscience send the pricks to their graves when I should be working to send absolutely everyone to their graves, and working towards extinguishing the whole human enterprise. This is what the true misanthropist—" His speech is interrupted when a shoe collides with his temple, knocking him unconscious. As Albert recovers, the military intervene, and arrange another democratic election for next month.

DECEMBER 2041

Public sympathy for the fallen pricks increases, as people repent at their shameful complicity. An opportunity for the pricks to seize power again presents itself, and the We Will Fuck You party is devised by Dan Groves, a prick formerly in hiding. Titled as a humorous tribute to the murdered, the party begins as a form of remembrance, however, a manifesto soon emerges, unleashing a series of tax breaks for the rich, cuts to benefits for the ill or dying, plans to bulldoze the partially completed affordable housing to build golf courses, and to charge entry fees to public parks and libraries. Caught up in the groundswell of sympathy, and alienated by the hard left, the people vote unanimously for the We Will Fuck You party, and entirely ignore the Albert Was Nuts, But Let's Try the Not Being Pricks Thing party. On the day after the election, small businesses are charged "brick tax" based on the number of bricks in their properties, primary school kids must pay tuition fees to enter state schools, cancer patients with a poor prognosis are refused chemotherapy, those earning over £500,000 per annum are permitted to have sex with whoever they like whenever they like, and all historical child rape investigations are scrapped. The people of

Kinross settle into their new reality, free from ritual executions, replete with policies that gradually make their bank balances smaller, their long-term health prospects poorer, their working hours higher, their human rights wronger, and their children more likely to suffer from chronic depression before their third birthdays. Albert Rye is sentenced to life imprisonment for mass murder, and the people, as they contemplate their horizonless futures, find themselves extremely confused as to precisely what percentage of pricks and non-pricks there has to be for the world to be less of a sad festering shitheap.

[From *Various Tyrannies: An Almanack*, ed. David Putz, Putterbum Books, 2042.]

"Tetris in Thurso"

[CAITHNESS]

IN 2034, TEENAGER Allan Gloop, enraged at having his gaming time cut short for inessential activities—taking a bath, attending school, pushing his used dinner plates back under the door—staged a violent coup. Storming into the Prime Minister's office with a bread knife, Allan caught the ageing leader Greg Rice unawares, causing the unstable 99-year-old to have a heart attack and collapse. Allan wasted no time in issuing the first order: that he be brought seven hundred Pepsis and the complete Nintendo back catalogue. After nine years, an aide recommended that more legislation be introduced.

I was completing the blueprints for a revenge building in Reno shaped like an ex-lover's penis when I received the commission. I was paid nine million pounds to turn Thurso into one enormous round of Tetris, a classic arcade game where a series of blocks, each consisting of four squares arranged in four formations—right- and left-pointing L-shapes, whole squares, and vertical lines—appeared from the top of the screen, forcing the player to rotate them at strategic angles to create a sequence of lines without any spaces. Each complete line would vanish and lines with spaces would remain on screen and pile up. The objective was to clear as many lines as possible and rack up the highest score. When incomplete lines reached the top of the screen, no more blocks would appear, and the game ended. To begin, I hired Tetris world record-setter, Matthew Buco, who achieved the maximum score of 999,999 with 207 lines, to advise me on the practicalities of this operation.

Our first challenge was to create the Tetris "blocks" from Thurso structures. The most useful were functional square-shaped buildings such as council prefabs or high-street shops, or vertical ones like office buildings and middle-class houses. For the average block, we measured four metres in width, nine metres in breadth, and eleven in height (we had the added problem of a third dimension). The Prime Minister sent a task force to each street, measuring each structure and suggesting alterations for those over our recommended dimensions. The most common "alteration" for homes was the removal of roofs, their triangular sloping shapes proving inadequate for the formation of the required shapes. Those larger homes, with a little shaving off either side, made perfect square-block shapes. Tower blocks were not suitable for Tetris without the structures being severed at various points. These were, of course, perfect straight-shaped blocks, alongside the various office towers in the area. Factories or warehouses required mass severing into squares. Each structure was either altered or welded to others to create the L-shaped squares required for the game.

This process took nineteen months. During this time, the affected citizens were relocated to camps. Once the structures had been made into Tetris blocks, the residents could return to their altered homes until needed for use in an ongoing game. A field was purchased from local farmer Robert Hobbes, where two 50ft metal supporting beams were erected, into which the blocks were to be lowered or placed by a fleet of heavy-load-bearing industrial vehicles. Whoever was playing the game would relay instructions to the crane operators, who would manoeuvre the blocks to desired places.

The first player, chosen in a raffle at the town hall, was Alison Weathers, a Tetris virgin. Her first few moves were terrible: two L-shaped blocks (one a cathedral) were placed atop each other, and two straights atop those, creating a huge space below. The execrable play continued, with the next ten moves sealing her doom in under fifteen hours. "Oh! That's not what I meant to do!" she said as the onlookers booed. The next player, Brad Orf, had experience with the original NES version, and conducted himself with more skill. Playing live-action Tetris was in varying respects harder and easier. Because the cranes took so long to position each block and the player could see what block was coming in advance (this was true of the original NES, which had a small preview of upcoming tiles for the quick-thinking to plan a next move), making the planning easier. However, unlike the original NES, the crane operators needed the angle in advance of lowering the block into place, meaning the last-minute angle-switching was not an option. You had to gauge how each block might fit into place.

Another notable change was that, unlike the NES, completed lines vanished from the screen: an impossible feat to recreate in the live-action game

without the demolition of individual lines, which would upset the whole balanced structure and ruin the game. And straight lines, if placed so that three
squares "hung" in the air, had a tendency to capsize, whereas in the original
these would remain unbothered by gravity. The cranes would be required to
keep these blocks suspended or "held up" while others were lowered, which
could be awkward and cause occasional inadvertent ruining of a game. So a
restriction was placed on the players' moves, meaning each would have to be
verified by the crane operators as to whether such a move was physically possible, and if it was, would be permitted. This slowed down play, but prevented
structures from becoming completely destroyed.

The victor of live-action Tetris would complete a faultless series of lines
with no spaces to the top of the beams, rather than a maintain a low level of
lines to achieve a high score. The first to achieve this was Max Moppingson
who had watched the seven preceding rounds and made notes as to which structures were liable to appear, those the crane drivers would refuse and when, and
achieved a perfect pile-up. PM Allan Gloop handed over the bread knife he had
used to seize power as the star prize. This victory proved bittersweet, as one
man who refused to leave his property ended up crushed during an accidental
capsizing of a hair salon as part of a post-game clean-up. His name was Dennis
Wilson.

['Report on Live-Action Tetris in Thurso', Frances Ursule, in *Tetris: A Global
Legacy*, Nintendo ibooks, p.39, 2057.]

"Quiz"

[DUNBARTON]

A RE YOU A REAL Dunbartonista? Do your hackles rise at the 50p price hike on malt loaf at the Auld Kirk Museum? Does the three-hour RSPB response time to a wounded mallard by the canal make you seethe? Would you wait until the pishing rain cleared the queue before pedal-boating? Do you order the cheapest thing on the menu even on your anniversary? Do you know your Baldernock from your Bellsmyre? Take our quiz to find if you are a real Dunbartonista!

Q: If you visit Lennox Castle and a wheelchair user needs access to ramp, which of the following actions would you take?

    a) Block the ramp with your capacious rear, and wiggle that rump in their wheelie faces

    b) Step off the ramp, apologise for your thoughtlessness, and tug their little cheek

    c) Move aside without comment and allow them to pass

Q: If you visit Campsie Hills car park and there are no spaces, do you . . . ?

    a) Accept the car park is full and explore something else

    b) Create a makeshift parking space by partially blocking two other cars with your Land Rover, leaving a barely navigable gap for others to pass through

    c) Park in a ditch by the side of the road

Q: If you visit a newsagent and your favourite newspaper is not available, what do you do?

    a) Purchase another paper espousing similar views

b) Strop out the newsagents muttering "bloody typical" under your breath, vow never to return to the premises ever again, and make a point of walking an extra twelve minutes to the next newsagent instead of the usual forty seconds

c) Lightly upbraid the newsagent in a tone that sounds friendly, but conveys real disappointment

Q: When passing through Renton, what do you remark?

a) "Looks like the backside of a horse, and I mean the backside of a horse that is excreting, and I mean the backside of a horse that is excreting a violent unrelenting stream of diarrhoea, following an ill-advised chilli in its sugar lumps"

b) "This deprived area could use an ample shot of investment so that locals can start businesses, improve the community, and make the place a cleaner and more welcoming conurbation in which to dwell"

c) "I'm so pleased I don't live here!"

Q: What is your philosophy of life?

a) Misery is the river of the world

b) I eat at a lochside bistro to avoid the hoi polloi, therefore I am

c) Live, laugh, love x x x

Q: If you are driving up a farmside road and spot a sheep stuck in a barbed wire fence, do you . . . ?

a) Stop the car immediately and free the sheep painlessly from the fence

b) Remark that it is a shame, but a farmer or somebody else will probably intercede

c) Drive on without helping the sheep, believing deep inside your heart that man's brutish nature is what makes him the most magnificent species, and woolly liberal acts of tolerance for foolish creatures are what is sending this country to the dogs

Q: If you were staying at a B&B for a romantic weekend, and the view of Loch Lomond was not as splendid as you had seen in the brochure, would you . . . ?

a) Ask to speak to the manager at once to demand an upgrade and, if refused, spend the entire romantic weekend in a huff, refuse to eat in the restaurant or order any drinks at the bar, spend as long possible outside the premises and, when inside the room, keep the curtains closed, leave all the towels out for washing, and refuse to have sex with your partner in protest

b) Accept that the views in the brochure are photoshopped somewhat to improve the B&B's trade, and that this is inevitable part of the business

c) Maintain an aloof attitude to the staff for the entire stay, transmitting your irritation through a system of shrugs and nods

Q: What is your opinion on Lennoxtown?

a) "It's like having fishhooks in your eyes, fishhooks that remove your eyes, then maim the underside of your brain through your empty eyesockets, then rip your brain from your head and feed the maimed mush to a rabid alsatian"

b) "It would be radically improved by a phalanx of gendarmerie thrusting their French truncheons into the inhabitants, shooting up the buildings with their automatic weapons, and flooding the streets with the blood of puppies"

c) "It is the sort of crumbling village where hope is bundled into a sack, driven to the woods, clubbed to death by four soulless mob killers, set alight with paraffin, then poorly covered with nearby twigs and lazily shovelled mud"

Q: What is your preferred method of exercise?

a) Far into the forest away from other mortals, where I can listen to my own thoughts and opinions ricocheting around my superior mind, where I can avoid families, dog walkers, and other irritating presences to whom I would have to affect being pleasant

b) In a running group, where I can socialise with likeminded people, have a tremendous laugh and shed pounds in beautiful locations

c) On a treadmill in a local gymnasium, preferably one overlooking a pretty forest trail

Q: What is your opinion on youth hostellers?

a) One or two of them are polite, but they are basically not to be trusted

b) They are constantly traipsing with their backpacks around my forests, making loud European noises, muddying the old trails with their clodhoppers, clogging up the village taverns with their self-satisfied faces, asking for directions to Inchmurran Island, which isn't even in this country, and rubbing their youthful energy in my face

c) They enliven an otherwise quiet rural location every spring and summer with their enthusiasm, humour, and provide a necessary kick to the local economy

Q: If a family of refugees moved into a vacant house next to yours, what would you think?

a) It is wonderful that these people who have suffered unimaginable horrors can find refuge in a safe, welcoming community like Twechar

b) They are simply replacing the misery of their war-torn plutocracies with a lifeless, mundane plutocracy so tedious, eventless, and drab, that the sound of an approaching exocet missile would bring huge relief

c) I would live in fear that one morning I would awake to my children's heads on spikes, the whole village lying in rubble, and my wife turned into a sex slave as I walk at knifepoint into a hospital with a timebomb strapped to my arse

Q: What is your opinion on literature?

a) I only read travel books with pictures of hills in mist, hills at dawn, hills with snow, hills in bloom, and hills at dusk

b) I love the dark and twisted crime novels of Ian Rankin, he's a terrific storyteller, always writes compelling plots, clever scenarios, and his characters become part of your life, deserves every penny he's made

c) There are too many people wanting to write, and there's no money in the book trade, these kids are throwing their lives away with their degrees in books, the future lies in wholeselling, whaling, and trouser-stencilling

Q: If eternal darkness descended on your village, how would you react?

a) I would leap up, fistbump the air, and yowl "Finalleeee!"

b) I would accept the upcoming extinction of all life with a resigned sigh and allow myself to slowly backslide into the hornèd hindgut of oblivion

c) I would cry horribly, weeping for weeks, if I had weeks, for the loss of such a wondrous and spectacular planet, wailing "O poorest Earth! Woe is thee!"

Q: You have the power to punish the kids who vandalised Balloch Castle. What do you do?

a) Have their fingernails removed with pliers, their necks nailed to trees, and their knees chewed raw by hogs

b) Administer a verbal caution and ask them to remove the graffiti

c) Arrange for a furious front-page headline to appear in the tabloids with the culprits' names and faces, have their homes surrounded for months by loud-speaker abusers, their mobiles sent a constant stream of violent and graphic texts, and hound them through a sustained campaign of hate to their graves

Q: If a friendly retired scholar moved into the house next door, what would you do?

a) Say hello politely at first then make sneery, sarcastic remarks about how uppity, smarter-than-thou the man thinks he is, and that intellectual snobs are among some of the worst people on the planet, and refuse the many invitations to his evening soirees, where he would no doubt sit around quoting philosophy, and make you feel like an ant cowering before his colossal brain

b) Smile politely at his stories while partaking vast quantities of the kind man's port

c) Welcome a distinguished man to the community with a homemade apple crumble

Q: It is sundown and you are stood before a beautiful sunset at the basin of Loch Lomond. What do you remark?

a) "What an incredible reminder that we live in the midst of rare natural wonder, and how salving these precious, painterly scenes are to the soul"

b) "We had better head back before it gets too dark"

c) "At last, the sun buggers off behind the horizon, and we can cool off and escape this irritating heatwave for another eight hours, before the sticky hell resumes for another long long day"

Q: You are born. What's your first thought?

a) I will probably only tolerate sixty-four years of this

b) How wonderful it is to be anything at all

c) Sweet infant Christ, push me back into the womb and spare me from this accursèd life, this pig-swill planet with its seething cauldrons of boiling excrement in which I must bathe from birth to death

Answers:

1. a), 2. b), 3. b), 4. a) 5. a), 6. c), 7. a), 8. b), 9. a), 10. b), 11. b), 12. c). 13. a). 14. c). 15. a), 16. c). 17. c).

If you scored between 0-7, sorry, you are not a true Dunbartonista! Your outlook is too positive and open-minded, your horizons are too wide. Try shutting the blinds, not returning your phone calls, and changing your news feeds!

If you scored between 8-13, you are on the way to becoming a true Dunbartonista! Your face is locking into the required scowl, that spring in your step is changing into a slow, weary shuffle along the pavement of resignation!

If you scored between 14-17, you are a true Dunbartonista! You awake to watery porridge, you begrudgingly drag yourself into your socks and shoes everyday like a prisoner on the morning of his execution, and you inflict your smelly life's failures on everyone unfortunate enough to encounter your repulsive face. Well done!

[From *The Dunbarton Herald*, June 12, 2044.]

"Aleatoria"

[NAIRN]

MARCH 30
Citizens vote for acts of parliament to be picked at random from a thousand public contributions placed in a stetson hat.

MARCH 31
Sandra Kennington to be bulldozered and replaced with a crocus.

APRIL 1
The coronation chicken sandwich to be recognised as a knight of the realm.

APRIL 2
All citizens to listen to The Fall for twelve hours straight.

APRIL 3
Public urination into kittens' eyes mandatory.

APRIL 4
An hour's silence to be observed for Arnold Wilson's stubbed toe.

APRIL 5
Banks to dispense unlimited £100 notes to men named Eäåmðn.

APRIL 6
Public holiday for those with helical avatars.

APRIL 7
A state of emergency to be declared if one happens.

APRIL 8
Sprechgesang banned.

APRIL 9
Friends who convince you to attend an opera version of Kafka to be barbecued.

APRIL 10
Brutal merciless violence to be replaced with cress.

APRIL 11
All citizens to draw the homeless a picture of a house to boost their morale.

APRIL 12
Politicians to cough on occasion.

APRIL 13
A mild slice of unease everywhere.

APRIL 14
Pixel rate to increase by 300dpi.

APRIL 15
Desiccated corpse chosen image for national flag.

APRIL 16
All bald men required to have tattoo of a man with a full head of hair on their heads.

APRIL 17
Swamp to replace bog in the phrase 'bog-standard' as benchmark of ordinariness.

APRIL 18
Potato milkshakes to be a thing.

APRIL 19
Derek Cookson has to run across a farmland to the point he can't continue any longer, then run for another four minutes, to the point he thinks he might collapse and drop dead, then stop for a breather. He can return home after.

APRIL 20
Cress to be replaced with brutal merciless violence.

APRIL 21
Sexier kerning on letterheads.

APRIL 22
All vocal chords to be fitted with autotune.

APRIL 23
A complete restructuring of the economic model, with the means of production to be replaced with pelvic thrusts, and inherited wealth to be replaced with a mild korma.

APRIL 24
Semiotics taught in primary schools.

APRIL 25
The outdoors to be abridged.

APRIL 26
The firing squad introduced for children who excel at mathematics.

APRIL 27
The winter fuel allowance replaced with one tank of propane per OAP.

APRIL 28
Curt Easterman's cottage repainted in cerise.

APRIL 29
Alligator sperm to replace tap water.

APRIL 30
Men under 40 will bow down to "The Stick".

APRIL 31
Successful meetings to end with the inflating of balloons.

MAY 1
Gated communities, please!

MAY 2
Potted plants, never!

MAY 3
Scabbed lips to be kissed better.

MAY 4
A slow, inevitable slide into oblivion to replace basketball.

MAY 5
Currency to be renamed "Drip-weasel."

MAY 6
Liveliness appreciated but not mandatory.

MAY 7
Sunburned mammals permitted.

[From *The Aleatoria Almanack 2034*, Mitchell Apse (ed.), p.23-25, Nairn Government Publishing, 2034.]

"Textual Dysfunction"
[GLASGOW & RENFREW]

IN 2020, GLASGOW & RENFREW *was absorbed into the ongoing novel of a disillusioned fiction writer, composing a lengthy self-referential "nonbook" about a writer trying and failing to start a satisfying literary project, who ends up waffling about his past lovers and nonexistent role in the book business, and making flippant remarks to the reader and other unnamed persons. The following extracts are a random selection from this insufferable and relentless "nonbook" which remained unfinished at the time Scotland was destroyed. It is believed the citizens of Glasgow & Renfrew were suspended in some bardic state, cursed for decades to read the indulgent ramblings of this unknown and extremely arrogant writer. —Ed.*

The original opening has been deleted.

[ ]

I and you and they, we all feature.

[ ]

AN OPENING:
Beryl bounded along the beach in open-toed sandals.

[ ]

You were a florist.

[ ]

A SECOND SENTENCE:
The noontide sun, sizzling her pale skin, would not abate. She sloshed into the sea and said his name: "Xerxes, Xerxes!"

[ ]

I kiss your face, pretty reader.

[ ]

There's a weak simile somewhere in this nonbook.

[ ]

I remember you fingering my bookshelves a few minutes before we had sex.

[ ]

THIRD SENTENCE:
She stepped from the sea, her feet soothed in the salve of brine. She sat on the shore and said: "Fuck me, I have a headache."

[ ]

Fuck me, I have a headache.

[ ]

"Write a little each day, and you will have a shitty novel in a longer time than if you'd sat and worked on the thing properly." —My quotable quote

[ ]

This not a comedy.

[ ]

My laptop has only 17% battery remaining.

[ ]

And nausea. And wrist cramp. And some kind of untitled internal suppurating wound that I am trying to make manifest on the page.

[ ]

They want "honesty", the reading public?

[ ]

One time, at the writers' group, an Irish bisexual man with strong political views, whose stories about growing up bisexual in small-town Ireland were called "heartwarming" and "moving" by the others, criticised me for overusing adverbs and "ten-dollar words".

[ ]

FOURTH SENTENCE:
She scratched her sunburned feet, leaned back, and ate an aposiopesis.

[ ]

If you saw what I've been doing for the last 40 minutes, you'd be like wtf.

[ ]

A release, like the lingering fingering of a morning's masturbation.

[ ]

"Your specialist subject," you would have said.

[ ]

Are you better at this than me?

[ ]

Is there a more potent way to launch this lamentive sniffle into the sorrowful stratosphere?

[ ]

I remember you saying that no one wanted to fuck you because you were fat.

[ ]

What is this?

[ ]

I should get the apologies in early.

[ ]

They couldn't care less about you, really, those perpetually perky avatars.

[ ]

I have fictionalised everything you said for my own amusement.

[ ]

Two weeks have passed, I have written nothing.

[ ]

And two further.

[ ]

What?

[ ]

"Keep me separate from your seditious scribbling, buddy. The lovers of littéra-teurs always end with their love lanced," you said, more or less.

"Fear not. My words are swords pointing straight into mine own guts," I said.

"Lucky me, to secure Scotland's most prolific self-eviscerator."

"Can I lick your knees?"

[ ]

OPENING OF AUTOBIOGRAPHY:
I stumbled out of bed and crunched my cereal in a huff. My mother queried:
"Written anything, darling?"

[ ]

Better to express frustration and rage than nothing at all.

[ ]

I might have cancer.

[ ]

It's more than likely that no one will ever remark on that sentence you spent
two hours refining.

[ ]

OPENING SENTENCE #32:
He awoke, unfortunately, in the same unfortunate body. He checked the mirror for new sores, growths, or wrinkles that might spur his imagination into
imagining a slightly different person, and found nothing.

[ ]

I remember saying that I couldn't care less if you were fat, and that I wanted
to fuck you, and feeling that I had badly fudged that reply.

[ ]

My inner critic thinks this sentence is a pile of steaming hippo excrement.

[ ]

My outer critic thinks the works of Lee Child are a pile of steaming hippo
excrement. (And no, he hasn't "read" them.)

[ ]

Q: Who is the audience for this work?

A: Myself.

[ ]

"This isn't writing!" my inner critic howls.

[ ]

Times New Roman is to blame for the dwindling powers of my prose.

[ ]

"This is *minor* writing!" my outer critic howls.

[ ]

One time, at the writers' group, a metrosexual man with an Oxford degree and two shirt buttons undone remarked that he wasn't able to "understand the intent" behind my story, although conceded it was "very well-written."

[ ]

This is the perfect form for the sort of writer who prefers surfing the internet and reading articles on late nineties indie to penning award-winning prose. That sort of writer is me.

[ ]

I can't remember having sex with you for the first time.

[ ]

I'm the sort of person who stays up into the wee hours making infinitesimal adjustments to perfectly acceptable sentences for no logical or aesthetic reason.

[ ]

This makes me lonelier than you.

[ ]

Mediocrity is a state of mind. A very mediocre one.

[ ]

This is not a flip book. This is a flip-off book.

[ ]

This project is deliberately designed to be abandon-proof. All my doubts and gripes will simply be sloughed into the text.

[ ]

What if no one appreciates or understands my intentions?

[ ]

OPENING SENTENCE #61:
He had returned to his parental home, located in the sort of provincial town that has never featured in a haiku, to mope. A ten-year stint trying to become a writer had sucked the hope from his knees.

[ ]

I should probably make allusions to the "novel of no", i.e. Melville's *Bartleby*. I'd rather recommend *Bartleby & Co.* by Enrique Vila-Matas.

[ ]

I probably have cancer.

[ ]

This may all seem very droll to you, but you have no idea what is happening between these sentences.

[ ]

And I'm not going to say, except maybe obliquely, because my real life experience would render this literary experience banal.

[ ]

This isn't a "novel of no". This is a novel of fucking-cunting-christing-fucking-hell.

[ ]

My intentions, my wonderful intentions!

[ ]

This is "non-writing", or if you prefer, "meta-non-writing", i.e. non-writing chatting about itself. This doesn't make it any cleverer.

[ ]

I am simply a well-read man beleaguered by the book world. I am simply a well-read man pickled by the perfunctoriness of present-day prose. I am simply a well-read man stymied by the over-saturation of stylish and well-written prose pouring from a million MFA pens.

[ ]

I remember never kissing the skin tag on your left breast.

[ ]

I find it hilarious to attack and flay myself in print. That's rather odd.

[ ]

You burrow far enough into the navel, you find art.

[ ]

OPENING SENTENCE #79:
Richie Samsa awoke, flicked the bug from his bed [I have read Kafka!], fried his kidney [I have read Joyce!], had the howling fantods [Foster Wallace!], placed a pebble in his pocket [Beckett!], and so on and so what.

[ ]

I have an MFA.

[ ]

I hate the letter 'b'. I hate the letter 'd'. I hate the letter 'y'. I hate the letter 'g'. I hate the letter 'j'. I hate untidy, protruding letters that jut out on the line, like that 'j' there.

[ ]

This is a book about feeling like you have nothing to contribute to literature and that your efforts will make no impact on the world and that your writing will never reach anyone, and writing anyway.

[ ]

I remember offering you a fresh croissant and flavoured water after sex.

[ ]

This book is the sinewy fingers of the strangler around your neck after an hour's lovemaking.

[ ]

You are drawing way too much attention to yourselves.

[ ]

The reason I'm writing this is because I have a MFA (did I mention?)

[ ]

Leonard Cohen said something interesting on *Bookworm* that I didn't write down. The mention of Leonard Cohen here is not significant.

[ ]

A SENTENCE:
He spent a number of weeks listening to Rowland S. Howard and early Swans on a loop.

[ ]

You might be wondering. I am too.

[ ]

Less is not more.

[ ]

You weren't the one for me, fatty.

[ ]

If you are a minor celebrity with an offer to write a memoir, please bear in mind your effort is suppressing a far superior literary work. That matters.

[ ]

Only the best fragments have been chosen for you to read.

[ ]

Books should never be "cash-in" products for those who excel at an inferior artform.

[ ]

Meaning and intent are overrated.

[ ]

The ability to holler the loudest still determines who is read or not. Literature is not an egalitarian utopia. It writhes in the muck of cut-throat capitalism.

[ ]

I remember your weird hair, like a badly topiarised hedge.

[ ]

It's raining. I'm at my desk contemplating my next paragraph. I stare at the dull rain drizzling over rooftops and trees. I think about the market value of my next sentence. The whole morning is ruined.

[ ]

The everyday reader prefers a thumping good read with a zippy plot and love-able characters. To make that assumption, you would have to assume the reader was either a) a simpleton, or b) a four-year-old.

[ ]

Literary slap and tickle, with more slapping, and tickling that turns to violence.

[ ]

It amuses me to think of your bemusement.

[ ]

Quit the project. Add words to the project. Quit the project. Repeat.

[ ]

I remember you saying something sniffy about Will Self.

[ ]

When there is nothing to write about, there is always this.

[ ]

You never made me mixtapes.

[ ]

I had some terrific ideas on that windfarm. Fortunately, I forgot to write them down.

[ ]

If I despise every well-varnished and overworked sentence, the sort I have buffed with care over several weeks, then surely these speedily unspooled nano-thoughts are the antidote?

[ ]

If you think I'm writing any old thing here, you're missing the point.

[ ]

Where there is this, there is nothing to write about.

[ ]

And grasping the point brilliantly.

[ ]

You'd have thought.

[ ]

I hate this shit.

[ ]

If I hadn't opened that Flann O'Brien ten years ago, I might be a bestseller by now.

[ ]

OPENING SENTENCE # 57:
He opened his laptop after two weeks. Thought he'd better write something. He wrote "the short man moved an inch", rubbed his chin for two minutes, and went to sleep.

[ ]

All I want is a patronisingly supportive review in a broadsheet. Then I can die.

[ ]

I never carry a notebook. I don't want to read my pitifully derivative ideas in bed later.

[ ]

I remember putting my head between your enormous breasts.

[ ]

I deleted something.

[ ]

Confidence, self-belief, and motivation. Without these, you have this book.

[ ]

How do I decide which fragments stay, and which are wiped?

[ ]

I picked up a Nick Hornby novel in the library, and felt a violent stabbing pain in the heart.

[ ]

There are too many writers. Please, do the decent thing.

[ ]

The world doesn't need another novel about a concert pianist's osteopetrosis.

[ ]

I remember you eating melted chocolate in your van, and feeling slightly repulsed.

[ ]

I want you to feel increasingly irritated, depressed, and resigned.

[ ]

The world doesn't need another novel. Perhaps we should publish on Venus.

[ ]

Most male writers I know struggle to resist the urge to masturbate while writing.

[ ]

SAY SOMETHING SIGNIFICANT HERE!!!

[ ]

Most female writers I know aren't interested in masturbating while writing.

[ ]

I'm reading Tom McCarthy and Rodrigo Fresan. And you wonder why my every sentence wheezes and splutters to the floor in a pathetic crying heap?

[ ]

Remarks are not literature, said G. Stein, except when those remarks are slamming with unrestrained vitriol the published works of rivals.

[ ]

I'm not a genius, and neither are you (unless you are). The best we can strive for is elegant mediocrity.

[ ]

I want to say nothing.

[ ]

I'm a genius in my imagination. I prefer to live there.

[ ]

NEXT SENTENCE:
He wrote "the short man moved another inch" and wondered if he might compose a novel about a short man moving in inch-size increments from one side of the room to the other, like in Beckett's *How It Is*.

[ ]

I tickle your little chin, ugly reader.

[ ]

I wrote nothing for two hours because I was too busy fantasising about being a totally radical infamous endlessly talented genius.

[ ]

They monetise your every fleeting pleasure.

[ ]

The first few notes of an early Beatles track has more artistic value than every-thing I have and ever will write.

[ ]

INSERT A PERTINENT QUOTE HERE!!!

[ ]

I blame you for this.

[ ]

I want to say everything.

[ ]

I want to crawl inside your brain and live there.

[ ]

I attended a friend's book launch and felt nothing but unbridled happiness for her success.

[ ]

I might go back to bed.

[ ]

Mornings when trying to squeeze a coherent notion from one's head takes Herculean effort.

[ ]

"You're punching above your intellectual weight," you said.

"Correct. However, my plan to compose lightweight comic novels in unremarkable prose was long ago scuppered by the reality that to write such things was to relegate myself to mediocrity," I said.

"But you *are* a mediocrity."

"Yes. But fiction offers you a chance to pretend otherwise. Everyday, you awake in the same fattening and failing mediocre body, your mind slowly rotting, your horizons ever narrowing, and you turn to fiction for a temporary respite, where you can arrange your words in such a manner you appear smarter, wittier, and better educated than you are in the merciless light."

"The truth will always leak out. In the sloppy syntax of your sentences, in the notably absent rigour of your themes, in the continual reversions to familiar tropes, in the two-tone tenor of your dialogue."

"But in any kind of artform, the underwhelming human being can pull magical work from his or her rear end, and serve up delicious platters of fucking brilliance completely at odds with their dullness."

"True. But in this room, in any room, with me, or with any other people, you can't spend two hours tinkering your sentences to appear smarter than you are. In the merciless light, as you say, you will always be a mediocrity."

"I want to marry your mouth."

[ ]

If you ever come and live inside my brain, be sure and pack a cyanide capsule.

[ ]

Facebook statues, tweets, click-bait articles, text messages: you are sucking the pleasure out of language.

[ ]

When people ask me what I write, I reply "spiteful feuilletons brought up from the throat like strings of bloody phlegm."

[ ]

TODAY I WILL DELETE EVERYTHING I WROTE YESTERDAY.

[ ]

I definitely have cancer.

[ ]

I don't know if I've told you this, but I have omitted a lot of material.

[ ]

I met a beautiful woman for a coffee. We chatted with ease on the vagaries of modern politics. I asked to see her again. She expressed an interest in my writing. We met for the second time, and our mutual attraction became clear. After dinner, we took an evening stroll in the park, and we kissed. On the third date, we swiftly repaired to my flat to express our passions. I asked her after making love if she wanted me to read an excerpt from my novel. "Nah," she said. Inside, I died.

[ ]

Don't worry, the omitted material will be available on my blog.

[ ]

I'm losing faith in this project.

[ ]

I wrote something here, wiped it clear, scratched my bestubbled cheek, scratched my chin, thought about how my face is falling off, and that I will soon be dead, and wrote this in pain.

[ ]

I'm only playing. The omitted material will never be published.

[ ]

When you sequentially write and delete stuff, you ride a very unsatisfying see-saw.

[ ]

These days, every blurb I read is followed by a theatrical eyeroll.

[ ]

I deleted arrogance.

[ ]

I deleted moaning.

[ ]

Everyone is my rival. From Shakespeare to the five-year-old who wrote a well-received story about their cat's latest furball.

[ ]

Why not call this poetry?

[ ]

I only write this out of love.

[ ]

"You revel in obscurity, in being a pinched outsider," you said.

"I know," I responded.

"Your neediness is your only subject," you said.

"I know," I responded.

"You are amused at being a self-created victim," you said.

"I know," I responded.

"Your sham worthlessness is a facade," you said.

"I am in vomitous love with you," I responded.

[ ]

What *is* this?

[ ]

It isn't poetry.

[ ]

There is no virtue in concision.

[ ]

I deleted three pointless haiku.

[ ]

I would step across the road to avoid another writer.

[ ]

I CANNOT WRITE IN THESE CONDITIONS
I DEMAND A FRESH BRAIN AND BODY

[ ]

I am choking on the cat hairs in my throat.

[ ]

I only write this out of hate.

[ ]

I am dying.

[ ]

If you feel like you're getting nowhere in the literary world, and that you should seriously reconsider tirelessly fighting for your place in the literary world, you are now a part of the literary world.

[ ]

I remember your enthusiasm about the songs of Yoko Ono seemed a little forced.

[ ]

EVERY IDEA IS ABANDONED IN UNDER TWO SENTENCES

[ ]

Perhaps the ephemeral and miniaturised nature of online text has created an incurable torpor of distraction, setting in at a line of text longer than this one.

[ ]

Write a sentence. Shrug at its failure to be the best thing ever written with a pair of fingers. Write a second sentence. Realise that further writing of that calibre would be futile and close the document. Try again tomorrow.

[ ]

Fortunately, beauty, popularity, and riches do not mean you can spray a semi-respectable hose of prose.

[ ]

Wake up. Remember that my previously published works were treated with indifference, and that even friends and acquaintances didn't bust a blood vessel to read or comment on them. Back to bed.

[ ]

I remember you always asking me if I had been paid for my published short stories before not offering to read them.

[ ]

Life is much more pleasant without the pressure to construct six-sentence paragraphs of three or four per page, across 300 or more pages.

[ ]

Minute by minute, second by second reminders of what you said, what you do, who you know, what you like, who you are.

[ ]

I am chained to the internet with tight and unyielding manacles.

[ ]

I would rather be having sex with you than writing this sentence.

[ ]

You would rather be having sex with anyone but me than reading this sentence.

[ ]

I remember thinking about whether I was in love with you, and concluding I probably was, but that I was too emotionally barren to properly feel any love for anyone.

[ ]

This is not a "twitter novel". This is a novel chronicling a serious and potentially fatal nervous breakdown, caused by a mildly amusing florist.

[ ]

OPENING SENTENCE #189:
Andrew walked into a bar. (My God, I am bored.) The barman, Skip, asked him what his preference for alcoholic beverage might be in the idiom native to wherever this paragraph is set. (My God, I am tired and achy.) Andrew failed to reply. (My God, what a boring sentence.) At this point in the story, the author's wrists began to ache from the act of typing. (And his fucking fingers.) His head was throbbing at the prospect of skipping ahead to try and contrive a coherent end to what he had started. He loathed the ham-fisted hackneyed opening to the story, kicking himself for such a pathetic and obvious set-up. (And for having started in the first place.) He decided the best thing to do was to stop. (Writing. For good.)

[ ]

I am teabagging your mind.

[ ]

You might think that writing about not writing is a waste of time. I reply: "Sir, you have no idea. If I cease writing altogether, I might end up never writing again. The fingers must be fulsomely flexed, even in inconsequential paragraphs of increasing vapidity."

[ ]

I loathe most of the paragraphs in this nonbook. But I won't delete them.

[ ]

Sometimes a sentence, even perfectly sculpted, looks hideous on the page before you. The way the letters jut from the line, the way the curly cursives poke their partners, the way the font frames things. There is no end to the ways an author can despise his own words.

[ ]

Do I hate writing? No, I hate not writing.

[ ]

"How can a writer end up as constipated as you?" you asked me.

"Penguin released a novel called *The Ministry of Utmost Happiness* today," I replied.

"That proves . . . ?"

"I exist in the infected hindgut of the marketplace."

"And . . . ?"

"I exist in the diseased anal cleft of the commercial world."

"And . . . ?"

"These things can constipate a writer."

"You're probably completely dried up in terms of ideas. Or you've long reached the pinnacle of your talents and are in dreadful denial about entering the long twilight of your literary career."

"I utterly adore you."

[ ]

I have, on several occasions, attempted to rewrite a novel entitled *The Reason Not to Jump*, a 600-page epic about three generations of misanthropic men who opt out of suicide. This rewrite will never occur. This fleeting mention here is the only legacy of these years of sweltering and fruitless toil.

[ ]

I haven't revised this sentence.

[ ]

You only criticise the literary mainstream if you are not part of it.

[ ]

Total loser, as a former President would say.

[ ]

Isolated fragments give the illusion of profundity.

[ ]

You are eating a cheese bagel. Somewhere, a smug writer is finishing his final paragraph with smug satisfaction. You are on a stuffed commuter train en route to an office. Somewhere, a rich writer is lounging in a cafeteria musing on the internal lives of his fascinating characters. You are in your office staring at a spreadsheet. Somewhere, a cool writer is preparing for the evening launch of his already well-reviewed third novel. You are tolerating inane chatter in the staff room. Somewhere, a thoughtful writer is penning an observant article about a worthwhile political cause. You are staring at a clock that appears to have frozen. Somewhere, a novelist, his fingers reflexively on his chin, is musing on the potent metaphor he has created. You are cooking a readymeal in the microwave. Somewhere, a writer is having cocktails with his equally talented friends. You are watching *Little House on the Prairie*. You have no one but yourself to blame.

[ ]

A prominent Scottish writer once praised a short story of mine. I cling to that seven-year-old praise far too tightly.

[ ]

Some people, born beautiful, simply have to pose in their pants to be adored. Some people, born weird, write beautiful 700-page masterpieces of refined and erudite prose, and no one cares. People are not to be trusted with the beautiful.

[ ]

Your remarks at the writers' group were met with polite tolerance, and forgotten a nanosecond after your long prayed-for final clause.

[ ]

Aren't you tired of the savagery of coherence? Don't you sometimes want a book to scream at you, howl at you, scratch your prissy little eyes out? Don't you need a book sometimes to claw at your mind until your thoughts are bursting and bleeding and finally illuminated?

[ ]

David Markson is better.

[ ]

I bought you flowers. You knew instantly their price, and the cheap insignificance of my gesture.

[ ]

This is a book about feeling shat on by the literary marketplace, and becoming so fucking fagged out by the business, the only form of release is to scribble inane manic gibberish, the sort you sometimes see behind the bedroom walls of lunatics after they've blown their brains out.

[ ]

Q: Why don't you write something beautiful?

A: I am only capable of the monstrous.

[ ]

I'm not taunting you, I'm tickling you.

[ ]

You'd better check your phone.

[ ]

It isn't that I loathe all writers [I do], or that I despise their success [I do], or that I am repulsed by the literary marketplace [I am], or that I hate what literature has become [I have], or that I am sickened by the dwindling numbers of readers [I am], or that I crave more success and attention [I do], it is more that everyone else in the universe except me is a fucking idiot [no it isn't].

[ ]

You'd better check in case you have a text.

[ ]

I deleted what was written here.

[ ]

Your unread text is much more important than this.

[ ]

Waking up is the strongest argument for full-blown misanthropy.

[ ]

Are you going to leave that text unread for much longer?

[ ]

£10.99 is a reasonable price of admission to my nervous breakdown.

[ ]

FOR GOD'S SAKE, READ YOUR TEXT!!!

[ ]

Write a proper book, you whiny dung-muncher.

[ ]

I HATE THIS PROJECT
I HATE THIS PROJECT
I HATE THIS PROJECT

[ ]

I stepped on the bus. [This sentence has MARKET VALUE! We can all relate to buses. Everyone has seen or boarded or heard of a bus in their time, apart from some people under six months old. Continue with our approval.] The driver was a blue rhinoceros. [This has NO MARKET VALUE. No one can relate to a bus driver being a blue rhinoceros. There is no such thing as a blue rhinoceros, except perhaps in a children's cartoon. Even if blue rhinoceroses existed, they lack the skills needed to power a bus through the streets. They would merely grunt and writhe in the driving booth and defecate on the seat. Delete this sentence at once.] A short, fat passenger boarded the bus. [This has MARKET VALUE. We have all encountered a short, fat man or woman in our lives, and the spark of recognition will spur the reader onwards. Continue with our approval]. The passenger retrieved a shotgun from his satchel and blew the rhino's brains out. [This has NO MARKET VALUE. The sudden act of brutal violence against a brightly coloured and innocent rhinoceros will repulse readers at once. No one will tolerate this random slaughter. Delete this sentence at once.] Someone in the bus coughed. [This has MARKET VALUE. We all cough from time to time, to clear our airways of phlegm or catarrh, so people will react to this observation warmly and happily. Continue with our approval.] Someone else in the bus coughed up a small baby turtle, ribboned in sick. [This has NO MARKET VALUE. The common reader adores baby turtles, and seeing one emerge from a someone's throat covered in vile bile is a complete turn-off. Delete this sentence at once.]

[ ]

In the event of my death, I authorise the distribution of this nonbook in every school classroom, and on every school and university syllabus, in the world. Because the little fuckers have to know.

[ ]

Self-pity ain't pretty.

[ ]

I validate myself.

[ ]

"What's your new book about?" my mother asked.

"It's not a book, more of a splurge," I replied.

"What your new splurge about?"

"It's an act of immature literary vandalism. It's as if, after having read thousands of the great masters, I learned absolutely nothing, and proceeded to urinate on their graves one by one."

"Is it something I might read?"

"It's the literary equivalent of syphilis in your right eye."

"Have you heard of Dean Koontz?"

"Until next time, Mother."

[ ]

I was thinking how the pressure to compose pristine, musical prose is lessened by the freedom I have to spend time composing pristine, musical prose.

[ ]

If you finish this book despising me, I have achieved something.

[ ]

I choose not to socialise with other writers.

[ ]

Other writers ask you what you are working on as a prelude to describing their own boring works at length.

[ ]

I don't like to discuss what I'm working on.

[ ]

All writers despise each other. Let's not pretend otherwise.

[ ]

You might be the sort of writer who loves to describe their works to their friends, seeking laughter and approval for your brilliant ideas.

[ ]

This business of stitching words together in a coherent order to seek approval from others.

[ ]

Short, yes, but it feels much longer.

[ ]

Please review me.

[ ]

I remember my ambitions for this nonbook being vaster.

[ ]

Woke up. Remembered no one is interested in fiction. Back to bed.

[ ]

I don't care what you are working on.

[ ]

Woke up. Remembered no one reads any more. Back to bed.

[ ]

Thank you for reading. Seriously, I adore you.

[ ]

Woke up. Remembered society doesn't care about me. Back to bed.

[ ]

Basically, in this nonbook, I am like a clingy, drunken lover, screaming "I don't need you" before storming off, then hastily calling at 2AM and weeping down the line that I love you, and always have, and that I never want to lose you, and I will do whatever it takes to make it work.

[ ]

Fuck you for reading. Seriously, fuck you.

[ ]

How can I overcome my immaturity, my burning desire to spoil a scene by introducing a camel at the most inappropriate moment?

[ ]

I can't write a sex scene without using the word "lubricious".

[ ]

Everyone has a novel in them, "they" say. I have a novel in me, only I am vomiting it up and splattering my carrotty chunks across the page.

[ ]

Bitter? Yes please, with lemon.

[ ]

For every sentence included in this nonbook, at least three have been deleted.

[ ]

"I am rebelling against the literary marketplace," I said.

"By deliberately writing a completely unpublishable nonbook?" you asked.

"Yes."

"But you will, of course, try to sell your unpublishable nonbook, and use your nonbook's anti-commercial stance as a pull for the sort of anti-corporate reader that you crave, who will purchase your anti-corporate nonbook for the cheapest possible price on Amazon?"

"Probably."

"Then your project is utterly useless, and you are a bumbling hypocrite."

"Kiss me."

[ ]

OPENING #86:
The sun came up, like the fucking sun always does at the beginning of fucking cliched opening fucking sentences. A character with a fucking meaningful name appeared and began to fucking speak and perform actions that kickstarted a fucking thrilling and powerful plot full of fucking stuff. This irritating fucking behaviour continued for another interminable four-hundred fucking pages.

[ ]

OPENING #43:
The hero set out on his adventure. Sadly, he was blocked in your country.

[ ]

OPENING #30:
The hero set out on his adventure. Hey there! If you'd like to read more of the hero's adventure, become a premium subscriber. Please review our payment options.

[ ]

Not even literature makes waking up desirable.

[ ]

I take that back.

[ ]

The writer wants paid for her work. The reader doesn't want to pay for books. The writer wants to be paid to keep writing her books. The reader doesn't want tax money to be handed to writers in the form of grants and stipends.

[ ]

You desperately want to keep literature alive. Yet you refuse to pay full price for a novel, rarely attend literary events, and secretly believe that writers should write and hold down full-time occupations.

[ ]

I flung myself into reading and writing with insane, clawing passion. Over the years, my passion for literature has never soured. Before my cardiac arrest, I will utter the immortal words: fuck the philistines.

[ ]

The nagging, aching, excruciating reality of other writers writing.

[ ]

This book isn't supposed to upset you, it's supposed to comfort me.

[ ]

If this book upsets you, I take comfort from that.

[ ]

Woke up. Remembered I am still an overgrown child with no self-sufficiency. Back to bed.

[ ]

If you long to become a writer, and you read very little, then abandon your dream.

[ ]

If you're a non-reader reading this nonbook: put this down, it isn't for you.

[ ]

If I have ensnared you with the subtitle "nonbook", in the hope you were seeking a read you didn't have to read, then who is the loser among us?

[ ]

Writing without writing.

[ ]

Reading without reading.

[ ]

I remember you thinking I had written you into a story, and your annoyance when I insisted I hadn't.

[ ]

This an epitaph for my ambition.

[ ]

You want to know more about my ex? You'll kick the plot habit one day.

[ ]

An editor's criticism of a novel I wrote aged nineteen: "tends towards the banal".

[ ]

Literature should never be presented in gaudy, pastel covers.

[ ]

Those hours before a first kiss, that might be the best thing.

[ ]

Why can't a writer's nervous breakdown make for a fun-filled literary form?

[ ]

OPENING/CLOSING #4:
My literary construct says: "I want a name." My literary construct's name is Faeces Dungheap. "I hate that name," he says. Faeces Dungheap leaps into his name. "This is revolting!" he cries. I kill him off.

[ ]

Do I contradict myself? Very well then, I don't contradict myself.

[ ]

OPENING/CLOSING #98:
My literary construct wants something to do. "I am bored," he says. I remind him I invented him one sentence ago. "And you still haven't given me anything to do," he whines. I launch him head first into a pile of steaming faeces. "That's better," he says. I kill him off.

[ ]

I used to think writing was a way to escape life's painful insignificance. But when the books are published, read, received, reviewed, and several weeks later no one cares, back we go again to that void of you.

[ ]

What wit, man?

[ ]

I have plans for a trilogy of unwritten novels.

[ ]

Oh, the plans I have for unwritten novels!

[ ]

What is *this*?

[ ]

If have you reacted in any way to this, I can probably relax.

[ ]

Who are "you"?

[ ]

I prefer to read.

[ ]

The sad thing is, I can only do this once in my "career".

[ ]

Is it better to release a perfectly sculpted novel in which you take no emotional risks, or release a raw, embarrassingly upfront document comprised of nothing but emotional risks?

[ ]

I think my face is falling off.

[ ]

This is a work of fiction. Any resemblance to reality is completely unnecessary.

[ ]

I remember you left your blue cagoule in my cupboard.

[ ]

Q: Where do you get your ideas from?

A: What ideas?

[ ]

Q: How do you have the patience to write a novel?

A: I could punch you.

[ ]

If you marry me, I promise to never write about you.

[ ]

I can't promise anything.

[ ]

Thanks for honouring your promise to read and review my book.

[ ]

I am talking to multiple people in this, but mainly myself.

[ ]

This is a nonbook about opening your word processor to a blank page and weeping for hours and hours and hours.

[ ]

I simply haven't made the effort.

[ ]

What do I want from you?

[ ]

I said I would write until ten o'clock. It's only 9.19.

[ ]

I remember you reading a few sentences of my story and severely wrinkling your brows.

[ ]

AN ENDING:
Perhaps all that remains of love, in the end, is a blue cagoule with the market value of £8.27.

[ ]

I deleted a better ending.

[ ]

No, what do you want from *me*?

[Excerpts from the "nonbook" of a failed novelist into which Glasgow & Renfrew had been absorbed, transmigrated into the mind of and transcribed by Dennis Pottix, circa 2034.]

"Appendix: The Isles"
[SEE ABOVE]

BARRA

Licked clean by Marie-Anne O'Duffy, September 2021.

CANNA, RÙM, EIGG

As of 2045, these had been acquired by the Russians to store mayonnaise.

COLL & TIREE

Turned into a landfill in 2034.

COLONSAY

Bought by Facebook to store historic status updates.

ISLAY

Islay had not been informed of any political change since the election of James Callahan in 1976. As a result, life there remained the same.

JURA

Towed to Iceland and claimed by that country in 2029, following a secret referendum.

LEWIS & HARRIS

Forgotten in the scheme of things.

LUING

It is still widely upheld that the Isle of Luing is a myth.

MARRAN

It is believed this isle was ruled by brutal tyrant nicknamed "Peppy Tim" who enslaved the populace and culled seven million sheep. By whom this believed is not known.

MULL
Acquired by Paul McCartney in 2020 for last date of the Wings reunion tour. The island was trashed by Keith Richards, following a wild aftershow party, and lapsed into disuse.

NORTH & SOUTH UIST
These items were found by holidaymakers in 2039: an electric kettle, a blood-stained bandage, two litres of kerosene, and a picture of Miley Cyrus. No other human life was found.

SCARBA
It is believed this man (page right) was venerated as a God here. The reasons, and the man, are unknown.

M.J. Nicholls is the author of *The 1002nd Book to Read Before You Die*, *The House of Writers*, *The Quiddity of Delusion*, and *A Postmodern Belch*. He lives in Glasgow.